MURDER
IN THE
MEADOW

MURDER
IN THE
MEADOW

AN IT'S NEVER
TOO LATE MYSTERY

DONNARAE MENARD

LEVEL
BEST BOOKS

Historia
ESTABLISHED 2011

First published by Level Best Books/Historia 2021

Copyright © 2021 by DonnaRae Menard

This novel is entirely a work of fiction. The names, characters and incidents portrayed in it are the work of the author's imagination. Any resemblance to actual persons, living or dead, events or localities is entirely coincidental.

DonnaRae Menard asserts the moral right to be identified as the author of this work.

Library of Congress Control Number: 2021941976

First edition

ISBN: 978-1-953789-88-4

Cover art by Level Best Designs

*This book was professionally typeset on Reedsy.
Find out more at reedsy.com*

To my péperè, Arthur Fortin who taught me to love the soil, the animals, and the bountiful farming smell.

Chapter One

Mr. Wilkins, Attorney at Law and executor for the estate of Irma Moore, paused at the end of his reading of Irma Moore's will. There was one other person in his office. Katelyn Took, Ms. Moore's only granddaughter.

"As briefly mentioned in Ms. Moore's will, Ms. Took," Wilkins explained, "there is one stipulation to the transfer of Ms. Moore's estate to you." There was the shadow of a sneer on his face. The young lady had projected a bored, disdainful façade since her arrival and he was going to enjoy pouring vinegar on her ice cream sundae.

"It's pronounced Tuke, with a long U, not took, like I stole something." Katelyn gazed across the steel and glass expansion of Wilkins's desk with distaste. Her first impression of Wilkins was overbearing, judgmental, and rude, all capped off with a large dose of he was so important, and she was not. "Why would my grandmother, after all these years, willingly leave me anything?" she asked. It was a question burning in her mind for the entire ride from Illinois to Vermont. She'd left home on bad terms and ten years later still felt the sting of her grandmother's anger. Katelyn's first reaction to the news of Irma's passing had been a shocker. Irma had made it clear her granddaughter was not a person she could willingly accept, and Katelyn hadn't expected the feeling of loss. She'd had a momentary visual of an astronaut floating in space and the terror when the tether broke sentencing him to an eternity alone.

"It is not my place to question her motives," said Wilkins. "She left a letter." From within the oxblood folder, he withdrew a standard white 9 ¾ inch envelope and held it out to Katelyn. In his other hand, he offered a gold-tone letter opener with a raised monogrammed *W* on the hilt.

Katelyn didn't want to accept the envelope. Once it was in her hand, she flipped it over to examine the seal, willing herself to stay in control. Though her guts roiled, the only outward show of distress was the tightening of her jaw. Ignoring the proffered opener, she slit the flap with her thumbnail. Inside was a single sheet of paper. Holding it below desk level where Wilkins' would not see the slight tremble, she read:

July 6, 1976

Dear Katelyn,

Though it may surprise you to receive this missive and the summons to receive it, even as I write these words, I realize this is not how I wanted to do this.

Please know that regardless of everything that has happened, you were always greatly loved, both by your mother and myself.

Everything I have is yours, though it's mostly just a patch of dirt, it is what it is. I have only one request and that is that you not abandon, leave to die, or reject the poor old cats I rescued and shared my last years with. I am asking you to give them a home until their demise, please. There is a voice within the house who will tell the tale.

I love you, girl, yesterday, today, tomorrow, and I will never be far.

With all my heart, Gram, Irma Roser Moore.

Katelyn folded the letter deliberately, taking her time as she fought to control the sudden rise of tears behind her eyes initiated by reading the handwritten note.

"And the stipulation," she finally asked, voice huskier than before.

Wilkens, who did not know the letter's contents, said, "Ms. Moore had, at her death, house cats. It was her wish that you provide them with a home until they passed away in a natural manner."

"And if I don't?" asked Katelyn, realizing Wilkins had not known Irma

2

added her own personal appeal to the legal documents on the desk.

"Ms. Moore had a contingency plan which I am forbidden to share with you." The smirk had grown.

"Well." Katelyn, who was both unemployed and on the verge of homelessness, shrugged. "I like cats."

"That's good." The smirk was now full-blown. "Because there are seventeen of them."

* * *

With the key inserted in the door lock, Katelyn took a moment to exhale. *Sort it out,* she thought, *sell it, and get the hell out of Dodge She threw away, for god's sake.* It was a simple plan which would provide the needed capital to find a good place to stay and the finances needed to get started fresh. Part one of that plan included a large fire in the driveway. From the day she had come here to live at age three after the death of her mother from breast cancer, and her father driving drunk on a cross-country big rig run, the house had always been the over-filled cluster of a life's collection. The addition of seventeen cats could only have turned a claustrophobic atmosphere into a suffocating nightmare. Katelyn tightened her already tense muscles, hardening her resolve. *This is not my place,* she thought, and the black crack in her heart shed a single crystal blue tear.

The door swung open on the faint squeal of rusty hinges. Katelyn gaped, the emotional quagmire of a moment before forgotten. The room before her was almost barren. There was an old fashion wooden rocking chair, low with a wide seat and a thin pad softening the back, a crate furniture sofa, coffee table, and one end table. The lamps were tall, spindly, and simple. There was nothing here that she remembered. Katelyn stepped inside.

"Okay," she smiled, "so a smaller fire and a plan to move the cats along fast."

Her eyes swept the room. It was almost homey, the way she'd want and what she had first expected when she'd come here to live. At the base of her throat, there was a thickening, a yearning for a more stable life than she'd had in years. She immediately coughed it off, scoffing at the sentiment. She had a plan.

The curtains were clean and starched. In the corner was a covered cat-box. Nothing else. In the kitchen, Katelyn found besides the normal appliances, the old wood cook-stove and a tiny dinette table with two chairs. The space between the cabinets and the ceiling was empty. All the brick-a-brack was gone. There was also a cat-box.

In one of the second-story bedrooms, Katelyn found an elaborate kitty play yard and another cat box. The open door to her grandmother's bedroom showed the maple bed Katelyn remembered, the tall-boy dresser and matching bedside table with Gram's eyeglasses folded near the lamp, and the inevitable cat-box. The bed was made and there was a jar of flowers on the table as though her Gram had just left the room. Katelyn closed the door afraid she'd lay on that bed and shed tears she didn't believe were deserved.

The last door opened to Katelyn's old bedroom. Once more she was awed. The room looked exactly as it had when she had run away four days before her eighteenth birthday. There was no cat-box. She stepped into the room, inhaling. The air was stale and dusty, but there was still something familiar there. A movement in the corner inviting her in, but she returned to the hall firmly pulling the door shut behind her.

Katelyn called back the memory of her plan and wandered back down to the kitchen. "I don't get it," she said, opening a cabinet filled with canned goods, "where are all these cats?" She opened the door to the panty, expecting to be mobbed, but found only that the one wall of shelving had been replaced by a washing machine and dryer, and another cat platform. Hidden in the corner, a cat-box. She was just turning to leave when she heard the murmur of a female voice. Remembering Gram's reference to a voice in the house, Katie stopped short, the hair standing up on her arms. Silently she moved to the connecting door which led to the garage always storing the over-flow, never a car. It was ajar. Katelyn pushed gently.

As the door swung wide, Katelyn faced several pairs of rounded or slanted, green, yellow, or burnished ochre eyes. There were also the generous buttocks of a person whose upper body was inside one of the sixteen shelter-style housing crates attached to the wall.

"Now I expect you all to remember what I told you," said a muffled voice. "Behave yourselves, don't be too demanding, and remember that Irma said Miss Katelyn would keep us all safe."

"Katie," said Katelyn, frowning.

There was a sharp yelp followed by the solid thump of the kneeling woman's head on the crate before she shot backwards and landed on the floor. Cats scattered in every direction. The elderly woman, whose head was covered in uncontrolled steel-gray curls, looked up at Katelyn, gasping for breath and with fear in her eyes.

"Katie," said Katie, clearing her throat. "My grandmother is the only one who calls me Katelyn."

The woman recovered her senses quickly scrambling to her feet.

"Hello Katie, I'm Ruthie, er, Ruth." She was shorter than Katie, round but not heavy, and at closer inspection younger than Katie had thought. "I've been taking care of the cats while we waited for you." More cats scurried away, some taking refuge in the open cages.

"Is this where the cats stay?" asked Katie. There were several cat-boxes here as well.

"Heavens, no," said Ruth, ushering the younger woman back through the pantry. "Normally they pretty much roam at will, this is where they're fed."

Once the women were seated at the dinette with cups of tea, Katie asked her first question.

"So, you're a friend of my…Gram?" At the last moment, Katie decided that calling her grandmother by her first name would indicate she and Irma were not on good terms. It might behoove her initially to not alienate someone who was probably a friend to her grandmother. The use of the endearing term caused a small pain, like a stitch taken in her heart.

Ruth ladled three heaping spoons of sugar into her mug as she spoke. "We were girls together."

"I don't remember you; did you move away?" Katelyn allowed herself a tiny smile at her correct assumption this was a friend, not someone hired to help.

"Not far. My late husband didn't approve of your grandmother. For several years we exchanged the occasional letter, Christmas card." The look on Ruth's face said the subject was closed. Katie moved on.

"The house is different. I don't remember Gram having this affinity for cats." Katie looked around, eyes landing on the partially opened cupboard door. There was another thing, Gram prided herself on being a scratch cook. "I mean, we usually had one that lived in the barn, sometimes in the house." She couldn't take her eyes off that slightly ajar door.

"She always loved them," said Ruth. "The rescuing came later, after you left. She was lonely. Most of the stuff that was in the house, Irma put in, ah, storage. You know, to help keep everything clean."

Katie's eyes swept around the room again, landing on Ruth. The young woman could see sadness, but what was that around Ruth's eyes? Fear?

"So much has changed," Katie began, clamping her lips tight. She also felt fear. Memories were shaking off cobwebs, she pushed them back.

Suddenly one cat jumped on the table.

"Get down!" Ruth ordered sharply. "You know that's not allowed."

The cat hit the floor with a solid thump, scuttling behind the cook-stove to hide. Ruth's tone surprised Katie who had pinned Ruth as passive, meek even.

"Irma always said you have to let them know you're the alpha or they'll walk all over you," Ruth explained. After a moment she added, "You're probably finding this overwhelming, aren't you?"

"To say the least," Katie admitted. The steel rod in her backbone softened ever so slightly.

Ruth read Katie's reaction in a different way.

"I tried to make everything ready for you." The meek was back. "You know, nice and clean. I got lots of groceries, swept up." There was a pleading note in her voice.

"Thank you."

They were silent for several minutes with Katie studying the chart that covered the entire front of the refrigerator. Each line started with a photo of a cat followed by its name, gender, age, special needs, and at the end a D, T, or R.

"Dropped off, trapped, or rescued," Ruth said without prompting. She had been watching, all the time chewing the inside of her lower lip. So much depended on Katie, and the older woman had no idea where to start making this feel like home.

Once again, they were silent until a small voice broke in on Katie's jumbled thoughts.

"Katie? Is everything okay here? Did I do it right?"

Katie turned a questioning eye toward Ruth.

"Will you stay, at least for a while?" Ruth's voice got softer. "At least long enough to find out why your grandmother was murdered?"

Chapter Two

Katie's jaw dropped. "What?" she gasped, sure she'd heard wrong.

"She didn't just die." Ruth's voice got stronger. "Someone ran her down, with a car or more likely a pickup truck. It wasn't an accident."

Folding her trembling hands together, Katie said, "Tell me." Suddenly cold, she crushed down the urge to shiver. *This can't be,* she thought. *My grandmother? Murdered?*

"We were pulling boards off the barn," said Ruth. "Out of the blue, we heard a truck roaring around in the high meadow, had to be ruining the hay. Irma told me to stay put, and she headed off that way. Maybe an hour or an hour and a half later, I got a bad case of nerves and followed her. By that time, it was getting late. I found her body in the meadow. She was laying in the crushed hay. She didn't just fall down; her limbs were all weird, twisted up."

Ruth was looking out the kitchen window toward the north. A large tabby laying in her lap licked the old woman's hand.

"I ran back to the house, called the sheriff. We went back to the meadow. It was close to dark. The doc came out and picked up her body. He said she'd probably had a heart attack. They took her away along with the envelope taped on the 'fridge that said LAST WISHES. They sent her body to be cremated. I walked into town the next day. The sheriff said it was just as Doc said. But, Katie, I saw her body while there was still light. It wasn't right." Ruth turned directly to Katie, eye to eye. There was no sniveling, no tears, just anger and something Katie read as certainty.

8

"That afternoon the sheriff showed up to seal the house," said. Ruth. "I told him I'd already called Mr. Wilkins, just like Irma had told me to do and he was on his way. The sheriff called me a meddling old woman. Mr. Wilkins arrived maybe ten minutes later; said he'd gotten lost driving out. I was standing right here when the sheriff told him it was common knowledge that I was crazy, not right in my head and he was going to call the animal control to catch the cats."

"Mr. Wilkins pulled this file out of his briefcase. You could tell the sheriff was mad, but Mr. Wilkins didn't get upset. He said he had a notarized notice that at the time of Irma's death, he was to contact you and I was to stay in the house taking care of the cats until you arrived."

Katie lifted her mug, but it was empty. Chills still ran up the sides of her jaw. Why hadn't Wilkins told her any of this?

"The sheriff just left?"

"He took the letter with him. Mr. Wilkins said that was okay because Irma left several copies."

"I need a few minutes, Ruth," said Katie. When she was alone in the kitchen, she filled a glass from the tap, sniffing the water before she drank. When she'd heard about the cats, she thought it was a tiny hiccup in her plans, and she only had to make a small revision. When she met Ruth, she'd made up her mind to play along, eventually swinging her future back on course. But hearing Irma had been murdered? That was impossible. She should call the sheriff, or maybe Wilkins. Somebody. Get a second opinion, verify Ruth was straight and, and then Katie didn't know what. She drank another glass of water before turning away from the sink feeling closer once again to control.

She found Ruth seated on the couch with three cats. There was no television, but the radio was playing '60's music. The front door was open and Katie could see a cat snoozing in the sun on the top porch step. It was so normal. Why did she feel warped, or was it only confusion? Her stomach knotted. Taking a moment to exhale, Katie calmed the rising surge within her guts. *One step at a time,* she thought. It had been her mantra when she was running from one catastrophe to another on her way to Illinois and had stayed with her throughout the years.

"What's the sheriff's name, Ruth?" she asked. There was a little shake in her voice, but she cleared her throat, swallowing her turmoil.

"Martin Lewis, but you can't call him." Ruth's voice rose shrill enough for the cats' ears to jerk up. "He wouldn't listen to me. When I told him he was wrong, he threw me out of his office and the nurse at the doctor's office said he wouldn't see me either. In the envelope that said FINAL WISHES, Irma had written she wanted to be cremated. I was there, in town, not more than twelve hours after the medical examiner hauled her body off, and they had already sent it to be cremated. Shouldn't they have verified that with someone first? They never asked me about family. We didn't have any real funeral, only a gathering here. She's buried in the family plot beyond the orchard where Fred is. I stayed up nights while I waited for you because I was so scared."

"I'm so sorry you had to deal with all that," Katie sat in the rocker. One of the cats surrounding Ruth climbed into the woman's lap. "I can't call Wilkins, he's so snide."

"He doesn't like cats."

"Ah." It had been a surprise to be summoned by Wilkins, and hearing of her grandmother's bequeath. Now she felt confused and somewhat unsure about remaining in the house. She'd spent years telling herself Gram didn't give a fat rat's patootie. Irma's short letter gave her cause to wonder if Katie's own thoughts, or even her memories, weren't jaded. As Katie considered this, her thoughts were clear on her face. Ruth seated on the couch felt her heart dip. So much depended on Katie, even just to stay on at the farm.

While Katie mulled over what she had already heard that day, her eyes roamed around the room. A small smile on her lips as she realized what she had thought to be a pristine and sterile environment contained obvious handiwork by the cats. Though there were scratch posts throughout the house, there was also scratch marks on the furniture, cushions, and door frames. Despair and her own needs had brought Katie back to Parentville. On the drive across country, she considered that with Gram no longer here, there was no reason to stay in Vermont. She'd liquidate, take the money, and stroll away. Gram had told her repeatedly she was a stubborn child, then a difficult teen. Katie knew once she'd left home necessity had forced her to grow a hard candy shell which remained intact until the one episode where someone else had crawled in with her. Then Julian had burned Katie up from the inside, used all she offered, and dumped her. Katie had grown a new shell, even harder, less dependent on anyone else. If someone reached out in friendship, Katie took it, but rarely gave of herself in return. She'd learned a lot being on her own, but what she found at the farm didn't fall into any of that knowledge. Exhaling, she considered her next option. Selling the farm would have to wait until the last feline funeral unless Katie came up with an alternate game plan. There was no way she was just going to walk. Ruth had to be wrong. A good night's sleep, some food in her belly, by tomorrow Katie would have it all worked out. The three cats in the living room had grown to seven. They all watched her. A shiver ripped down her spine. Katie bit down hard on her lower lip.

"I need to think," said Katie. "I'm overwhelmed with what has happened. I need time to figure it out."

"I'll go," said Ruth, wiggling toward the end of the couch.

"Where do you live?" asked Katie. "I'll give you a ride." The only vehicles in the drive were her Subaru and what she assumed to be Gram's dust-covered pickup.

"No," said Ruth, quickly getting to her feet. "I live in a little house down the road and walking is good for me."

Katie was also on her feet. The cats scattered around the room watched her, ready to run at any sign of hostility. She took a step toward the front door, then turned toward the kitchen where another cat watched from under the table, before turning back toward the open door to the porch. All the while, she was rubbing her hands. Ruth, like the cats, watched and waited.

"Okay, here's the thing." Katie began, sure she was babbling. Everything that had happened since she'd walked into the lawyer's office felt like a soap opera. "I like cats, but I've never owned one. I don't have the vaguest idea how to care for a single cat, let alone seventeen."

"Sixteen," said Ruth. "Mo passed away two days ago, but don't worry I took care of everything. I didn't think you'd want to find a shoebox in the freezer with his body in it."

Katie gulped. Her stomach flipped again.

"Exactly what I mean." Her voice squeaked. "I'd like to hire you to stay here with me for a few days, help me get my feet under me, you know?"

Ruth was silent.

Katie rushed on. "I know you don't know me, or I you, but Gram must have trusted you. It's been a long time since I was here, I'm unfamiliar." *Yeah, that's it, play the pity card.* She exhaled, shoulders drooping. It wasn't a lie. Katie didn't like the feeling of dependency on this old lady she didn't know from Adam. "I need you to tell me about Irma, ah, my Gram, and why you believe someone murdered her. I just need a few minutes to get my act together. Will you stay?"

Ruth smiled. "Oh yes, Katelyn, I can sleep on the couch." Fighting the impulse to hug Katie, Ruth squeezed her hands together. Even though Katie looked like she'd just stepped on a poisonous snake, or was going to puke, Ruth was sure everything would work out.

"You can sleep in Gram's room," said Katie. "And, please, Katie."

Katie didn't understand the transformation in Ruth. Before the older woman had appeared deflated, gray, and sagging. Now she was Mrs. Christmas, a petite ball of golden yellow butter. It was Katie's turn to gape.

"Why don't you bring your things in," directed Ruth, brushing the cats aside to stand up. "I'll make lunch. I'm not the cook Irma was, but I make a mean grilled cheese."

Katie's belongings were few; a knapsack, a box of books, and two boxes of miscellaneous household items. There was also the thick oxblood accordion file Wilkins had given her.

"This," he'd said, "contains all the material your grandmother brought in, plus the pages of transfer information my office has put together for heirs. If you have questions, call."

With the knapsack and boxes stowed behind the firmly closed bedroom door, Katie took the file down to the kitchen, intending to read the contents after lunch.

Ruth had the table set and a cast iron fry pan on the gas range. The inviting aroma reminded Katie she hadn't eaten that day, and the sizzling sputter made her want to stick her face right in the pan. Once she sat down Ruth put a plate in front of her with two thick sandwiches, golden and oozing, German potato salad, and dill pickle wedges. Katie dug in, barely noticing Ruth's plate held half as much.

Halfway through her second sandwich, Katie slowed down. Embarrassed, she had wolfed down the meal; she drew a deep sigh.

"Sorry Ruth, that was rude. I just didn't realize I hadn't been eating, and it smelled so darn good." Smiling at the other woman, she added. "That had to be possibly the best grilled cheese I've ever had."

Ruth pinked. "The secret is mayonnaise, not butter, and three kinds of cheese."

While Ruth put the dishes in the sink, Katie sipped lemonade, one hand on the folder. Before she flipped it open, Ruth sat down again.

"I think we should talk about the dog in the room," said Ruth.

Katie quirked an eyebrow. So far, she had seen no evidence of a dog. "Are you talking about the cats or Gram?" she asked.

"The cats are simple, what happened to Irma wasn't."

Just then the sound of a souped-up truck roared past the windows. The cats scattered. The truck screeched to a halt, turned, and sped back the way it had come.

"Instance number one," said Ruth, motioning Katie who had risen out of her seat to sit back down. "About the time Irma rescued me, this man from the city started dropping in to see her. First, he was friendly, talked to her about how he knew she didn't have any family and how hard it must be for her to keep the place up. She told him she was fine, but he kept coming back. He would be here early in the morning, late in the day, and sometimes he just called, like at suppertime. After a while, she told him point-blank to stop coming out or calling."

"I'm kind of a country girl and I chidingly remarked that this guy was interested, like a beau. Irma said the only thing he was interested in was the land. Specifically, the ledges and the lower meadows. These sixty acres were Irma's world and she wouldn't part with a square inch. Even though she doesn't farm anymore, the Dean boys plant, harvest, and cut hay so the land keeps open. What they pay for rent covers the taxes." Ruth was making lines through the sweat ring from her lemonade glass, watching as the swirls lengthened and thinned.

"The man didn't come back but stuff started happening. Irma got one flat tire after another, some here, some elsewhere. This is a town road, but other than the people dropping off cats, no one comes up here. Now it's the highway. They get this far; they roar back the way they came day and night. Mailbox got wiped out a few times, stuff was stolen from the back of the truck while she was in town. It was all just nuisance kid stuff until the day some fool decided to tear up the meadow." Ruth got up from the table slowly, as though suddenly her age was heavy on her bones.

Katie stretched a finger out to a gray tiger that had been watching her eat. If she kept one, this would be it. She smiled at the picture of her driving away with the cat riding shotgun.

"That's LG," said Ruth as she walked out of the kitchen. "She bites."

Katie slowly withdrew her hand, reaching instead for the paperwork Wilkins had provided. Once the red file was empty, the table was covered with instructions for Katie and accounts that would have to change to her name.

Why bother, she thought, *if they don't get paid, they can shut it all down and try to figure out where to get their money later.* In the back of her head, a shadow man was shaking his head. It was the remembered image of Poppa, reminding her right was right. Katie concentrated on the instructions, shutting the memory out. There was also a checkbook with a few thousand dollars listed. Katie re-read the instructions while trying to devise a list for getting everything done. When she gave up shoving everything back in the file, she found Ruth dusting and chatting with the nearest cat.

"Ruth, I didn't find a check to pay for Gram's final expenses," Katie said.

"She had a paid account at Saint Jude's church. I have one too. Neither of us had someone to step forward. The reverend set up a trust for people like us. What it didn't cover, her friends volunteered."

Katie studied the floor. Irma knew everyone and was the first one in line when someone was in need. God knew she had dragged Katie toting a casserole to the homes of enough strangers. People remembered. Katie's throat filled again, while just below a hollow place ached.

"I'm going for a walk," Katie said.

Ruth watched Katie step off the porch. She knew exactly where the young woman was going and equally sure Katie would turn down an offer for company.

Scooping up the cat, Ruth said, "Just this once I wish you were a dog. I'd send you with her."

Chapter Three

At the end of the overgrown lane just before the woodlot grew up the side of the tall slate ledge her grandfather always referred to as the shale mountain, Katie stood in the middle of the high meadow. The hay was ruined. There was evidence of the joyriders having circled the outer edges, but in the middle where it was still horribly flat, she found the painted circle where her grandmother's body had lain. Katie turned, feet pacing in place. Gram had been her height, a tall woman. There was no way she could have been standing here and not seen by the driver. It appeared Ruth had been right. Irma's death had been no accident. Katie waited while the hot sun burned the part in her hair. She expected anger, grief, the certainty of being alone, but other than a slightly hollow feeling at the bottom of her rib cage, there was nothing. She waited for another tear to fall, but she was bone dry without and within.

The walk back was quicker. Just before she stepped out of the green tunnel shading the lane, Katie saw the rural mail carrier coming up the road. She could see the man intent on getting ready to make the drop, but as he pulled ahead ready to back into the driveway for the return, he spotted her car. The mail vehicle slowed perceptively while the driver craned his neck looking for someone new. Katie recognized this stranger as a curiosity seeker, an ambulance chaser, someone who got a little thrill from somebody else's misfortune and wanted to know all the grisly details. Gram's business was now Katie's business, and she felt violated. Now she was angry. She waited until the mail vehicle was out of sight before walking across the lawn.

Starting her car, she pulled it around the back of the house, leaving the lane that traveled down to the barn to cross the side lawn. She parked the Subaru close enough to the building to make it invisible from the road. When she got back to the porch, she found Ruth hanging onto the railing with a death grip. The old woman's eyes were filled with tears.

"What's wrong?" Katie demanded, rushing up the steps.

"I heard the car," Ruth whispered. "I, I thought you were gone."

"Not gone," said Katie, patting Ruth's arm. "But I have questions, and I don't want to stand around outside and ask them." Once inside, she put the teakettle on the stove. "You said the sheriff blew you off, and the doctor wasn't any better. Look, Ruth, I'm not trying to be all pessimistic here, but if what you believe is right, maybe we should play it a little low-key until we figure it out. You know, if no one knows I'm here yet maybe we can get a clue to what happened." *And not alert the bill collectors.*

"What about the lawyer?" asked Ruth.

"Gram went all the way to Burlington to get a lawyer," said Katie. "Obviously she didn't trust whoever is local. I think tomorrow morning, I'll drive into the city and talk to the man."

"You could call."

"No, I want to be looking in his face when I ask my questions. I'm going to use Gram's truck. It runs, right?"

Ruth nodded. "Yes, but if someone recognizes it in town, they're gonna know."

"Okay, that's true. I'll take my car and you're to stay right here in the house with the door shut and locked."

Ruth's eyes widened. "I guess I'd better take the cover off the cat door."

"That reminds me," said Katie with a casual sigh. "Wilkins was talking about the cats passing on, he alluded to the fact he'd know if someone bumped them off. How could that be?"

Ruth who was filling a wicker basket with cat toys said, "I don't know, other than he asked me questions about Mo, and told me if a cat died, I was to call the vet before disposing of the body."

Of course, he did. Katie frowned. It looked like Wilkins was destined to be another wrench in her works.

Katie made supper, discovering the reason for so many cans of store-bought food in the cupboard was because Ruth didn't cook. At bedtime, it took a lot of persuading to get Ruth to sleep in Irma's bed. Then finally the day was over, and Katie could collapse on her own. The door was shut tight keeping the cats out but she could still hear their muted mews and the occasional scratch on the wood signaling one was knocking, hoping for entry. Sometime later a slight weight jumped up on the bed, settling into the curve on the back of her knees. One sneaky feline had breached her defenses.

Sleep didn't come, but old memories did. Being little and helping with the milk cows who traveled to and from the grazing land through the orchard, gathering eggs, Poppa teaching her to drive the tractor, and there was that one time, that long ride down the lane.

"We own this side of the road," he said, "Deans' own the other. Neither owns the lane. It's a fire road and belongs to the town though it ain't been cleared in years." They rode along bumping over rocks and rubbing against trees up through the woodlot, over the stony mountain, then through a boggy area on the far side. Finally, Poppa stopped the truck. "This is the end of us," he said. "That's Kittredge Road ahead."

Katie remembered thinking they weren't on a road at all but parked on a tall spot in the drainage ditch.

When Gram took on the responsibility of Katie, she wanted a daughter like the one she'd lost, all pink and white ribbons and lace. That wasn't Katie and no matter the lecturing, frowns, or punishment Gram dropped on her; she couldn't change. Poppa took Katie as she was letting her play in the barn, mess with the equipment, or scamper up the mountain. When Katie was thirteen, Poppa had a heart attack in the night and was gone. Gram took it badly, blaming herself for not waking up when he needed her. She got hard, stricter with Katie, dictating who could be a friend, what the girl would do. When Katie couldn't take anymore, she left, headed toward Illinois where her two much older brothers lived with their father's family. It took her three years to get there.

She'd hitch-hiked out of town with a romantic dream about a comfortable trip across country and the welcoming arms of siblings she hadn't seen in fourteen years. The getting out-of-town part went well, but after that romance gave way to a more sinister fact. She'd had a few dollars in her pockets, $1.18 to be exact, and her theory of living by her wits died when she met others that were smarter, slyer, or more dishonest than she was. She'd slept in ditches, unlocked cars, and periodically in the beds of demanding owners. It was not a story she would willingly share. She'd been hungry, stoned, and filthy beyond imagination. A begged for job milking cows, one of her few skills, had pulled her up by the boot-straps and left her in a world gray with need, but no longer black with despair. In Illinois she'd met with another disappointment. False pride had kept her from coming home.

"If I could tell a ten-year younger version of myself anything," Katie said to the cat hidden in the dark, "I'd say be grateful for what you've got and work at fixing what's wrong there before taking on the world."

Her hand reached out to the spot where Poppa would sit and read as many stories as it took for Katie to fall asleep. Her roving hand encountered a soft, warm body with sharp teeth that took hold in warning, then let go. Katie couldn't stop the tears each consecutive memory brought. She wanted to hug the sneaky cat who had gotten in before the door closed, but it was clear the cat didn't want that. It was enough to not be alone in the dark. Katie slept until the rubbing of whiskers on her face signaled the feline wanted out.

* * *

Ruth had been right. Even though Katie waited until there would be a lot of traffic traveling Main Street, she watched heads turn to look then ignored her when she wasn't recognized. She was wearing an old flannel shirt of Poppa's and his John Deere bill cap. In the lawyer's office, she pushed past the secretary entering Mr. Wilkins' private office unannounced. She didn't want him warned.

"Sorry Mr. Wilkins," she demurred. "I can't begin to tell you how tough yesterday was and while I'm here going to the, ah, bank. I thought I'd take you up on your offer."

"Offer?" he asked. His suit jacket and tie were laying on the back of his chair, there was a cup of coffee in one hand and a large jelly doughnut in the other. He didn't look anywhere near as snarky at that moment.

"Yeah, I have a few questions like why did Gram hire you? Did you have any conversation with anyone else in Parentville about me? Did my grandmother have a savings account?"

To his credit, Wilkins didn't back down from the change in Katie's attitude from simpering to demanding though he did set the doughnut on a napkin before proceeding.

"It was clear Ms. Moore didn't trust whoever the local legal person was in Parentville. She seemed to have issues with several people there. I've only been to Parentville one time when the woman Ruth called me. The only information I gave was that a member of Ms. Moore's family would handle the disposition of the property. I don't remember anything about a savings account. I only had the check register she gave me ten days before her death."

"You didn't think it was odd, her being here, then dying ten days later?"

Wilkins walked around Katie to shut the office door. When he turned to face her, his brows pulled together, and he was frowning.

"I found it completely odd. My research turned up only the news report of an unfortunate accident and the coroner's report of a non-suspicious death. I put both items in the envelope marked *Copies Death Certificate*. I didn't know how to broach the subject with you, so I let it go. To be honest, you didn't appear to be overly interested in Irma's passing, just about the inheritance. The day I spoke with Ruth she was very emotional. I wasn't sure if she was speaking from her own mind or from her heart, or maybe fear because she had nowhere to go. My decision was to give you a few days on the farm, then call and see how you were doing, maybe you'd have drawn your own conclusions."

Katie was silent.

"I can't direct your actions; I can only warn you to be careful as you go. Ruth hinted there was more going on than I would know about. You don't know me, and I can tell you don't want to. But crusty as she was, Irma Moore had a passion. Sometimes that sort of thing makes you blind. If you need me, call. Maybe make an appointment or try not to piss off the woman who makes my coffee." He gave a small smile.

"Deal," said Katie, smiling in return. She left knowing she would have to trust that what he told her was what he knew, even though he hadn't provided any real information. Mr. Wilkins wasn't someone she'd invite to dinner, but maybe he was the person to call if she needed legal advice.

"Yeah, maybe next time I'll bring him a cat," she said, walking to her car.

In Parentville Katie went into Beauregard's General Store for bread. At the cash register, a woman about her age asked if there was anything else Katie needed.

"Nope, that's it." Katie raised her head and realized the woman was studying her closely.

"Do I know you?" the woman asked.

Katie blanched, quickly turning her face away. "No, thanks, have a good day." She hurried out the door, glad she'd parked far enough away so the clerk couldn't see the car.

She had one more stop, Baldwin's Feed and Hardware.

Standing in line, she recognized Stan Baldwin behind the counter. He had been a junior when she was a freshman.

High school jock. Football? She mused. *Had a fancy name Stanley the third? Pompous family of jerks.*

"Can I help you?" asked Stan.

Startled, Katie stepped up to the counter. "Ah, yeah, I need two large bags of kitty litter please."

"Sure." Stan smiled. "I'll even give you the cat lady discount. Though usually I have to deliver too."

"What?" Katie tried to make her face blank. "A discount would be nice, but who's the cat lady?"

"I don't know Miss Moore, you tell me." Stan wasn't speaking quietly, and he had this poop-eating grin on his face that was just inviting someone else to ask what was going on. He knew exactly who she was.

21

Katie tried one more time.

"Well, I'm sure the Moore lady is happy with the discount, but I'm a Took and on a time schedule here."

Suddenly from across the room behind her, a voice said, "Hey, Sheriff, how's it going today?"

From right behind her a second voice said, "Just fine."

Katie went rigid. Had the sheriff heard her announce to the world who she was? Stan's eyes narrowed. The young woman across the counter seemed to become shorter and thinner before his eyes. Katelyn wasn't moving or speaking, but her eyes were like brown soup bowls. It didn't take Stan half a second to realize she was looking for a way out that didn't involve the front door.

"Well, ma'am, we can get the paperwork done pretty quickly," he said. "Why don't you step into my office? I'll be with you in a sec." He pointed to a windowed door directly to his left. Without raising her head, Katie walked into the office and found a place to stand out of sight. While she waited, she chewed her cuticles and studied the wall of photos of three generations of Baldwin children.

Stan came through the door and pulled the shade down before he motioned her to sit.

"Ruth was in town last week, getting groceries. I gave her a ride back out to the farm and she told me you were coming," he explained.

"She walked?"

"Always does, she doesn't have a car. But that's not the problem is it?" Stan asked. "She told me about her fears. Irma and I used to work together on the cat project with Doctor Veronica."

Katie's eyebrows shot up.

"Veronica is the vet; you haven't met her yet?"

"I've barely been here a day," said Katie.

Stan studied her for a moment. "From your reaction to the sheriff, I'm willing to bet Ruth told you not to trust him."

"Do you?" she asked.

"I don't have a reason not to. Your situation is different."

Katie decided if Stan had so easily identified her, she should give him some information.

"I only have what Ruth said to work with, and I don't have any experience with this type of thing or know what direction to take. I was hoping to check around without being recognized." She sighed.

"To be honest," Stan said. "I worked closely with your grandmother, you kind of look like her, and Ruth told me you were coming."

Who else did she tell? Katie looked out the window. She could see the creamery building on the other side of the parking lot.

"If you go out back to pick up the litter, Rick is going to recognize you," said Stan. "He was sweet on Irma. I tell you what, how about if I drop you off a half dozen bags on my way home? That'll keep you for a while, give you some space to figure out what you're up to."

"How much is that going to be?" asked Katie. Her wallet was empty and the woman at the main branch of Irma's bank in Burlington had told her it would take six to ten days for Gram's money to be freed up.

"I'll bill Irma's account," said Stan jumping up when the door swung open and an employee stated they were getting backed up out front.

After verifying the sheriff had left, Katie high-tailed it back to her car and out of town. At the turn onto Fire Lane 61 and a mile down the slope from the farm, Katie glimpsed a small building hidden in a forest of Sumac and Bittersweet vine. This was the corner edge of the farm property and according to Poppa, the one-room school he had attended up to the eighth grade, the end of his formal education. He had spoken fondly of the little building and during his lifetime maintained it. It saddened her to see it lost in the weeds. She parked the car and walked around the schoolhouse. It wasn't nearly as derelict as she expected it to be. Beyond the school three-quarters of the way to the farm was the Dean house, which sat much further back from the road and were the only buildings she'd pass before arriving in her own yard.

Back at the farm, she found the front door locked but the house empty. The back door was wide open. There were boxes of splintery plank wood stacked near the wood cook-stove that hadn't been there when she left.

23

Stepping outside, Katie yelled Ruth's name.

"Over here." A faint voice called back.

Katie rushed to and around the back end of the barn and found Ruth pulling loose a board from the collapsing rear corner of the structure. Dismay at the falling building pinched Katie's face together.

"Damn," she said.

Ruth looked up. "Careful where you go." She moved back from the buckling wall, cats following her. The corner, a low spot built up with stacked rocks, had given way. "We've been cannibalizing broken boards for the stove." Grunted Ruth hefting a box off the ground. Katie stepped forward, taking it from her. "Gonna rain tomorrow," Ruth explained. "We might want to take the damp off."

"What's that pile for?" Katie nodded with her chin to a neatly stacked pile complete with risers off the ground and spacers every four or five layers up.

"We were going to have a chicken coop," said Ruth sadly. "Raymond Dean said he'd build it once we had enough lumber cleaned up."

Katie stopped, eyes searching the area east of the barn. "What happened to the old chicken coop?"

"Burned last winter." Ruth kept walking. "Irma said it was winter lightning, caused by a Bic."

"OK Ruth," said Katie, dropping the box on the floor and sending cats scurrying. "You keep talking about all this bad luck crap, but you don't seem to have any evidence to back it up."

"You want evidence?" spate Ruth. "Besides the fact no one gave a fat patootie when Irma died, or the trucks tearing up the lawn on a regular basis, two pairs of footprints and an empty gas can out by the chicken coop, hm, let's see, oh yeah, there's the ruined hay that actually belongs to the Deans."

Ruth stomped off into the living room. Katie watched the old woman go, wondering if there was a grain of truth in what Ruth was saying.

"Is she angry because I'm not head over heels believing what she's saying," Katie asked the cats at her feet, "or is she scared?" Deciding to give Ruth a few minutes, Katie grabbed the stack of pots on the woodstove. If they were going to light a fire, the pots and pans needed to be moved. Yanking open the bottom cupboard; Katie released an avalanche of magazines and newspapers.

"What the heck?" she exclaimed. She had opened the upper cupboards previously checking out the food and looking for plates and cups and everything looked normal. She opened a second lower door and found more of the same in the way of unorganized paper.

"Ruth," she yelled. "What's all this?"

Ruth returned with a shrug she said. "Irma's stuff."

"You mean like her filing?"

"Nope, that's in her dresser. This is just stuff she kept." Ruth picked up a handful and shoved it back in the cupboard.

"No, don't put it back," said Katie. She gathered an armful and dumped it on the wood they had lugged in. Ruth was looking at a scrap that had dropped out of the mess and landed at Katie's feet. It was a ten-dollar bill. Both women stared open-mouthed.

"Oh crap," said Katie. She dropped to the floor, lifting one magazine from the wood box and flipping through it one page at a time.

"Katie," said Ruth in a small voice. "There's more." When Katie looked up, Ruth added. "Paper. In the closets, down in the cellar, and maybe in the attic."

Waving Ruth away, Katie slumped against the cupboard. A week ago, she had been alone with no job, no money, no prospects. Now she had a place to stay for a while, maybe even over the winter if she could learn to manage the herd of cats, but that thin thread of security seemed to be hour by hour bringing a lot of baggage with it. When she finished with the first magazine, she picked up a second. By the end of that one, she'd found two more tens and realized she would have to go through every piece before she could throw it away. The red folder beckoned. Katie decided that should probably be her priority. Just as she got to her feet, she heard a tractor roll up and voices in the front yard. Curious, she moved to a front window.

At the edge of the road, Ruth was talking with two of the adult Dean boys. One sat on a familiar green tractor, the other was leaning on a dusty pickup truck. One idling machine towed a plow, the other a harrow. They were coming from the direction of the high meadow.

Knowing these guys were neighbors who would notice her eventually, Katie bit the bullet and walked out to the threesome. The two men were the oldest of the five Dean boys. The fourth, Steven, had been in Katie's high school class.

"Hey," said Katie.

"Raymond," said Ruth, pointing to one, "Paul," the other. She left it to Katie to explain who she was.

Before Katie could volunteer information, Raymond jumped in.

"Katie…" His hesitation letting her know her last name wasn't Moore, but he couldn't recall what it was."

"Took." She smiled, extending her hand. Raymond reached out, giving her arm a firm shaking.

"Good to see you back," he said. "We want to offer our condolences and anything you need, we're right down the road."

A lump grew in Katie's throat. Her reaction to people's concern or maybe it was to references of Irma's passing distressed her. She nodded her thanks. "Mess up the road, huh?" She finally got out.

"Yeah, we got it seeded and ready to go," said Paul. "A little light rain tomorrow will give a head start." With a metallic hum of switching gears, he pulled the tractor ahead. Just as he passed the driveway a yellow pickup decorated with the feed store logo pulled up and backed up to the door leading into the converted garage now cat quarters.

Stan waved a greeting to Raymond before dropping the tailgate. Katie excused herself to talk with Stan.

"I've been thinking," she said, "about the account bill."

"I know where to find you," he laughed.

Katie had only a wan smile in return. Watching Stan's back, she sucked her teeth, tapped her foot. It embarrassed her to admit even just to herself she had expected to find ready cash among Irma's effects. Earlier she'd emptied the worn cloth bag Irma had used as a handbag and found several used tissues, bills waiting to be paid, and two dollars in change in the bottom.

"You know," said Stan standing behind the truck with a hand on the yet unloaded sacks of kitty litter, "Ruth would have been in a rough spot if Irma hadn't swooped in like a big ass bird and rescued her."

"What?" Katie laughed. The change in subject took her by surprise, but the analogy offered a very accurate description of her grandmother's habit of taking control of anything she was involved in.

Stan didn't notice Katie's humor and continued with his thought.

"The bank was taking the house back so George's cousin stepped in and bought the loan. He wanted Ruth out before the closing. She was pretty frail, you know, in her mind at that time. Irma didn't even hesitate. She took Ruth home with her like Ruth was another stray cat and helped her get past the whole episode."

"It's hard losing someone you care for," said Katie.

"I don't know how much affection there was there, George was known for having a heavy hand if you catch my drift."

Katie stopped walking. *Heavy hand? Like in he smacked her around?*

Stan hefted a fifty-pound bag up onto his shoulder. "There were a lot of people in town who weren't convinced she couldn't remember anything what with her waking up next to him in the morning, and him having that eleven-inch knife buried in his chest."

Katie's arms fell to her sides. If she'd been holding a bag of litter, it would have landed on her feet. Her jaw also dropped. Turning, she looked across the yard where Ruth was still discussing the hen-house with Raymond Dean. Thoughts ran through her brain, conversations, maybe casual references. Nothing. Ruth hadn't talked about her husband's death, only that it had happened, Katie had assumed natural causes. Eleven inches of steel didn't seem all that natural.

Maybe it's time for me to live here by myself, Katie gulped. *Change the locks, get a big dog, sleep with a loaded pistol, any of that.*

"Do you think six bags will hold you for a few weeks?" Stan was back.

"Yeah." Katie nodded following Stan's example and shouldered a bag. "The weather is nice, most of the cats go out during the day." A quick flash of light on the horizon followed by the rumble of thunder had Stan laughing at her forecast.

"Are you all set?" he asked. From the worried crease between his brows, Katie guessed there was a deeper concern than his words bespoke.

"Actually," she said, once again taking her lip between her teeth, "I saw a help-wanted notice in your store. Is the job still open?" She hadn't pre-planned the question. It had just jumped into her head that maybe she could work off her account balance.

Stan hesitated, rubbing a hand along his jawline. "It's part time, temporary until my guy's back heals."

Katie nodded.

"Requires heavy lifting."

"I'm brawny," she said.

With a sigh Stan said, "You'd have to work with Rick."

"I'll figure it out." She let go of her lip, straightening her back. She'd been self-sustaining for a long time. This wasn't the time to go soft.

"Tuesday through Saturday, eight to one-thirty, day after tomorrow, eight sharp." Stan climbed into the truck, and with a wave backed out.

When he was out of sight, Katie turned to find Raymond and Ruth gone. Walking around the house, she found them returning from the far end of the barn.

Ruth called out to her. "I told Raymond he needed to check with you about the chicken coop." There was a wide smile on her face.

"You people have enough planking cleaned up," he said. Stopping in front of Katie, he continued. "The deal with Irma was she'd pull the planking, get the windows and doors down at Chet's Recycle, and I'd frame it out down at the farm and finish it here. My brother who is a sawyer at the furniture mill has been pulling out decent two-by-four seconds, cheap money, and we've got tin pieces left from re-roofing the barn. Whole deal will probably run you forty or fifty dollars."

"Including labor?" she asked. The offer seemed too good to be true.

"Irma helped with some sickly calves earlier in the spring. It's a tradeoff. You give me the say-so; I'll call Chet and tell him what to pull out for you to pick up."

Ruth was bobbing in place, hands clasped together, as she grinned at one person then the other.

"Okay," smiled Katie. She offered her hand to seal the deal. *Well Gram, now I know why you let me find that thirty dollars.* Suddenly she realized what she was doing. This wasn't part of her plan. She wasn't supposed to be creating a better environment here, but getting ready to move it along and get out. It was on the tip of her tongue to call Raymond back and cancel his plans.

Raymond, already waving goodbye left with the promise to call Chet and maybe get started during the next day's rain.

* * *

While Katie browned ground beef for spaghetti, she considered Ruth's housing. If, no, *when* Katie sold the farm, Ruth would have to go somewhere else. *Better she considers her options sooner than later,* thought Katie. There was, as Ruth had referred to before, another dog in the room.

Ruth filled small bowls on a tray while cats meowed their impatience. She explained the cats got fed in the cat room and the door left closed until the people finished eating.

"They get supper at four-thirty with a bite of tuna. They come in special for it and then I close the door so they're stuck inside for all night," said Ruth. A parade of felines followed her through the laundry room.

"I'm short one cat," said Ruth, carrying a single bowl back with her.

"Which one?"

"LG maybe." Ruth put the bowl into the sealed tub where the food was stored. No insect, mouse, or nosy cat could sneak an extra bite.

Katie cleared her throat as she pulled the rubber seal to open one of Irma's quarts of canned tomatoes.

"So, Ruth, Stan kind of told me this morning about George's death." *Might as well get right on it.*

"I didn't kill him," said Ruth. Her voice was thin, low, and had a tired edge to it.

The skin on Katie's skull crawled.

"I never said you did," she coughed to clear the shake in her voice out. Her nerve was broken, and she bypassed that thought and went to door number two. "What I was getting to is that Stan told me Irma brought you away from there. You told me you were living in a house down the road. As far as I can tell, the only two houses are this one and Deans." She poured the pasta into the boiling water.

"Except," she turned to face Ruth, "the schoolhouse."

Ruth didn't move.

"I stopped by there today." Katie spoke softly. "Poppa loved the place, and I wanted to check it out. I found where someone had pulled the Bittersweet away from the side door. There's cardboard covering the broken windows and," she stepped forward, ignoring the sizzling pans behind her. "Inside I found a cleared space with a bed and clean blankets. How long have you been living in the schoolhouse, Ruth? Since before Gram died? Since I arrived?" She waited.

Ruth slid into a chair. There were tears on her face. She rubbed them away with her sleeve.

"Mr. Wilkins said you were coming," she said. "He didn't know when exactly, but I wanted to be ready so I moved my bed figuring I could stay there 'til I found something else. I was afraid if you found me here, you'd go away, but if there was no one to take care of the place, maybe you'd stay." The old woman pulled the sleeves of her sweater over her hands, rubbing them together.

"After supper," said Katie, "before it rains, we'll move your bed back upstairs. God knows where the cat furniture goes." Pulling toast from the toaster, she spread the garlic butter she'd mixed. It was make do cooking, but she'd lived that way a lot of years.

"If scramble cooking was an art." She'd told her last girlfriend. "I'd be Picasso."

The climbing posts upstairs proved to be classified as living room furniture. Grunting and hauling took longer than knocking the bed back together. Katie left Ruth making the bed while chatting happily with the cats. Across the hall, the young woman wedged her bedroom chair under the door handle.

Chapter Four

After a night of tossing and turning, Katie woke late to the splatting of raindrops against the window glass. She stood in the bedroom window looking over the one-time garage, now cat dormitory. The far side of the building provided a support wall from Irma's huge Hollyhocks and Dinner Plate Dahlias. Beyond that the hill sloped gently downward to the low meadow and four miles past that end, the outskirts of the village. Down in the kitchen, Ruth had already fed the cats and stoked a small fire in the wood cook-stove.

"It'll keep the damp off," she explained. "We've been using the cook-stove for a few years since the price of oil went through the roof."

"Even in the winter?" Katie turned to look at Ruth, who didn't seem fazed with the idea of two elderly women taking apart a barn to heat a house. "How can that be Ruth? It's a house."

"We closed up the upstairs and the cat room when we had to. Then we'd pull and chop up downed trees from the woodlot." Ruth laid a hand on Katie's shoulder. "Irma and I lived close to the belt, not extravagantly. The biggest bills we had were from the vet." With a pat, she turned away. Though she appeared unconcerned, it chilled the older woman to think anything she might inadvertently say would cause Katie to leave. She had peeked into Katie's room and saw that Katie was still living out of her backpack. If Katie wouldn't unpack, would she stay?

Katie sat at the table with the contents of the red folder spread around her again. Ruth scrubbed the top of the gas stove, played with the cats, and finally sat knitting and listening to the radio in the living room. She looked up in surprise when Katie explained she was going to start work the next day at the feed store. "It's only part-time," she said. "When I get done, I'll pick you up and we'll take the truck down to Chet's Recycle."

"If you're driving your car around, people will notice the out-of-state plates."

"Yeah, but they'll notice a stranger in Gram's truck too, which by the way hasn't been registered since April."

After lunch, Ruth retired for a leisurely rainy-day nap. Katie pulled out another armful of papers and newsprint from the kitchen cupboards. Though she didn't find more money, she did notice a lot of newspaper articles highlighted or circled in pencil. Many of them had to do with a Burlington company called L&F Construction or the owner, Lawrence French. French had his fingers in a lot of development projects as well as being a high-profile member of the monied social set. Katie stacked all the articles to the side along with a deed dated October 1969 and the tax records from three years before that.

"I'll ask Ruth about these later," Katie said to LG, who with a few of her friends watched the woman work. Every time she reached out the small cat let her get within a few inches, then snapped her sharp white teeth and Katie withdrew. LG made it clear she could touch or sit in Katie's lap at her whim, but Katie had yet to earn that privilege. When Katie got bored shuffling paper, she collected all the cat toys that had apparently been knitted by Ruth, and teased the cats with them. Because of the rain, except for two brave souls, all the cats lounged around indoors. Katie found it unnerving to see a cat every time she turned around. Only a husky orange fellow and a skinny senior approached her. Instead of looking them up on the refrigerator map, Katie called them all Kitty. With only the radio to keep her company, it didn't take long for Katie to start looking for projects. By six o'clock she was cooking supper and looking forward to bed.

"Thanks for helping out, Katie," said Ruth, shutting the cats away in the cat room while the people ate.

"It's not much," said Katie. "I don't mind." It surprised her to realize she didn't.

CHAPTER FOUR

The next morning Katie considered her resources, which were low. She had arrived with a backpack containing her entire wardrobe of two pairs of jeans, three t-shirts, and a single hoodie. Rummaging around in Irma's belongings, she found a pair of work boots that fit, socks, and some flannel shirts that were one size larger than needed, but would do.

"Huh," smiled Ruth when Katie came down the stairs, "It would please Irma, you didn't just throw her stuff away. I packed you a lunch and there's oatmeal and toast to hold you."

When Katie pulled out to go to work, LG sat on the front step watching across the puddles left from the rain that had stopped a few short hours prior. When the Subaru was far out of sight, the cat climbed the staircase, nudged the door to her bedroom open, and settled in for a nap on Katie's bed.

At the feed store, Stan directed Katie to the office.

"There's paperwork," he said. "My wife Cindy is in there doing the payroll, she'll give you what you need."

Cindy proved to be a bouncy woman with honey-colored hair. Three small children played at her feet and were instantly attracted to Katie. Having had little experience with youngsters, she was relieved to discover smiling at their giggling greeting was all she needed to do.

"Don't let them bug you," said Cindy. "As a herd, they can be overwhelming. I only do payroll and it seems foolish to get a babysitter for the short time I'm here."

"That's true," said Katie, bending over the employment and tax forms.

"Stan says you're a friend of Ruth?"

Katie's shoulders tensed.

"I only just met her after I got married and moved here," said Cindy, suddenly blushing. "I'm not trying to be nosy; it's just not being local; I don't always know. You know the story. The full back doesn't get the college scholarship or the cheerleader, so Stan went to Champlain Business College. That's where we met."

Katie felt the need to answer. "He's a nice guy."

"He is." Cindy blushed again. "He's a little concerned about the changes in

33

Ruth, that's why I asked."

While Katie considered Cindy's words, the littlest child, a girl, fell down. The child was still tearful and sniffling when Katie left.

With obvious trepidation, Stan led Katie out to the feed shed.

"This is Rick," he said. "He'll show you around, teach you the ropes, such as they are."

Rick was a tall, good-looking older man. He wasn't shy about taking a good look at Katie. Right about the time she felt her hackles rising, Rick smiled. The round apples in his cheeks appeared, moving up to push the bottom of his sparkling blue eyes into crinkly laugh lines.

"I know you, Katie Took," he grinned. "You were your grandpop's pride and joy, a tomboy that drove your Gram up a tree."

She wanted to be cool, stand-offish, but Rick had been Poppa's great friend and she had too many fond memories.

"Hey Rick, you haven't changed a bit."

"Hah!"

They worked until noon with Rick explaining the layout before giving Katie time to read labels and signs. Her memory was sharp and the old man smiled the first time she took off with the two-wheeler to collect grain sacks without his direction. When the lunch whistle rang, they settled on hay bales to eat. Katie opened her paper sack and found a cold grilled cheese sandwich and a can of baked beans. Rick laughed aloud.

"What did you put in your thermos?" he asked.

"Lemonade," she answered after a sniff. "Ruth packed my lunch. I told her I was just working half a day, but she insisted."

Using his pocketknife, he cut an apple in half handing her one section. "She tries, it's just sometimes when she gets stressed or confused, she's not in the right place." His words were gentle.

"Rick." Katie licked her lips. "Did you know Gram sent for me to come back? I'm finding a lot of things I don't understand and well, if people figure out who I am or that I'm even here, that is what it is, but I'm not advertising the fact. I need time to get my feet under me, you know?" It was the same thing she had told the Deans' and just like them, Rick appeared to understand

34

Katie's confused thoughts.

"Not a problem," he said. "But you'll take it easy on Ruth, right, and all them darn cats? They were important to your Gram."

"I will," Katie said. Her eyes followed his to the barn doors thrown wide with dust motes playing in the bright light. Suddenly there was Ruth. Katie knew it was an illusion even as the figure walked toward her. Then Stan appeared.

"I told her you were out here." He followed Ruth into the storage barn, then stood watching Ruth and Rick nervously.

Katie shook her head clearing her thoughts.

"How did you get here?" She asked Ruth.

"I walked. That's how I always get into town." Ruth bent to give Rick a hug.

"Cindy can give her a ride home," Stan said.

"We're going to Chet's," said Ruth, a petulant frown on her face as she looked at Stan. "Right Katie?"

"I have to work until one-thirty, then go back and get the truck." Katie looked from Ruth to Stan to Rick. She didn't miss the quick eye contact between the two men.

It would be nice, she thought, *if you guys would share information.*

Stan took Ruth's elbow, steering her toward the door, his voice like cotton candy. "Come on Ruth, Cindy is taking the kids home for lunch. You can help and she'll bring you back later."

The thought flickered through her mind that Irma might have been Ruth's caregiver, not a job Katie wanted.

Before Katie could say a word, the PA announced shoppers were coming back to pick up feed. Later Katie punched out and found Ruth sitting near the employee entrance. Katie elected to wait for a time when she wasn't trapped in the car to discuss her concerns with Ruth. Chet's Recycling turned out to be a shed area at the dump where the town employee, Chet, sold items he had rescued from the landfill and burn heaps. Katie loaded the five window sections and door Raymond had requested and a four-drawer metal file cabinet she found.

"Cash only," Katie laughed. "I wonder if the town gets a cut of Chet's business. Speaking of the town, with any luck Sheriff Martin won't catch us out here cruising around uninspected and unregistered."

"Take a left here," Ruth directed. The indicated turn-off was barely a lane, but the dirt road swung west toward the Charlotte town line, avoiding the drive through the center of town. Once they crossed onto the Parentville-Charlotte Road, they were only a few miles away from Fire Lane 61. As soon as the truck turned on to their road, Katie exhaled. Ruth seemed unfazed.

Katie pulled the truck behind the house, parking near the stack of cinder blocks Ruth and Irma had gathered to use as supports under the chicken coop.

"That's it," she said. "The truck stays here until it's legal, I just sweated ten pounds off."

Ruth wasn't listening. As soon as the wheels stopped rolling, she threw open the passenger door and was hurrying back toward the front of the house. Unsure what was happening, Katie followed. She found Ruth holding a small cardboard box and cooing to whatever was inside. Peeking over the top, Katie found three tiny orange kittens, possibly three or four weeks old. Her heart fell. Three more mouths to feed and kittens were sure to have a longer life expectancy than the cats already in the house.

"They need to eat," said Ruth. Katie followed amazed at the gentle, calm way Ruth took control mixing baby formula, filling three tiny doll bottles, and swaddling the kittens in warmed washcloths. She handed one kitten and a bottle to Katie, then sat on the couch feeding the other two at the same time.

"Easy," she cooed, "slowly. You're don't want to get a bellyache. That's a good baby. I've got you, you're okay."

Katie followed her example, holding the kitten securely against her chest and offering the bottle.

"She can hear your heartbeat," said Ruth. "It makes her feel safe."

"Ruth, these are very young kittens, I doubt they'll survive without their mother." It was on the tip of her tongue to suggest taking them to the vet, but the referrals to Irma as the cat lady probably meant they'd end up back here, anyway. *If the vet is the person telling Wilkins what's going on here, then she's the last person to tell.*

"Maybe not all of them will make it," said Ruth, rubbing the kittens' bellies with her fingers, "but we have a secret weapon."

With Katie following, Ruth carried the small box into the cat room all the time calling out. "Sashie, 'mere Sashie. Come to me." Ruth placed the kittens in a larger box lined with a clean towel in one of the double cages. To the far side was a cat box and a water bowl and food dish she filled. Right about then an older Tortoise-shell cat strolled into the room. Scooping her up, Ruth held her to the open door of the cage.

"Look Sashie," Ruth crooned. "See the babies? Oh, what pretty babies. Where's their mamma, Sashie? Huh? Where is she?" Tiny mewing noises came from the kittens as they crawled around trying to find the warmth of their missing mother. The big cat struggled to get free of Ruth's grip. Her head was stretched as far as her neck would allow, ears forward, and the irises of her eyes were large circles of black. Sasha's whiskers danced as she sniffed the new scents. "See the babies, Sashie," said Ruth one more time before she let go.

"What now?" whispered Katie.

"She'll either accept them or kill them," said Ruth. "But she's a consummate mother."

The cat took one slow step after another. Katie couldn't take her eyes off the cat, ready to lunge if the kittens appeared to be in danger. Sasha placed one foot into the box, then another. She sniffed, nudged, then licked a kitten, rolling it over before settling down among them.

Ruth smiled. "That's my girl," she said. Closing the door without latching it, she turned to Katie. "She won't be able to feed them, so she'll come and get me. This is what we do; Sasha, me, and Irma, take care of the babies and the injured, the lost. We find them new homes or give them a life with dignity." She walked away leaving Katie behind feeling slightly lost and unsure herself. Life on the farm had changed in her absence. A feeling akin to a spider web touching her face caused her to stop short.

Run.

Get out now.

Run.

Suddenly Ruth's startled voice called out. "Katie!"

Katie hurried into the kitchen they had just walked through. Ruth pointed toward the window over of the sink. Neither had noticed the round hole in the glass moments before. Now Katie couldn't miss the shards in the sink, the overturned mug on the table, or the tennis ball size rock laying on the floor. Ruth bent toward the rock.

"Don't touch anything," Katie ordered. Startled, Ruth yanked backwards.

The only telephone in the house hung on the wall next to the living room door. Katie yanked the receiver off the hook and reached toward the dial. Then she stopped. The only person to call was the sheriff, the same man who had denied her grandmother had died suspiciously. While Ruth watched, Katie considered her options. Clearing her throat, Katie asked,

"Is there a camera here, Ruth? One with film?"

Ruth produced an Instamatic. After finishing the roll of film, Katie drew a sketch of the room on notebook paper, wrapped the rock and mug in a hand towel, and sat Ruth at the table. "Write out what happened ever since we got home, time, date, and exactly how we found everything here. Sign it and seal it in this envelope," Katie directed. "I'll clean this up, then I'll do the same." While Katie wrote, Ruth used masking tape to attach a piece of cardboard over the hole.

"You don't think this was an accident, do you, Katie?" Ruth asked. Fear added a shaky timbre to her voice.

"You'd have to be standing in the side yard to hit that window," Katie replied. "Why would someone stand there and throw rocks?"

After supper Katie hauled the filing cabinet inside, explaining to Ruth. "Among the paper trash, Gram had pieces I think she wanted to keep. I'm going to put everything in here and sort it out later." She walked over to lock the front door. Never in all the time she had lived here as a child had they locked the door. It felt alien, even though life away from Parentville had taught her it was best. Wilkins had taken her key from the file folder, Ruth had one. Where was Gram's?

38

"Ruth, is there another key to this door?"

"Yes," said Ruth, "under the geranium pot on the porch."

Katie retrieved the key from outside. "This stays inside until I say different." While she was tossing the key from one hand to the other, Ruth went upstairs. She returned with a large ring filled with several styles of keys. Handing the ring to Katie, Ruth told her there was a key outside that would open the kitchen door. Without being told, she went out and collected that one as well. There was fear in her eyes, and a wariness Katie found unnerving.

It had been a taxing day for Katie. Focusing on either the file folder or the hidden stacks of paper proved impossible. There was the added distraction of her fingers continually reaching for the keyring.

"Oh, my god," she told herself. "Look them over and get past it." Among the dozen keys were two different vehicle keys, an odd round one that she knew locked the freezer in the basement, a shiny one with an overlarge finger grip, and some old fashion skeleton keys. Ruth was feeding the kittens so Katie took the bundle with the rock and mug and the keyring upstairs. She separated the skeleton keys and tried one after another on her bedroom door. One of them twisted the inner mechanism and a satisfying click locked the door. She left everything locked in her room and headed toward the staircase, deciding if Ruth questioned the locked door, Katie would tell her it was a habit she'd picked up while living on her own.

"Katie," called Ruth from downstairs, "could you grab the blue sweater in my room?"

"On it," Katie called back.

Moving Ruth's few furniture pieces had taken more time than Katie had expected. Though few, they were heavy wooden pieces, plus the air had been heavy with the approaching storm and the mosquitoes vigilant. Besides the maple twin bed, a mate to Katie's, there was a tall-boy dresser, a bedside table, and a ladder-back chair Ruth said once belonged to her mother.

"It's my most prized possession," Ruth declared.

It hadn't taken a genus to realize Ruth was a person of rigid habits. She always made her bed before coming down in the morning, cleaned the house starting with the bathroom, swept daily, washed the dishes as soon as the meal was finished, so there was no surprise Ruth's bedroom was neat as a pin. There weren't many personal items there, but a mason jar of wildflowers sat on the windowsill and a woven basket on the caned seat of the chair. As Katie leaned to pull the folded sweater off the chair back, she saw the basket held several prescription bottles, most of which looked empty.

Downstairs Katie realized there were more jars of flowers and throw rugs that had been missing before, were scattered across the floor. The windowsills were free of dead bugs, dust, and cat hair, even though the windows were favored resting places for all the felines.

"You do a good job keeping everything up, Ruth," said Katie.

Ruth blushed.

"It was my part," she said. "Irma cooked and was good with all the outdoor chores. I've never been much for that stuff, except maybe weeding. When I was married, cleaning house was what I was supposed to do and heaven help me if I didn't do it right." Realizing she'd revealed more than intended, Ruth hopped up and started herding the cats toward the cat room. "Okay all you lazy tubbies, time for you to go to bed."

Katie, standing at the window overlooking the side yard, let her go. On the far side was the pile of blocks for the hen-house and the clothesline. Ruth had done laundry that day comprising of pieces of blankets and towels used for cat bedding. The wash hung on the two remaining stretches of rope hanging between the poles. Each piece knotted and drooping toward the ground. One end post tilted toward the center and the other listed severely starboard.

That's on its way out. sighed Katie.

Chapter Five

The next morning after packing her own lunch, Katie drove to work. It was another day of hot, still air filled with dust and grain chaff. By mid-morning Katie had given up the flannel shirt and was wishing she was wearing shorts.

"You Katie Took?" asked someone behind her.

"Who's asking?" said Katie, grunting under the weight of a fifty-pound sack of oats.

The person asking wore a sheriff's uniform and a frown.

"Sorry," said Katie, "long day already."

"How is it you got a job like this?" the sheriff asked. He was about forty, barrel-chested, and about her height. He stood with his thumbs hooked in the belt holding his holster.

"Well." Katie smiled weakly. "Stan had an immediate need and so did I. It just worked out."

"Martin," said Rick, walking up.

"Must be difficult having a girl here doing a man's job," the sheriff spoke to Rick, ignoring Katie.

"The only difficulty is me having to tell all the gents to stop doing my job and let me do it," growled Katie.

Rick nodded. The sheriff opened his mouth again, still facing Rick, but the old man turned on his heel and went back to what he had been doing. The back of the sheriff's neck darkened as he turned once more to Katie.

"I hear you're some family to Irma Moore," he said. "You here closing up the house, getting rid of all those damn cats? You planning on being here long, getting a job and everything?"

"I am here at Irma's request," said Katie. "There's stuff that needs to be sorted out. I'm sure you know what I mean." She was careful to not sound more abrasive or to give him more information than he had given her. The sheriff nodded in agreement. Bending at the knees to get under the sack of oats, Katie added. "I left my job behind and I need to eat. This job is temporary until the injured employee comes back." She dumped the sack into a pickup backed up to the cement loading dock.

"Well, I was just going to say, if you're staying, you'll need to register your car. If you need something, you can call the office." Without another word, the sheriff walked away.

"Word gets around," said Rick.

Having not heard him coming, Katie jumped.

"For crying out loud Rick, I could have knocked you silly." She rubbed her naked arms. "What brought him here?"

"I was going to ask you the same thing," Rick said.

"What's his name?" she asked. *He's got to be the sheriff that came out when Ruth called.*

"Martin Lewis," said Rick. "His dad is Al Lewis, lives over in Monkton."

Neither name meant anything to Katie. For the rest of the afternoon, she was edgy, but the biggest surprise waited in her own yard.

Raymond Dean's pickup was now parked next to Irma's. A tractor with a low-bed trailer attached was pulling out of the side yard. And settled on the cinder blocks, was an almost finished chicken coop. Raymond and two teenage boys were busy sawing and nailing planks onto the framework.

"Holy cow!" Katie couldn't help smiling. Ruth came running out of the further field carrying a large box filled with hay and long grass. From a string hanging around her waist, a pair of long-bladed shears bounced.

"Whoa. Stop." Katie ordered. "This is no way to carry scissors Ruth," she admonished untying the string.

"Sorry. Sorry," said Ruth. Her face glowed like Christmas morning.

"You guys!" Katie beamed at Raymond. "My gosh. What can I do? I can help."

"How about some cold water?" Raymond wiped his forearm across his face. "You don't need to do anything. This is a 4H project for Davy and Bill is earning his scout badge."

"Two," smiled the younger boy. "Community service and woodworking."

"Come on Ruth," Katie laughed. "Let's see what we can rustle up."

From the overfull cupboards, they found lemonade mix and a package of chocolate chip cookies.

"We'll have this finished up tomorrow after church," said Raymond. "All that's left is the roof." He showed Katie how they used the six pane window sections and made hinges of discarded leather harness, rehung the door, and added a ramp for the hens to go through their little door.

"So, make sure you're holding onto the windows when you turn the wood latch 'cause the hinges are on the bottom so they'll fall downward. Instead of buying hardware, everything has a wood turn latch. I made a section of four nesting boxes I'm just going to nail them up before I leave so Ruth can stuff them. After that, all you need is the roof and chickens."

After Raymond and the boys left, Katie and Ruth inspected the tiny building. Having been raised thrifty, Katie appreciated the time spent figuring out how to use what was on hand as opposed to running to the hardware store. She couldn't help smiling.

"We should paint it," said Ruth.

"Huh?" said Katie, suddenly aware of what she was doing. It wasn't in her plan to get involved in anything more permanent than selling and getting out. Painting was approving. She turned away. "That, lady, is on you."

Katie had put a roaster on to cook. While she basted and peeled potatoes she watched Ruth going in and out of the hen-house. The cats followed investigating this new phenomenon. Katie wondered where someone got chickens.

"Ruth," she called out. "Can you look around and see if you can find me two old buckets or pails, or even three-pound coffee cans? Just leave them out there and come in to supper." It was past feeding time for the cats. Several had abandoned Ruth to sit in the kitchen watching Katie expectantly. Shooing them away didn't work. Katie was sure they knew their silent stare made her nervous.

"You have to wait," she explained. "It's not my job."

While they ate, Ruth reported she'd found pails in the barn and left them outside. Also, the kittens were holding their own. When she finally quieted, Katie told her about the sheriff's visit at the feed store.

"You didn't say anything to anyone did you?" she asked.

"No." Ruth carefully laid her knife and fork down. "He drives out here every couple of days." She looked over her shoulder toward the road. "I think he always makes sure I see him, you know, racing the engine just loud enough to be heard, driving down the barn lane and then back. That sort of thing."

Katie also laid aside her utensils, her appetite was gone. When she had asked Stan why Rick would specifically mention Al Lewis, Stan had replied Al had a reputation.

"Al's got a nasty temper, did time at Windsor State Penitentiary," said Stan. He leaned against the counter, considering the open doorway. "Maybe Rick's trying to tell you that sometimes the apple doesn't fall far from the tree."

* * *

At dawn, Katie was out in the yard with a wheelbarrow and a shovel digging up the clothesline post. She was wiggling the second one free when she smelled wood smoke. Startled, she looked from the woods to the barn to the house. A curl of smoke rose from the chimney.

"Breakfast," Ruth called. At Katie's raised eyebrow, Ruth nodded toward the gas range. "Out of gas." Another expense she didn't want to contemplate.

Katie dug the post holes wider and deeper, placed the buckets in the holes and the poles in the buckets. Then she mixed Sakrete she'd picked up the previous day at the feed store. With Ruth's help, she got the poles upright, surrounded by Sakrete and tied down. Katie had also bought a new coil of rope.

Ruth was rescuing clothespins from the line Katie had cut off and tossed to the side when Raymond Dean pulled in. He parked beside the clothesline, his truck filled with pieces of corrugated tin and ladders.

"Hope we're not parked on the septic system," he laughed.

"It won't be a joke if we are," replied Katie. She stayed to help pass tin up to Raymond and Davie, who had arrived with him. While they worked Raymond talked about Irma. The fond memories made Katie's heart swell with longing. Her eyes drifted to Ruth, still near the clothesline and examining rocks. Periodically she'd drop one in her sweater pocket. *What the...,* Katie's thoughts were cut off by something Raymond said.

"I'm sorry Raymond," she said. "Say that again."

Raymond was just coming down the ladder, and he turned toward her upturned face. "I said, I wasn't sure if Irma paid the taxes before she passed. I'd just given her the money a few days before and taxes are due the end of the week."

The heart, so full a moment earlier, shriveled. She was willing to bet the money that was in the checking account she had been banking on for bills was the tax payment. Raymond missed the crestfallen look on her face because he'd turned toward the blue and white pickup that came to a stop next to where they were standing.

Seated in the driver's seat was Rick, a wide grin on his face. On the passenger side Ruth was looking through the truck at him.

"Looks like I got here just in time," he said, climbing out. "You said you were getting a coop, and I went to the livestock auction last night. Guess what I bought?"

"CHICKENS!" yelled Ruth. Releasing the tailgate with a bang, she grabbed the wooden crate by the side and tried to drag it toward her.

"Here, here," laughed Rick. "Let me get that." Raymond's boy ran over to grab a side and they carried the crate into the coop. "Well, seeing as there's already hay in the boxes, all we need is water and we're setting up housekeeping."

Ruth had rescued a metal basin the same time she'd gotten the buckets and using the hose still stretched across the grass filled the basin then slowly carried it into the coop.

"Open the crate, they'll get out by themselves," said Raymond. "Don't let them outside for three or four days so they'll know where they live." He and his son drove off.

Katie reached in her back pocket for her wallet.

"Nope," said Rick. "Not happening."

"Lunch then?" she asked.

"Lunch it is."

After washing, Katie made a small hot fire in the woodstove to heat vegetables and brew coffee in Irma's old metal percolator. Outside she could hear Rick laughing as Ruth extracted the hens from the crate which went back in his truck.

"We got three Rhode Island Reds and one Plymouth Rocky," Ruth announced when she came in.

"Gonna be hot in here with a fire," Rick said.

"I think we're out of gas," said Katie. "I'll let it go out as soon as the coffee perks."

Rick went outside. Katie heard him taping the gas cylinder with a stone, then he crossed by the window. She heard a deeper clunk, clunk from the lean-to covering the two-hundred-and-seventy-five-gallon oil tank.

"No oil either." Rick came back in the kitchen.

Katie wasn't fast enough to stop her shoulders from bowing.

"How bad is it?" he asked.

"Bad." She was saved from going on as Ruth came rushing in.

"One hen is already in the box," she enthused. "I'm going to call her Gertie."

Sunday dinner was cold sliced chicken and hot Bisquick biscuits Katie mixed up. Rick carried in one of the porch chairs and they talked about antics he and Katie's Poppa had gotten into.

"Remember when we replaced the hopper?" he asked. Turning to Ruth, he said, "There was a small crack in the toilet's base, and the floor had rotted out. We got a new toilet, figured it'd only take the afternoon to fix the floor, swap out the toilets, and install the pedestal sink Irma wanted. A week later we'd replaced the whole bathroom floor, laid new linoleum, and put down new kitchen floor right up to those cabinets." He leaned back, laughing

46

loudly.

Katie laid on the table, tears running down her cheeks as she laughed. "Even the kitchen sink had to come out while they worked. Gram was so mad."

"She was," Rick agreed.

Without warning, Ruth jumped up and ran through the house to the front porch. Katie watched her go while still holding tight to a stitch in her side. Rick was faster.

"Car out front," he said.

They arrived at the front door just in time to see the sheriff backing his car in, his eyes on Ruth holding onto the railing. From this angle, neither Rick's truck nor Katie's car was visible from the driveway. The sheriff jerked upright when they appeared. Pushing past Katie, Rick went down the stairs.

"Can I help you, Martin?" Rick's big voice boomed.

"Nope," stuttered Martin. "Just out riding around." He pulled back onto the dirt road, raising dust as he went. Rick had stepped out into the middle of the road. Katie was sure Martin could see him in the rearview mirror.

Standing on the step below Ruth, Rick put his hands on her shoulders.

"Listen girlie," he said, voice softer than before. "He comes back, or someone else you don't know pulls in the drive, you don't come outside, okay? Promise me?"

"I promise," she whispered.

"Okay then." His smile was back. "How about a cup of coffee and pie? You do have pie?"

"We have chocolate chip cookies," said Ruth.

"Then we'll have that." Rick waited for Ruth to go back into the house. "Something's not right there," he said, nodding after Ruth. "She has medical needs, prescriptions."

Katie thought about the empty pill bottles telling Rick about them and Ruth's careless act with the scissors before going upstairs to get the basket. Rick put the three bottles in his pocket.

"I'll take care of these," he said. "I need you to promise me when she runs out, you'll tell me. This silly confused woman that you're seeing now, isn't

Ruth. Not the woman I know."

"Gram would be pleased you were taking an interest in someone she'd taken care of."

"Irma and Fred were the best friends in the world a man could have," said Rick reaching for the screen door. "I loved them dearly. But Ruth, well, she's the one who got away. Picked a guy from another town and I wasn't smart enough to rescue her. All these years she's been here and I've been trying to court her. It's like trying to kiss the moon."

Katie watched Rick's back move away across the room. She had thought from the way Stan talked Rick had been chasing Irma. All the time, his interest had been Ruth. A smile crept back onto her face.

Guess you just never know, she thought.

* * *

During the late afternoon, while the Dean's and Katie had been working on the hen-house, another pair of eyes watched. From the other side of the orchard, the watcher lowered binoculars, irritated to see the ruined coop replaced. When Rick appeared, the watcher stamped in disgust.

"I know where you work, old man," cussed the watcher. "What are you doing here? Can't stay away from where your girlfriend used to live? Idiot."

The watcher slunk away, knowing the more people hanging around the farm, the more care they were going to have to use.

Chapter Six

"If the sheriff and heaven only knows who else is going to be checking on us here, we'd better get our ducks in order," Katie told Ruth at breakfast. "I'm leaving a list of people for you to call this morning, electric, telephone, stuff like that. Tell them I'm settling Gram's estate. There's a list of questions to ask so I'll know what to do."

Ruth paled.

"You can do this, Ruth," said Katie. "I know you can. Just tell them you're helping me collect information because I'm at work, okay?" Though to Ruth, Katie's request sounded like a plea for help, for Katie it was a chance to test the other woman's abilities. It would also signal to anyone who checked that she was doing exactly what she had told the sheriff. Later, she would compare Ruth's results with the comprehensive instructions Wilkins had provided. If Ruth couldn't follow simple instructions then Katie needed to be ready to find a home or facility to move the older woman to.

Katie had her own list of tasks to complete. At noon she drove over to the old high school, which was now the town hall. Multiple municipal offices shared the building, including the sheriff's office. She parked where the sheriff could see the car from his windows. The town clerk was sympathetic to Katie's loss and helped get information regarding the taxes, change of ownership documentation, and providing vehicle registration forms and the form for a driver's license transfer. Katie's head was swimming at the number of forms, but she wanted to be ready when it came time to sell the farm.

"I knew your mom," said the woman who was the same age Katie's mother would have been, "and your grandmother. You come from good stock. It was a terrible shame and there was…some talk." Her eyes drifted to the door that Katie had already considered as being the second entrance to the sheriff's office. She waited, but the woman didn't say anymore.

"I tell you what," said the clerk once again the efficient town employee. "You take these forms, get them filled out and dropped off. I'll get started on the deed paperwork. I'll call if I need anything else. Here's your tax receipt. Hold on to it."

"With both hands," said Katie as she left.

She only had a few minutes left for lunch. When she opened her bag, she found three prescription bottles and an apple had been added to her lunch. She thanked Rick and worked silently beside him until her shift ended at one-thirty.

As soon as she got home, she started Ruth on the medicines.

"You didn't need to get these Katie," said Ruth, eyeing the bottles lined up on the table. "I'm fine without them, I don't even need to take them every day."

Katie listened to Ruth but remembered what Rick had said. If the cost of the medicines had been the reason Ruth was no longer taking them, then her reference to needing them only occasionally was a lie. Having already read the labels, Katie knew the instructions were daily with food. Perhaps she should keep track of how often Ruth would take the pills.

"Let's keep these in the kitchen cupboard for a few days until it's a regular habit for you," Katie said.

Ruth agreed. With that out of the way she presented her notes from the telephone calls, all written in clear cursive. While Katie was looking over the pages, Ruth took a small bowl from the refrigerator and placed it in front of Katie. Two speckled brown eggs lay in the bowl. At Katie's surprised gasp, Ruth danced around the kitchen. Cats disappeared in all directions.

Katie spent a boring afternoon sorting through the list of duties and paperwork in Mr. Wilkins's file folder. After reading the last notice, Katie sighed in relief but didn't give herself a moment to think before she pulled the final stack of Irma's papers out of the kitchen cupboard, dumping it into a box. Sitting in the living room with the cardboard box in front of her, she went through the stack page by page. By the end of the evening, she had found another forty dollars, mostly in five-dollar bills. There were also several more newspaper articles, including a recent photo of a tall, wide-shouldered man smiling at the camera. He had his arm around a brassy blonde who leaned into the photo over his paunch. The caption identified Lawrence French and his wife.

"He doesn't look like he does much real work, does he?" she asked LG, who was lying at her feet. Wetting her lips, she addressed Ruth.

"Were you collecting rocks Sunday?" she asked.

"Yes," said Ruth, extracting Simon from her ball of yarn. "I wanted some smallish ones to put in the bottom of my flower pots, why?"

"No reason," said Katie. *Fist size isn't exactly smallish,* she frowned. Just before dark, she walked down through the orchard to the family cemetery.

She had been there many times in the first years after her grandfather had passed away, then one day decided it was too painful to stand before the granite stone. Now, here in the tiny fenced area, she could see a small place where new grass and tiny wild violets were just beginning to grow back in. She had returned to the hayfield a day prior. There Katie had also found points of new hay breaking the ground, covering any clue that might have remained.

"Your letter surprised me, Gram. I admit it," she said aloud. "The whole mess feels like you knew something bad was going to happen. How can that be? Were you just scared? I can't figure out how to sort this out, and I don't want to stay that long. Ruth says the sheriff and the doctor can't be trusted, and to be honest, I'm not sure about Ruth either. I don't know what to do. This isn't anything I know about." Sudden unwanted tears flowed down her cheeks. "I love you, Gram. I never expected to not see you again. Please don't desert me. If you left some kind of clue, why can't I find it?" Unable to stop herself, she gave over to grief, allowing tears to flow and finally kneeling on the ground reciting the half-remembered prayers learned at Sunday school back when she attended Saint Jude's church. It had been her natural spot to sit between her grandparents. She knew then that was where she belonged.

Behind her, Ruth's voice carried on the wind calling her name. Katie, rubbing her face dry, as she trudged back up the rise through the waving grass and the sweet smell that evoked memories and made her feel like a child again.

"You didn't say where you were going. I got scared." Ruth's shoulders bowed; her hands clung to each other.

"It's okay, Ruth. I was just taking a little walk."

"Did she tell you what to do?" Ruth asked.

Shocked at the other woman's question, Katie could only stare, her knees quaking.

"I ask her too," said Ruth gently. "I'm sure she'll let us know when she's ready." After patting Katie's arm, she took the doll bottles into the cat room to feed the kittens.

* * *

When Katie returned the next morning after having worked only four hours, she noticed small white popcorn-shaped flowers covering the lawn. Bending to pick one, she realized the grass had grown tall. She constructed a sliced chicken and spinach sandwich for lunch, which she followed with an argument with the lawnmower. The machine was old, dirty, and didn't want to start. The late summer heat was relentless, and she was sweating profusely by the time she started mowing. At mid-afternoon, Raymond's wife, Grace, walked up the road with a woman whose resemblance was striking, and a small child.

"Hi Katie," she called. "My mother wants a cat, we heard you had kittens."

Ruth had shown the kittens to the boys the day the hen-house had been installed, one of them must have told their mother.

"Yes." Katie smiled, relieved someone was interested. "We have kittens."

"I get to pick out Grammy's new kitty." The little girl smiled, showing the loss of both of her front teeth. She was a healthy-looking farm girl with tight braids of dark brown.

"This way to the kittens," said Ruth. "Their names are Marmalade, Tangerine, and Zest."

Katie laughed. This was the first she had heard about the kitten's names.

"Well then, there you go." Katie pointed the way for the little girl into the cat room.

"The garden is coming in fast," said Grace. "I brought you some vegetables. I hope you're okay with that?"

"Fresh vegetables? How could that be wrong?" asked Katie.

Grace handed her a brown paper bag containing summer squash, zucchini, and tiny beets with greens. Katie could feel green beans stuffed in the bag's bottom.

"Holy cow," gaped Katie. "This is a lot of just extras."

Grace moved away from the table where Ruth and the little girl were writing a note giving ownership of Marmalade to Grace's mother.

"Ruth has been coming down a few hours almost daily and helping me in the garden. She always does. I usually pay her with vegetables, eggs, sometimes butter and cheese from my goats. She told me she won't need eggs anymore. She was very excited."

"You have goats too?" Katie had never given a thought to how Ruth spent her time. She believed it was the other woman's private business. But this was another way the two older women had survived.

"Yes, they started as a 4H project and now they're a thriving business. The cheese I make in my churn house sells in two different stores." Grace blushed at her own obvious plug. "My mom helps me out. Ruth wants to learn but lately she's been sort of, I don't know, vague."

Turning away to put the bag on the sink drainer, Katie said, "There was an issue with some medicine she was supposed to be taking. I think we might have it straightened out now." It was almost the truth.

"That's good," Grace was smiling at her niece whose chin lay on Ruth's arm as the older woman read the note back.

"Ah, Grace." Katie nervously wet her lips. "I tried to convince Ruth to visit the doctor, she won't go. If the medicine doesn't make everything right, I'm not sure what to do."

Grace moved a step closer, lowering her voice she said, "The doctor here in town, right? I know she had an argument with him after Irma died. And, Katie, she told me what she thinks happened. Raymond and I are wondering if she might be closer to right than people think. There's been a lot of traffic on the road this summer. We take the kids to a younger doctor in Monkton. How about I make an appointment for Ruth? If she won't go with you, maybe she'll go with my mother. They get along well together."

Katie could only nod because the girl ran over and threw her arms around Grace's legs.

"We have to go home," she said breathlessly, "and make a bed and get cat food and toys. In three weeks, Marmalade is coming to live with Grammy!"

"One down, two to go," smiled Ruth waving goodbye.

"Which reminds me," said Katie. "I've been watching that old black cat you carry around. The skinny one. Is something wrong there?"

"That's Shade, she's just old, maybe sixteen, and her vision is fading fast. I don't let her go outside because I'm worried that she won't be able to find her way home."

"Is that why she yowls like a banshee?"

"She does that when she can't find me, or someone else to comfort her." Ruth's whole frame shook with her sigh. "Time for her is short. She shouldn't be alone. None of us should."

"That's true." A shudder ran along Katie's arms as the cold finger of a breeze touched her. She looked over her shoulder, but found nothing.

"Remember, most of these cats are old, eventually they pass away." Ruth spoke as though Katie were a small child who had never experienced death. While Katie wondered for the umptieth time if Irma's cat rescue project had actually developed into a feline nursing home, Ruth sorted the vegetables.

"You know with what we have here and what I brought home yesterday, I bet we could can some pints." Her eager happiness was infectious.

"Sure," agreed Katie grinning. She was still smiling as she added, "I have no idea how to do that."

"I'll teach you. And Irma has an old Betty Crocker Cookbook that tells you all you need to know about caning and making pickles."

54

"I have to finish mowing the lawn before the lawnmower forgets how to work," said Katie, loath to finish the sweaty chore. She was even more unwilling to put it off and have to give up another afternoon.

"Okay, can you get the canning kettle and a box of pint jars out of the barn first so I can wash them? It's all stored down there off to the right if you go in the milking parlor door."

Money for groceries was tight, so Katie had gone through all the cupboards and inventoried the freezer contents and jars of vegetables in the basement. The number of pints and quarts had been surprising considering there didn't appear to be a garden plot near the house. Grace's garden explained everything. Humming a tune stuck in her head as it spun around like a carousal, Katie slid open the heavy plank door and walked into the milking parlor. Though the collection of boxes and bags surrounding her didn't faze her, the enormous piles of assorted junk she encountered entering the barn did.

"What in the world?"

Obviously, Chet was not the only person who rescued items from the dump. Irma must have as well. Household items, tools, bags of mixed discarded treasures were stacked between the stanchions. In some places, the piles reached nearly to the ceiling. Everywhere she looked stuff had been dumped in no apparent order. Over the top of the stacks, Katie could see cabinets and larger furniture crowding the wide barn doors at the far end of the barn. On the end that was collapsing, someone had nailed boards into place, sealing that third of the barn from the area where Katie stood.

Several minutes passed before she remembered to search for the cobalt canning kettle. By the time she walked into the house, she had decided it was time to have a talk with Ruth.

Ruth, however, had donned an apron and was industriously washing vegetables. There was a cutting board on the table with a long chopping knife beside it. The glint of the blade froze Katie's words in her throat. In all the time she had been going through the cupboards, she hadn't unearthed that knife. When Ruth turned, she took the stricken look on the younger woman's face as something else.

"You hadn't been in the barn, had you?" She wiped her hands on a dishtowel. "Irma collected things, she wanted to open a store, earn money for the bills. She used to say all that stuff came to us free so she could sell it for small money and take care of more cats, or maybe she said the vet bills, I don't remember."

"We're going to haul all that trash back to the dump," said Katie, anger in her voice. Setting down the kettle and box, she went back outside. With one vicious yank, the lawnmower started. Katie mowed until she ran out of gas, leaving a small area near the coop. If she couldn't finish it, maybe the hens would.

Sweaty and exhausted by the heat and still enraged, she stalked through the kitchen and into the bathroom.

"You can let the chickens out," she growled.

The bathroom in the farmhouse held what Katie considered the most wondrous tub in the world. Large, made of cast iron and perched on lion claw feet, it had a sloping back just right for leaning against while soaking in hot water and lavender bubbles. Irma's favorite. Forced to fill the tub because of the lack of a shower, Katie eventually relaxed and sank up to her chin. The only interruption was when the door opened a few inches and a hand reached in, dropping a cotton bathrobe on the floor. The open door also let in LG, who with a graceful leap, laid in the sink watching Katie through barely open eyes.

"What?" asked Katie.

LG blinked.

"I'm sorry," Katie said to Ruth when she emerged wrapped in the soft and worn flannel. "It just seems that I'm not making any headway and more crap keeps getting shoveled in my way."

The room was heating up because a fire had been lit under the canning kettle. Ruth had a piece of newspaper on the table stacked with food scraps for the hens.

"I should have waited to build the fire," said Ruth without looking up. "While it's hot, I'll fry some bacon to have with the eggs. We can have breakfast for supper." At the door, rolled newspaper in hand, she turned back to Katie. "Don't worry about getting a little steamed. Irma and I know you're trying. We'll figure it out. Oh, and you've got no clean clothes. The ones you've been wearing are starting to smell." She went out the door, leaving it open for the line of curious felines following her.

"Aargh," Katie said through gritted teeth. Upstairs she went through Irma's dresser. Because the closet was full of paper, her grandmother's one dress hung on a hook behind the door. Katie had moved all the files downstairs. Now the dresser was mostly empty. Then Katie took time to sort through Irma's private things. There was a small jewelry box she put in her own bedroom along with everything she'd be able to wear. Old underwear, items worn beyond use, and tattered hankies were in a pile to discard. Everything else including the too-big pants and dress went back into the dresser. Repacking her grandmother's things made the job seem a little less final. She was still wearing Irma's robe when she went downstairs. She could hear the washer thumping away.

Ruth laughed at her. "When I was a kid, we only got to wear our night things downstairs if we were so sick death was imminent."

"You're real funny, you are," said Katie, trying not to laugh. "Maybe I'll put on a pair of Gram's pants and use a piece of rope for a belt." It felt good to laugh until Katie remembered she wasn't supposed to be forging friendships, but instead getting ready to cut free.

Ruth laughed again. "That would be good for here, Katie, but you might not want to go into town that way."

Irma's pants were corduroy or duc. Katie went with duc which was still heavy and hot. She removed a narrow leather belt from one of Irma's drawers, and though she felt like a true hillbilly; she was at least wearing clean clothes. As she walked around the yard, she found other chores to do. Ruth hung out the laundry, then headed down the road to the Dean farm carrying a milk bottle. Katie sat on the kitchen stoop. Across the side lawn, the hens scratched around in the tall grass she hadn't mowed. When one of the stalking cats got near, the offended hen would lead a squawking retreat up the ramp into the coop.

Deciding the stoop was a comfortable place to sit for the evening and ponder, Katie returned to her grandmother's room, returning with two paper sacks of old newspapers. One bag provided nothing more than burnable refuse. The other contained not only a single month's worth of the Burlington Free Press daily's, but also the corresponding time period of a small local weekly covering Parentville, Charlotte, and Monkton.

An obituary for George Beauregard caught her eye, causing her to return to all she had discarded. Using the kitchen shears, she trimmed out everything relevant. With only those pieces before her, she read each article, placing them in chronological order. The front door opened. Ruth was home.

Katie walked into the living room carrying two glasses of lemonade. Ruth accepted one gratefully as she sat on the couch fanning herself with a magazine. Even with the sun sinking beyond the mountain to the west, the air was still sullen and heavy. Cats lined the window sills or lay with their bellies pressed on the cool linoleum.

"So, Ruth," Katie began.

Ruth lifted her hair off the back of her neck to press the cool glass against her skin.

"There have been things said to me, some by you, that lead me to wonder about George's death." This was the first time Katie had raised the subject directly. She expected Ruth to react sharply, but the older woman continued to sip lemonade. Lamplight created a shadowed field on her face, changing the emotions Katie saw there from moment to moment.

"And you want to know my side, right?" Ruth asked. She no longer sounded like the meek woman but spoke with conviction. "Don't get embarrassed, I figured eventually we'd get to this." She spent a few minutes collecting her thoughts. "I was working at the store in the center of town. Beauregard's. I'd been there almost a year working in the office some and out front. I enjoyed it. So much to do, ever-changing, lots of people all the time. There were three or four guys I'd go out with now and then, one I thought might be serious, but he never stepped forward. Then I met George. He and my boss were half-brothers and George had been off in the army. I didn't remember him at all though he said he'd seen me before."

"He was so, I don't know, debonair. He smoked cheroots instead of

Marlboros, sipped whiskey, not beer, his trousers were pressed, he was always, always clean-shaven. I was at a dance in the high school gym and he stepped up and asked if I'd like a coffee. Not a coke, coffee. He didn't dance, so we sat in the bleachers talking. He'd done his military time, gotten a job over at the furniture factory, and was ready to settle down. Then he came out and asked me if I wanted to marry him. Just like that. I said yes without so much as a second thought. We got married two weeks later by the justice of the peace. My mother was so angry."

"I kept working, and for a few years, everything was good. Then George suggested maybe the reason I hadn't gotten pregnant was because I worked so hard, so I quit. I never did get pregnant. Maybe ten years later George got hurt at work. Then again, a few years after that. The second time they let him go. His temper had been getting rough what with the pain and everything and he said I wasn't helping. The first time he hit me, he swore it was the pain making him do it. After the second time, the third time, eventually he stopped making excuses. I wanted to go back to work. He wouldn't let me. After a while, he didn't let me go out at all except to the clothesline. My folks had both passed away. I was alone."

Katie opened her mouth to tell Ruth she didn't need to say more, but Ruth was already talking.

"He broke my arm, my nose several times, and I think maybe cracked my ribs. Irma came across me when she was out trapping feral cats. She became my secret friend and urged me to leave. I wouldn't go. Irma didn't abandon me, she just kept coming back. The doctor gave me pills to help me sleep after I *tripped* and broke my arm. One night after a particularly bad fight where he'd punched me enough to blacken both my eyes and my guts felt like they were bruised to hell and back, I took some pills and went to bed. When I woke up in the morning George was laying there, dead. His eyes wide open and that knife stuck in his chest." Ruth held her hand against the place the knife had been. "There were police, the doctor, a lawyer I think, and Irma coming to get me. George had half-brothers and step-brothers he never seemed to get along with. His half-brother that owned the store held the note on our house. When the judge said I was innocent, he called the note. I had nowhere to go. I remember telling Irma I didn't want to taint her reputation with my bad luck and she laughed at me."

For the first time since she'd started talking, Ruth looked directly at Katie.

"I didn't kill him, Katie. I swear to God on Irma's grave, I didn't." She got up with Shade in her arms and left the room. Water was running in the tub and Katie went out in the twilight to bring in the laundry.

Chapter Seven

Taking the telephone number off the previous year's income tax form, Katie called Josh Burns Accounting the next afternoon, explained who she was, and made an appointment to sit down with Mr. Burns.

"It's slow this time of year," said the woman who took Katie's call. "Can you come in tomorrow around two?"

"Yes," said Katie. Stan would just have to understand. After getting directions, Katie called the feed store, telling Stan she'd have to leave a little earlier the next day.

"Sure," said Stan. "Take what you need, just tell Rick when you go."

"He's being nice, I feel I should give him a tip," Katie told Ruth who had been working down at the Dean farm.

"You got mail today," said Ruth. Fearfully she held up a business-size envelope with a green patch on the top signifying certified mail. "I signed for it," she added. "Should I have told the mailman no?"

"Don't worry Ruth, it's fine." Katie tried to laugh, but the tips of her shaking fingers were ice cold. Gram had always scoffed at the certified letters. She'd said registered mail was money, certified was trouble. Near the time Katie left there seemed to be a lot of certified and never any registered.

Gram's prediction proved correct. The letter was from the town of Charlotte informing Irma Roser Moore, there was now a lien in place on her property for back taxes.

"I don't get it," said Katie. "I paid the taxes; I have the receipt and I filled out all that paperwork to have the name on the deed and the tax bill changed."

Even though she didn't think she should be, Ruth was peeking over Katie's shoulder.

"Katie," she asked, "why would the town of Charlotte be collecting taxes for Parentville?"

"I don't know," said Katie. Sitting at the table, she read the letter again, running her fingers along the words. "Can I use your pencil, Ruth?" Katie circled the lien number, amount due, due date, and the parcel number. Tapping the pencil on the parcel number, she searched her memory.

"I don't think this is right. It seems to me the number on my receipt starts with RF, this is a ten-digit identifier only." She went up to her room, returning with the receipt she had received at the Parentville town office. "Well, there it is then; we somehow got somebody else's tax bill. It's a different number."

Ruth nodded in agreement. Katie put the letter in the folder with the information she had gathered to take with her when she went to talk to Josh Burns. She also confiscated a page from Ruth's three-ring binder to list questions she didn't want to forget.

At one o'clock the next afternoon, Katie drove past Fire Lane 61 on her way to Charlotte. Memory served her well. She had no trouble finding the village, and none whatsoever locating Mr. Burns' office. Main Street, Charlotte proved to be a step up from Parentville. On a central block across the street from the town hall was an old storefront where the hardware had been before they built a larger facility at the end of the street. One half of the building housed the accountant's office, complete with a tiny bell announcing her entrance.

"Everything appears to be here." Mr. Burns laid Katie's legal papers aside. "Where would you like to start?"

"With the money," said Katie.

"There is no money," said Mr. Burns.

"Exactly."

"Okay, let's see. After Mr. Moore passed away, Irma began liquidating her assets." Burns opened a side drawer and pulled out a file he must have prepared earlier. "If she could sell it, she did. Livestock, equipment, I believe she even had some old jewelry she let go. After that, it was tooth and nail. She had her earnings from the furniture factory. When they let her go, she was just old enough to collect early retirement, social security, which means at a lesser rate. She had her job with the town. I think as far as income, that was it."

"On the debit side, she made some serious errors." Burns read his notes. "She got a little cranky there for a while and wasn't open to any advice I gave her. Ah, and up to three years ago she spent a large amount of money on an investigator who I believe was tracking you."

"What?" Katie blinked.

Burns looked up closing the file. "I remember her telling me, she got quarterly reports on where you were or maybe what you were doing."

"I didn't know that."

"She also borrowed substantially to renovate the garage. Initially, she talked about opening a small cottage industry there."

"The cat room," said Katie.

"I don't know. The upshot is the loan was sold. The new owners raised the interest rate. According to Irma's last tax return, no payments had been made on the principal."

Katie's mouth went dry.

"I don't have any money. For crying out loud, I only have a part-time job." Katie stared at Burns, who stared back blandly. She had expected someone who would willingly share his wisdom or offer her some advice. The accountant appeared to believe she must have checked her smarts at the door.

Swallowing hard, Katie pushed the certified letter across the desk.

"I got this in the mail," she said, "but I paid the taxes already."

Burns looked over the letter. Holding it out to Katie, he asked, "Both of them?"

"There's two sets of taxes?" She couldn't believe what she was hearing.

"This is the Charlotte bill; did you pay the Charlotte taxes?" Burns was having a problem with Katie's inability to understand. When she didn't answer he sat back in his chair tapping a pen on the edge of the desk.

"How long has it been since you had any communication with Irma?"

"I was here about six years ago for, well, to be honest, I was just passing through. She didn't want me around. Maybe three years ago, I sent her a letter, she answered, I sent another. It was all pretty general. We corresponded every couple of months; how are you, I'm good. Then I got called back here and was told she'd been murdered."

"Couple of things," said Burns. "I'm willing to bet you've never owned anything more than maybe a car, probably never even lived in an apartment alone. There's a lot of responsibility being a property owner and you're going to be getting a crash course, because of a farm? That's a helluva lot more. Irma had two sets of property, one she got when her husband died, the other came to her as an inheritance when her brother died."

"In the fire," whispered Katie.

Burns shrugged, the reason for Maxwell's death didn't matter to him.

"There was a small amount of money and it went to inheritance taxes, funeral expenses, transfers, and I think maybe the property taxes for the first year. After that, it was all on her shoulders. I suggested she sell the property; she wouldn't hear of it. The letter you have in your hand is for that property. According to that notice, she owes for the last year and this year both."

"Ms. Took, unless you have some serious funds, you will lose the land unless you liquidate. There's a lot of new growth happening around here. There's a realtor right next door. Get someone to help you move the Charlotte property and maybe you can stay on the other one for another year."

"Also, stand up and face the facts. No one murdered Irma. I saw the police report. Someone destroyed a crop she depended on, and she succumbed to a heart attack. She wasn't young and the last time I saw her, she was pretty sour on life."

Katie stood up gathering her paperwork. She couldn't process everything Burns had said and felt confused and wanted only to leave. He allowed her to walk out the door believing like most people who have suffered a sudden tragedy. When she got her feet under herself, she'd be back. He replaced the file in the desk drawer and poured himself coffee.

Seated outside the open window at the rear of Josh Burns' office, someone else sipped coffee. The bench was a pleasant place to sit in the sun while enjoying a cigarette break. Today the voices coming through the screen had been enlightening, verifying a theory into fact.

* * *

Katie sat in the car for a long while. *Why didn't I know any of this?* She chewed on the inside of her lower lip. Her mind searching for any hint she might have missed. Then she remembered a deed dated 1969. Was that the transfer of Maxwell Roser's farm? That would have been about a year after his death, so the timing was right. At her first meeting with Attorney Wilkins, he had passed two deeds across the desk to Katie for her to look at. She had examined the top one only minutely and then, assuming the second one was a copy, hadn't read it at all. *Was that the Roser property?*

"You'd better smarten up and slow down, baby-cakes," she said aloud. "At this rate, if someone wipes out your pretty, young ass it'll be because you let them."

Outside the car, the day was hot, yet she was shivering. The urge to start the car and turn on the heater prompted Katie to move.

While Katie was sitting in the Subaru parked on Charlotte's main street, an individual exited the narrow alley between Burns' office and the post office. Snuffing out the last of a cigarette, the smoker made two passes by Katie's vehicle, noting the make of the car, the plate number, and getting a good look at Katie herself. Taking a seat on a bench near the park, the smoker lit up and waited until Katie pulled out. When the Subaru went in the opposite direction of the Parentville-Charlotte Road, the smoker left the bench. The smoker, aka the watcher, marched rigidly up the street. With clenched teeth and narrowed eyes, they entered their workplace and at their desk dialed an out-of-town telephone number.

"Okay," the watcher said. "I've run into a problem. There's a family member, a girl who's moved in and she's out asking questions."

Chapter Eight

Deciding to find the place where her grandmother had grown up before she left town that day, Katie turned on the directional and pulled into traffic. At the gas station, she got directions to Kitteridge Road, believing the site of the burned-out house would be easy to spot. It took two trips up and down the road to realize the sumac and goldenrod grove encircled with twisted wisteria vines was the remnants of a dwelling. Leaving the car parked in the vaguely clear driveway, and wearing Irma's barn boots, Katie walked around the grove. The fire had burned the house to the ground. There had been no real cellar hole, so when the vines and wild bushes took over, they covered the entire area. Turning away, she examined the out-buildings, finding the relic of an older sedan and an assortment of unidentifiable tools. A winding lane led back into the woods; Katie followed for a short distance. The lane ended at a sandy hole cut into the hillside blocked by felled trees.

Standing where the house had stood and then walking around the rest of the property didn't bring Katie any feeling of connection. She knew this was her grandmother's roots and dear to her, but for Katie, it was just an overgrown lot. She left and returned through Charlotte. No one noticed as her Subaru drove through. It was the best bit of luck Katie had all day.

Once in the house, she went directly to her room with no word to Ruth who stood in the entrance to the kitchen holding Shade. The door shut with a sharp rap, and leaning against it, Katie sank to the floor.

She'd come here ready to leave again soon after, yet the business end of the trip hadn't worked as quickly as she had imagined it would. Then somewhere after she had first crossed the town line into Parentville, her stony outlook had chipped. Without throwing a punch, Katie had fought to beat all semblance of emotion out during her time here. But familiar sights, remembered smells kept calling forth memories she'd suppressed years ago. She didn't want to care about what happened here, except that it should be over. There was no room in her plan for other people, old or new acquaintances. Ghosts haunted her, while live bodies stood in her way. She was losing her ability to see objectively. Since she had arrived, she had faced disappointment and heartache. Now despair wrapped its slimy fingers around her throat. She could feel the pressure of these unwanted emotions taking away her ability to breathe, bringing darkness into her mind, confusing the way to her objective.

At that moment, leaning against the door, Katie knew it didn't matter what she did, how hard she worked, she would lose. She'd lost before and lived through it just fine. Unfortunately, this time there was a whisper within herself saying the loss was going to be on multiple fronts, some of which she didn't yet know existed.

Above her head, the worn bronze knob turned slowly. Katie held her breath and leaned harder backwards. The door pressed against her, trying to open. She made herself a more solid obstacle. Finally, she heard the soft tread of steps moving away and the door to Ruth's bedroom close. Reaching up, Katie turned the key in the lock. On her hands and knees, she crawled to her bed and pulled the patchwork quilt off. Wrapped in the blanket that had covered her throughout her younger life, she rolled under the bed and hidden away against the wall, she wept until only sleep released her from the depression that obscured her ability to think.

Chapter Nine

Daylight came bright and shiny, but Katie felt the darkness around her keeping the glow at bay. With toast and coffee, she couldn't touch in front of her, Katie watched Ruth until the other woman sat down. LG had been waiting when Katie opened the bedroom door that morning, silently following the young woman downstairs. Now she lay draped across Katie's lap.

"Ruth." Katie cleared her throat. "The accountant's report was pretty bleak. Did you know Gram owned land in Charlotte? Maxwell's land?"

Ruth pursed her lips. "Yes, I think I did. We never talked about it. Too much pain, I think."

Katie nodded.

"Yeah, well, that seems to be a big part of the problem, that and the loan for the cat room."

"Isn't that paid off, Katie?" Ruth stopped buttering toast. She put the knife down carefully.

"Nope." The thought of mentioning money Gram had spent tracking her down hurt too much to bring up. "While I'm gone today, I'd like you to make a list of anything you can think of that Gram did to help pay the bills. It looks like I may have to sell the Charlotte farm, and even then, I don't know if I'll be able to keep this one." She hadn't meant to sound as though she was contemplating staying here. But at that moment she was too drained to explain herself.

Unable to face Ruth's stricken face a moment longer. Katie grabbed her lunch bag and left.

She hadn't been at work for more than a few minutes before Rick asked her how it had gone with Burns. Katie leaned on the forklift Rick was using to load the flatbed delivery truck and repeated what Burns said.

"It's all over, Rick," she said.

Stan had walked in while Katie was talking. Having heard most of her report, he felt his spirits falling as hers had. Cindy had spoken highly of Katie; sure, the other woman would shine in a positive light. If Katie had to leave, his wife was going to be disappointed. Now while Rick stared out at the loaded truck, and Katie up at Rick, Stan was at a loss.

"Katie," said Stan.

Katie jumped slightly, then turned.

"Get your gloves, you'll go with me for the deliveries. Dan, you work with Rick today." He went down the cement steps to the truck.

Dan, newly hired for delivering, looked after Stan. Katie spun around to Rick.

"Take your lunch," he said, never looking her way. Engaging the gearshift on the forklift, he backed away from the loading dock and the truck which was now running.

They left town via Shelbourne Road. Stan didn't address Katie's concern, instead of explaining the stack of deliveries he had handed her were in order to make a swing back to Parentville.

"From the back of the truck forward," he said. "You'll be up, tossing, make sure everything comes off. The right stuff. It all should be grouped together, but you'll be the last check."

They had finished more than half of the deliveries when Stan pulled into an empty lot. It took a moment for Katie to realize they were at the Roser property.

"Why are we here?" she asked flatly with no intention of getting out of the truck. Stan already had his door open.

"Don't take this wrong, you're a smart girl. Sometimes, however, everyone needs a second set of eyes."

They walked the same route Katie had the previous day; she pointed out what she had seen. At the sandpit, Stan climbed over the dead-fall and into the lot. He pointed. "Sand." He turned, pointing in another direction. "Mixed gravel." From there he walked further up the overgrown lot. The ground felt mushy under Katie's feet and the pine trees rose high above blocking out the sun and holding the moisture in.

"Well?" she asked when they were back in the truck.

"Thinking," he answered.

At the feed store, Dan took the truck out on another round of local deliveries while Katie returned to working with Rick.

"What happened?" he asked.

"Darned if I know," she answered. "We stopped at the Roser place."

She grabbed the top of a feed bag. There was a droop to her shoulders and the look of loss Rick hadn't seen before.

"What's for supper?" he asked. He needed time to think about what she'd said, and time to ask her candidly what her intentions were.

"I'm making meatloaf."

"I've got some venison hamburger in my cooler to stretch it," he said.

Chapter Ten

Katie left for work the next morning with a new list of errands to run, and forms to drop off at the town clerk's office before she returned home. The woman was too busy to chat and the sheriff nowhere in sight. Stopping at the doctor's office, Katie made a new patient appointment using a fictitious last name. She wasn't concerned the doctor would get angry and refuse to see her again because she planned on visiting there only one time. With Ruth's grocery list in hand, she wandered around Beauregard's until she located the owner. The man was too young to be George's brother, but maybe the brother's son. Not the guy she wanted to see. Katie considered driving by the furniture factory, but it was a sure bet no one there would talk to her if they even remembered George. Her grandmother had still been working there when Katie left home, and the girl wasn't sure how long Irma had continued with the heavy factory work. She had heard Ruth's opinion, and Rick's was no secret, what Katie needed was the insight of someone who hadn't been emotionally involved. She wanted to trust Ruth, but couldn't quite get there. All she needed was some independent third party to say the man was a brute. Or worse, that he wasn't. It was frustrating to feel as though every lead she could think of to the dead man was a dead end. Needing a few minutes to calm down before she pulled into the driveway, Katie pulled in beside the schoolhouse. She sat in her car sipping soda while trying to come up with the name of someone she could stay with when she returned to Illinois. It was a shortlist.

Her two brothers, five and seven years older than she was and raised in the home of her father's brother were, as referenced Katie, upper-middle-class white bread and milk. Her uncle hadn't been enthusiastic when she had shown up on the doorstep seven years prior. The boys were college jocks headed for jobs in the business sector where a trophy wife, two-point-five children, and a white picket fence were what they would need. There wouldn't be room in the silver-framed picture for a country high school educated, out of work, younger sister with a trashy mouth and a lesbian attitude. The uncle's wife let her stay ten days. On the last day, a taxi had pulled in to the Quiki-mart where Katie was hanging out, yelled her name, then dropped her stuff on the sidewalk before pulling away.

The Quiki-mart mama had taken pity on the girl, letting her work in the store for a few weeks until she had enough money to move out of the abandoned car in the alley and rent a room at the YWCA. The job and the room were supposed to be short-term. Katie had stayed with both for two years.

During that time, she had met Julian, who she had loved deeply and expected to spend the rest of her life with. They had flown back to New York to meet Julian's parents, rented a car, and driven to the farm. Katie had called and told Irma they were coming, but in hindsight realized she hadn't given her grandmother quite enough information.

Irma had opened the door, taken one look at the bleached blonde, African-American woman who was the love of Katie's life, and slammed the door without a word. Julian had laughed all the way back to Illinois, where she promptly dumped Katie.

"Oh child," Julian had smirked, "it just seems you're more like an appetizer than an entrée. And me? I need something more substantial."

"Well, I showed her, didn't I?" said Katie throwing the soda can in the back seat. "I was nothing then and I'm even less now." Her eyes went back to the schoolhouse and the empty place in her chest thickened. That cloudy gray place seemed to be returning more and more often.

Unwilling to face Ruth feeling the way she did, Katie drove back to the village and toward the feed store. Arriving almost at quitting time, she searched the deep, dusty shadows of the storage barn until she picked out Rick tossing bags of grain on the rolling deck for an upcoming order.

Knowing he'd be biased didn't matter. There weren't a lot of other people she could ask questions of. She walked back into the gloom.

"Rick, I need to talk to you about Ruth," Katie said.

He straightened up, looking at her, ignoring the man waiting to be tossed the next bag.

"This is a working place." He frowned. "If it ain't to do with that, it can wait till later."

So, Rick and Katie sat in his pickup in the empty employee lot. Everyone else had gone home for the day. They sipped from cans of lukewarm beer taken from a small and very dented cooler behind the seat.

"Yes, it's like Ruth said." Rick stared at the place his thumbnail tapped against the can. "I was there, I didn't ask for her hand, even when word got around that George had. I knew he was a bad seed. The bunch of them are. I didn't warn her. Years later I was at the docs when she came in all bruised, her arm hanging useless. Even then, I didn't step forward. Irma wouldn't let me, said it would make it worse. When he was found dead, we stood and waited, your Gram and me. If they had found Ruth guilty, the plan was for me to step up and tell them I did it out of love. Irma was ready to swear I'd carried on about loving Ruth for years, and after seeing her that way I was all but out of control. I'd say I got drunk and went up there, killed him, and in my drunken state had never even seen Ruth laying there. I'd keep it up until they had to believe me."

"But you didn't, right, Rick?" Katie asked. She could have been sitting in the truck with a killer, but she didn't believe she was. She trusted the old man and refused to believe he would hurt anyone. Rick had an old-fashioned way of talking when the subject was Ruth that Katie believed came from his heart. As sure as warm beer had a sour taste, Katie knew Rick would do anything for Ruth. She also knew he felt a tremendous amount of quilt because the older woman had endured so much bad when all he would have had to do was ask one question.

"No," he sighed. "I don't believe Ruth did either. Katelyn. George had a lot of enemies. He was a hard drinker, and a mean drunk. He got thrown out of every bar and tavern in the area. Blackballed by most. There were five brothers, they were all brought up nasty by a father who enjoyed beating his women. Even the boy that came to him with his second wife was an ass. There's only two left. Some of their sons are better, the one that runs the store now, but not all of them. I've learned to watch my back, you'll need to also, I bet."

Katie didn't miss the fact Rick used her full name in the weight of the conversation. She had thought George was Ruth's problem. With his death, it should have gone away.

What about revenge, fidelity? She started her car, worried she had uncovered another bucket of worms. Maybe Irma hadn't heeded the warning to watch her back. Had it been issued or had Rick just assumed she'd know to? How was she going to know? It was a cinch Ruth had told her everything she thought was relevant, and Rick was getting testy. There had to be someone else, someone who had lived here for a while, knew everyone, like, maybe... Raymond? No, too trusting. Stan!

Katie swung around in the seat to face the feed store. Stan had lived here all his life, but had gone to college in Burlington, living there, making different friends, meeting Cindy, and probably gaining a wider perspective than some of their neighbors. He had already attempted to share information. How far would he be willing to go? For the length of the ride home, she considered a conversation opener that would not alienate Stan before he divulged any pertinent facts he knew.

She pulled into the driveway, having decided to talk to both Raymond and Stan. There was a white panel truck backed into her spot, the lettering on the side declaring the owner to be Valley Wide Veterinary Services, small and large animal specialist.

The petite woman standing on the porch with Ruth had black hair that fell straight down to near her waist. When she turned, her almond-shaped brown eyes and rich brown skin tone further hinted she was not local to the area.

Ruth waved to Katie. "This is Doctor Ronnie, the vet. She came over to check the kittens and Shade."

"I'm glad you arrived to help," said the vet. "You can carry the food bags into Ruth's cat area."

Katie cocked an eyebrow. It was clear Doctor Ronnie didn't know who Katie was. And Ruth wasn't volunteering information.

"Go through this door." Doctor Ronnie directed. "You can leave them near the galvanized trash cans."

"Sure," Katie agreed. When she came out after lugging the last of the two forty-pound bags and dumping it in the can, the vet had left.

"What did she think of the kittens?" Katie asked.

"She agrees they'll be ready to go in a few weeks. She left worming medicine to use before they go." Ruth paused, then added. "There's also a copy of Irma's vet bill."

"Ew," said Katie, considering the worming. She'd deal with the bill later. "So, we owe her for the cat crunchies too?"

"No," said Ruth. "She's the holding area for the county if need be and quarterly she gets a donation of food, litter, stuff like that. Irma would take on the over-flow or special needs animals. When Doctor Veronica got her supplement, she always gave Irma two or three bags of cat chow. She dropped them off today because she was over this way. It's probably the last we'll see though."

"Then why the bill?" Katie asked. She was standing with her hands on her hips, the sun hitting the back of her head was hot, but not unwelcome. Across from her, Ruth stood, arms crossed and head bowed.

"Irma would collect extra animals, like the feral cats. She had an agreement for a rate on getting them fixed. Then she was supposed to turn them loose where she caught them. Several of them weren't feral and they're still here. Irma got behind on the bill."

Katie sighed. "Water under the bridge now." *Until I have to tell her a cat 'died', then she's going to remember I owe her money.*

Ruth didn't consider Dr. Ronnie a threat. However, whether or not Katie planned on staying, was still an issue. It was clear to Ruth; something had gone wrong that day. Katie's disappointment was on her face and in her voice. A tiny tremor of fear coiled a knot in the older woman's belly.

"Fact of life," said Ruth, hoping to move past the debt. "We should hang up some notices to let people know we have two kittens ready to go."

"Your job," said Katie. "Maybe mention we have others too. I want to walk down and talk to Raymond."

At the barn, she found milking in progress. Raymond was working in the milking parlor, so Katie took a chance he'd let her chat while following him around.

"Raymond, how soon after Gram died did you go up to the high meadow?" she asked.

"Same day," he said.

"Can you describe what you saw?"

"Do you want to know what I think happened?" Raymond stood in front of Katie; arms crossed on his chest. The gurgling milk moved through the filters unsupervised.

"I'm starting to believe my grandmother's death wasn't an accident. Ruth remembers differently than Sheriff Lewis." Saying the words elicited a chilly shudder along the outside of her arms. "You saw the same thing the sheriff, and the doctor saw, I didn't. They said she had a heart attack brought on by despair. If she got hit by a truck, there should have been broken bones, I don't know, cuts, bleeding. Even if they missed all that in a dark hayfield, wouldn't the doctor have seen that once she was in his office? And why would some idiot tear the field up?"

"Exactly my thoughts," said Raymond. "Okay, so what did I see when I got there?" Raymond rocked back and forth on his heels; head turned in the direction of the hayfield. "A vehicle with over wide tires, like maybe 285's or off-roads had been circling the field doing donuts, spinning out, jack-rabbiting. Had to be heavier than the average car. There were deep grooves, places where soil rooster-tailed away from trenches like you get if you stop then tromp on the gas to take off."

Katie nodded, watching his face while he was thinking. Raymond didn't move, not even his eyes, but he wasn't seeing Katie in front of him. A nervous tick appeared at the outer edge of his right eyebrow, and he seemed to pale under his summer tan.

"There weren't a lot of marks where the truck had gone in a straight line for any distance except right up to where Irma had been standing. The truck had been at the edge of the field, turned, the driver hit the gas hard, the truck jumped ahead, then slammed to a halt when it hit Irma. She flew fifteen or twenty feet, landed on her back or kind of sideways, her neck broken, so she died instantly." Sweat was beading on his forehead and upper lip.

"Thank you, Raymond," Katie said. "I know that wasn't easy." Her knees felt weak and her ability to walk home an impossibility. She wanted to reach out and touch his arm but was afraid she'd end up clinging to him for support.

"There's one other thing, Katie," said Raymond. He looked to the side as one of his boys entered the milking parlor. "Outside," he ordered. "Until I call you."

The boy looked confused but obeyed without hesitation.

"We knew where Irma was when she got hit because one of her boots was still standing in her tracks."

At the house, Katie mixed tuna salad, sliced fresh vegetables, and put their cold supper on the table. She also put out the last two biscuits, and Grace's goat butter. She had no taste for the food, but like her grandmother had to keep her hands busy. All the years she'd been on her own, she'd worked in and out of foodservice. She cooked with her heart, fed from her soul, and took comfort in her ability to satisfy the needs of others.

Unsure what had happened to Katie at the Dean farm, Ruth sat at the table chattering about her day, hoping to raise Katie's spirits.

"You know your poppa wouldn't eat tuna," she said. "He said it was cat food."

"And Gram wouldn't eat egg salad," said Katie, "because she thought it was a sneaky way to disguise bad mayonnaise."

"Maybe tomorrow we'll have enough eggs for egg salad. I think there's a jar of old mayonnaise."

They both laughed.

While washing dishes, Ruth saw Katie heading up the lane. LG and one of the tiger cats trailed behind. Though darkness was still hours away, varmints willing to consume a domestic cat would be on the hunt soon. Stepping outside, Ruth called the cats back, shaking a jar with treats inside to tempt them. It was a trick Irma used. The cats knew the jar held a yummy snack they would get if they came when called. Katie didn't stop walking until she was past the meadow and into the woodlot. The Deans only came as far as the meadow entrance to hay so where she was walking now saplings had grown in over the seventeen years since Poppa had stopped clearing. She had to walk around the larger ones, unable to bend them aside. It would be almost impossible for a truck to have driven in from over the mountain.

Twittering birds and sunlight nosing to the ground from between thickly leaved boughs carried her back in time. Poppa had come up here with the tractor skidding out hardwoods he would cut and split over the winter, keeping a year ahead on the firewood. In the spring they tapped a few of the maples. During the holidays they cut their own Christmas tree. Poppa let her scramble over the slate ledges, finding Lady Slippers, salamanders, and chasing chipmunks.

"Look," he'd admonish, "and leave. No picking or injury by your hand." In the fall he'd harvest a deer to feed them through the winter, but that was all. He was a gentle farmer, revering the land and honoring its bounty.

"I'll never be the person you were, Poppa," whispered Katie, "but I'll always know my place." She left the woodland chapel and stepped into the meadow's wide entrance.

Walking carefully among the green shoots, she moved to the center of the field. There was no way now to know where Irma had been standing. Katie could only hope the enlightenment she was expecting would find her. She turned like a windmill, waiting. Ruth said they'd heard a truck, but she said nothing about a vehicle driving past the farm. Was there another way?

"If it didn't come over the mountain from Charlotte, then from where?" She walked around the outside of the field and found a place where the ragweed and thistle had been crushed and though the weedy plants were righting themselves now, there were still places showing some damage. The track led to the north, angling eastward as she descended toward LaPlatte's Brook. The uneven ground made walking difficult. When she stopped to rest, she realized she could see an old granite marker to her left. Katie's jaw dropped. She was standing below the family plot and her own orchard. The trespassers had driven to the meadow along the northeast boundary of the farm. Not far past that point she could see a place just made for a truck to have crossed the brook. The area on the other side was woody but recently thinned, possibly all the way to the road beyond. She could see the frames of new houses going in, roofs of others. During Katie's youth, another farm had stood on the far side of the brook. That house and big red barn had been transformed into a housing development. Most likely from the proximity of one house to the other, for people from the city bringing their urban sprawl outward. She turned back, cutting up the hill past the cemetery and through the orchard. From the brook straight up the rise and into the orchard, deer had parted the grasses, leaving a faint path for her to follow.

As she walked along, Katie replayed Raymond's description of the site. Was it possible for only one vehicle to have done so much damage? Would Raymond be able to remember if there were two sizes of tire tracks? No one had mentioned photographs, measurements, or any other evidence collection. She groaned at the thought. How could the sheriff believe the destruction of the field and Irma's death were not connected?

Ruth had put the cats to bed and retired herself by the time Katie got back to the house. She took a bath and crawled between the sheets, wiser, but no closer to an explanation. Sleep took a long time to come with Katie tossing and turning. LG jumped up on the dresser to sleep in peace.

Katie's plan for the next day after she finished at the feed store was to decide what to do about the mess in the barn. Then if time allowed, finish the boxes of papers in Irma's closet. She arrived home shortly after Ruth, who had made egg salad sandwiches with thick slices of tomato for lunch. Determined to finish at least one project, Katie started with the closet and was just finishing the last box when the mail truck pulled in. The driver blew the horn. Ruth, cleaning on the first floor, went out to the box. She came upstairs with a manila envelope addressed to Katie.

"The mailman wanted to know about delivering your mail here," Ruth said. "There's a card for you to fill out if you want to receive mail."

"Yeah, I'd better do that," said Katie, opening the envelope. Inside she found a note from Wilkins and two certified copies of the farm deed which she read through this time. She found one was for the farm in Parentville and the other for the property in Charlotte that she felt would eventually be her undoing. "There's a court hearing on the transfer next week. If I want to contest any of the transfer, I should go. Why would I contest it?" She looked at Ruth.

"I dunno."

"Other than that, it all goes through, he contacts me via the mail, and the town gets what they need." Katie shrugged her shoulders. "It all seems cut and dried to me." She shoved the papers back into the envelope. Tossing the mailman's card on the bed, she picked up another magazine to flip through. She didn't find more money as she went along, but there was a newspaper article about the house fire that had taken Irma's brother's life.

"I remember visiting him," Katie told LG and her three feline friends, all of whom stretched out on Irma's bed. "We'd drive over to Charlotte, Gram always brought food. He was a quiet guy, worked in a garage or something, I think. He always seemed to smell like gas or motor oil, lived alone in the family home. Gram and I went to the funeral the last winter I was here. There weren't many there, pitiful, I heard someone say. We left right after that, never even went to the meal."

LG stretched out, open claws reaching in Katie's direction. Katie extended her hand, and even though the sharp tips touched her, they didn't hook in.

"Yeah," Katie agreed, "I guess that means we're family now, at least through the winter when we'll probably freeze our butts off. I bet you want to be the bossy older sister?" It took three trips down the stairs to take all the papers out to the burn heap. On the kitchen table was the rest of the mail. A Sears and Roebuck catalog, a grocery flyer, and some bills addressed to Irma. One was the shut-off notice for the telephone, the other the final notice on the electric.

Katie poured the last of the cold coffee out of the pot. Ruth was out of sight somewhere, probably in the barn, and the house was quiet. There were cats sleeping on the window sills and the porch. Little orange balls of fluff were curled up against their adopted mama in Katie's rocker. Taking the filled-out address card in hand, Katie went out to the mailbox. Just below the name Moore and above the flag arm, someone had painted **TOOK** in even block letters. The paint was still wet and shiny.

"I guess that makes it official," she said.

Chapter Eleven

Katie walked down to the barn, then around the outside, surveying the structure, looking for defects. Besides the sunken rear corner, there were some missing windows, lots of peeling paint, and high above the haymow doors were all open. She noticed the low door on the backside Poppa called the pig door was open, the top hinge pulled slightly out of the door frame. There was a short concrete ramp leading to the ground. Because the door was warped and hanging crookedly, the bottom was wedged in place on the ramp. At one time there had been a pigsty here and a space beneath the barn where the pigs could get out of the sun. Someone, probably Irma, had tacked boards over the opening. Around the outer side, the wooden fencing was tumbling down.

Ignoring everything on the first floor, Katie climbed the slatted ladder to the mow, pushing the trapdoor open and letting it drop with a bang that sent birds flying.

There were four mow openings, each set in a little peak. The heavy doors were constructed to slide in place if the weather turned. Each door moved slightly when she put her shoulder to it. Other than some rotted hay and piles of bird poop, the mow, two stories high and built to hold a winter's worth of feed for a milking herd, was empty. Katie left the doors open to vent. She climbed down and found a push broom to sweep the bad hay out. No reason to cause rot, she surmised. Having wasted all the time she could, she returned to the first floor.

The only place there seemed to be any organization was the milking parlor. On the deep end of the main barn near the free stalls, someone had dismantled one set of stanchions, stacking the metal pieces against the back wall. Rust leaked through the whitewash of the stacked metal. A cardboard box filled with bolts, screws, and small pieces lay disintegrating on the floor.

"And why?" Katie asked aloud, toeing a holding bar.

"To sell for the metal, by the pound," said Rick.

Katie swung around. "It's not five yet," she said. "Shouldn't you be working? And stop sneaking up on me."

"Slow day so I knocked off early," he said. "I brought supper for us and the squawkers, that is, if I get an invite. I didn't sneak, you just didn't hear me. I'm quiet like a mouse, or an owl, or I know, a wolf!"

Katie laughed at his attempt to look like a dangerous predator.

"You're always invited," she said aloud, then thought, *You did too sneak.*

"Come on up to the house, see what Santa brought you." Rick turned away, waving for her to follow.

Near the kitchen door one of the empty gas cylinders laid on the ground.

"I gotta take the empty back with me," Rick said. "I had to make a deposit on the one I brought. You also need to find something different for the cracked corn because the bucket belongs to the feed store."

"Rick," said Katie. "You can't do this. I don't have cash in hand to pay you back right now. Or for the corn either."

"Corn is the waste from a split bag. If I hadn't swept it up, mice and pigeons would have just eaten it all. We need fewer mice down there. Ruth's got her notebook out and is starting a credit page for me." Chuckling, he opened the kitchen door allowing Katie to proceed before him.

Sure enough, Ruth was sitting at the kitchen table with a 3-ring binder open before her.

"I'll light the pilot light on the stove, then we're going to have a business meeting," said Rick. "After that, I'm thinking we could cook up the pork chops I brought and some of those new potatoes in Ruth's tote."

Ruth had a collection of cloth tote bags she took with her when she went down to Dean's. When she came home, she always brought weeds she'd pulled for the chickens to eat, less than perfect vegetables, and often something from the churn house. Today a large section of chocolate cake with fudge frosting lay on a plate covered with plastic wrap.

"Oh my god, I could eat the whole thing," said Katie, eyeing the cake. "We need to come up with a way to pay back all this."

"It's for us to share," pouted Ruth. Katie patted her shoulder on the way to the bathroom and a wash.

"Now about this business meeting," she said when she returned, bangs still wet against her forehead.

"It's like this," said Rick before Ruth got started. "For years Irma went to yard sales poking around, taking the cheap and anything free. She picked up stuff left at the curb outside houses and collected from the dump when Chet wasn't looking. You've been in the barn, seen that mess, right? Well, there's got to be something you can sell in there. Look in the paper, people sell all kinds of stuff in the classified section."

Katie rubbed her hands across her face, considering Rick's words.

"Classified ads cost money and you can't write an ad that just says junk. To be honest, I have no idea what is out there, but most of it is, well, not worth a lot. You said the metal can go as salvage; I can take the stanchions apart after I get them unburied. You also said Gram went to yard sales. That would be easier. We could put a sign down at the edge of the road advertising a barn sale and just let people poke at will, make an offer, whatever."

Rick sat back, arms crossed on his chest while Ruth hovered over her notebook, pencil in hand.

"How about this," said Rick. "Two tent signs. One for the road, one for the end of the driveway that leads to the barn. That'll direct people. There's wood in the barn I can use to make 'em up quick. Gotta be old paint out there too. Some planks and bricks for shelves and you can put some stuff outside, maybe other stuff in the milking parlor, but I don't think I'd let people range freely in the barn. You might get some folks out for a weekend drive stopping in and a few bucks here and there."

"I can keep track of that," said Ruth.

Rick smiled at her. "Yes, you can. There's almost a pickup truck load of metal ready to go to the collection place in Monkton. Keep the copper, tin, cast separate. I have Wednesday afternoon off, we could use my truck, then you'd know how to find the place. You might get enough to register Irma's truck or transfer your registration. Both vehicles are old, it'll be fairly cheap. You heard Lewis; he's watching your plates."

"Another thing," Rick turned his attention back to Katie. "There's soft wood up on the ridge, virgin stuff, that you could sell. There were some guys at the feed store talking about wood lots they were looking to harvest. There are the oaks too, but I wouldn't cut the maples. I hear the Deans are negotiating for a piece of property on the other side of theirs that includes a twenty-acre parcel of maple forest."

"For?" asked Katie.

"One of Raymond's brothers is building a big sugar house. They're going commercial on the syrup business. If they rent your hayfields, maybe they'll rent your woods too."

"How long will it take to make some kind of profit on that?" asked Katie.

"Year anyway," said Rick. "Some of that depends on what's already out there for logging roads or whatever. The soft wood and oak were already cut out of the piece the Deans are looking at, so the tracks are already in there."

"Too long." She took the bag of potatoes to the sink to wash, then turned back to Rick. Her brain whirled as she tried to figure out how much time it would take to hire someone to cut the soft wood, sell it, and get paid versus how long the town would sit on its hands regarding the back taxes. No one in the local government was moving forward investigating Irma's death, but she knew if someone owed the townships money, the local government would be moving fast to collect.

"Tracks?" Katie spun around. "You mean like cleared areas where a pickup could drive through to get across from one place to another?" asked Katie. At Rick's nod, she added. "So, there could be tracks leading across Dean land to the high meadow, even left from when Poppa was out there?" Once again, Rick nodded. Katie turned back to the sink and the bobbing potatoes. *What about over the mountain?* She wondered.

After supper, she walked down to the barn with Rick and Ruth to see what they had put together. Rick had made two tall A-frame signs using

85

two-by-fours and plywood pieces while she was cooking.

"Either one will fit in the back of your car," he said. "You just need to paint them and get your junk ready."

Rick left for home, and Katie told Ruth to put two hours of labor down on his notebook page.

"If we actually make any money," she said, "he should get paid for his work."

Ruth nodded, scribbling in her notebook.

"Also, Ruth." Katie waited until the other woman looked up. "What happened to the stuff Irma was wearing or had with her at the, ah, accident?"

Ruth got up and went upstairs. Katie could hear her rummaging around but was unsure which room she was in. Ruth returned with a brown paper bag with the top folded over and taped down.

"I didn't open it," said Ruth. "I just put it under her bed, not mixed with her other things."

Katie took the bag. She felt an unusual heat where the bag bumped up against her leg.

"What about her boots?" she asked.

"You're wearing them," said Ruth.

The color drained from Katie's face. After covering the table with newspaper, she opened the bag. Inside she found a green-checked flannel shirt, rust-colored corduroys which were almost worn through, and underclothes. She discarded the underwear and bra, then spread the pants and shirt out. Everything was stained and smelled bad. The side seams of the outer clothing had been cut open.

"I'm surprised you got these back," said Katie.

"When I went into the doctor's office, the nurse brought them out to me," Ruth said. She was hanging back, eyes averted.

There were some three-corner rips in the shirt and pants. All on the front. Katie didn't like the thought circulating in her head.

"Ruth, I know this is hard. I need you to look at these and tell me if they look like they did when you last saw Gram."

With slow steps, Ruth approached the table. "Well, yes," she said. "And kind of no."

"Explain that." Frustration had Katie clenching her teeth.

"This," Ruth pointed to a hand-stitched place, "and this is a place Irma mended the pants. Just because we didn't have new, didn't mean we had to look like a bum. I don't remember those other rips."

Silently Katie folded the clothes, placing them and the original bag inside a new one. She took the paper bag into the laundry, tucking it high on a shelf over the washer.

Chapter Twelve

Katie left for work half an hour early to catch Stan, but he wasn't available. They were busy that day and Stan left during the afternoon. Dan came out and told Katie that Stan would need her to work through the entire day.

"Darn it," Katie said. By the time she came through the employee entrance, everyone was gone including Rick.

When she shifted into drive to pull ahead, her car wobbled to the left with a sickening thump coming from the back.

"No," she said. Climbing out, she walked around the back of the car and found the rear tire flat. A roofing nail was buried between the treads. Leaving the car where it was, she walked out to the street and stuck out her thumb. No one stopped for her on the short walk into the village, but a woman exiting the post office on the Parentville-Charlotte Road picked her up.

"Hitch-hiking is dangerous, you know," she lectured Katie.

"Yes, ma'am," said Katie. "I got a flat tire and there wasn't anyone around to help me. I'm just trying to get home." She had the woman drop her at the end of Fire Lane 61. The first half of the fire lane ran through a tunnel created by tall oaks lining both sides of the road. Though wide enough for two vehicles to pass, it was still a dirt road with a drainage ditch on the village side, which was also the bottom-most corner of her farm property. With only a glance at the schoolhouse, Katie plodded along, thoughts far away to the days when Poppa had a milking herd, four a.m. mornings spent leaning on warm, softly lowing bodies willing to give what they had and always ready for a good scratch, and then Poppa taking her to school on his way to the creamery in town. He had been a hold-out still using metal milk cans long after others had changed over to the more efficient method where milk flowed into one large stainless-steel holding tank and the milk tanker came to them.

"Hey," said Grace, stopping her station wagon beside Katie. "Are you out for a walk, or would you like a ride?"

"Actually…" Katie sighed. "I'd love a ride." She climbed inside, leaning back against the seat with another sigh. "I didn't realize how tired I was until I started walking."

"Car trouble? I didn't see your Subaru on the side of the road."

"Flat tire," said Katie. "It's still in the feed store parking lot."

Grace's head whipped around.

"How is it flat?" she demanded.

"There's a nail stuck right in the middle of it," replied Katie. Taken aback by Grace's tone, she leaned against the far side of the car. "You know, like a galvanized roofing nail, big head. There are carpenters working at the feed store and I must have just run over one that fell on the ground."

Nodding her head, Grace turned into her own drive.

That's all right, thought Katie, eager to get out of the car. *I can walk the rest of the way.*

"Do you have to go home right this minute?" Grace asked.

At Katie's negative response, Grace went into the house, returning in about six minutes. Once again in the driver's seat, she pulled down the barn drive to the tractor shed. Inside Katie could see the other woman rummaging around for a few minutes, then returning dragging a hydraulic pump jack.

Her younger son came out of the barn and Katie heard Grace instruct him to run up and tell Ruth, Katie had car trouble but they were getting it fixed. With the pump in the back of the car, Grace drove back to town.

"If you're going to live out here, you need to help yourself, or at least help the helpers," said Grace. She laughed at Katie's puzzled expression. "My brother-in-law is a mechanic in the village. I called him and he's going to see if he can put a plug in your tire."

89

When they arrived, Grace introduced Katie to Philip who already had the car jacked up and the tire removed.

"You left your car unlocked," Philip said.

"Driver's door doesn't lock, so it feels kind of foolish to bother with the others," Katie said.

Philip nodded. Grace shook her head.

"Waiting here, or coming with?" he asked.

"You'll have to come back for your jack anyway," said Grace, "we'll wait."

The wait took half an hour. The women drove to the store, returning with cokes and a half bag of chips.

"Don't tell my kids." Grace giggled like a young child.

"I think they're both good kids," said Katie.

"Boy, have they got you fooled."

Katie watched Grace, whose eyes wandered off, unfocused, while she chewed her lip. Something was wrong. Katie was sure it had to do with them sitting in town while there were things Grace should be at home working on.

"Ah, listen, Grace, I can't tell you how good this is of you. I'm sure you have stuff of your own waiting." Now Katie chewed at her lip.

"You would help me. I just feel like, I don't know, whatever was happening to Irma is coming to you. Raymond and I were talking the other day. He pointed out that if a car went up the road with no headlights on, we'd never know it was there. I mean, Bully barks, but he's old and might miss something if he's sleeping. With the fans on and everything, we might not even notice. I don't like it. I'm not one for secrets or skulking around in the dark."

"Does that mean you don't like Halloween; cause it's going to be here before you know it."

It was Grace's turn to be surprised. Reaching out to give Katie a shove, she laughed aloud.

The tow truck pulled in and Philip bounced the tire over to the Subaru.

"Nice straight hole," he said. "There's a plug in it, but these tires have a lot of wear. You'd better be thinking about some new ones before the snow comes." He handed her the nail which she pocketed, safer for another unsuspecting person.

Katie paid him, promising when she was ready for tires, she'd come down to the garage. Just as she passed the Dean farm, Raymond stepped outside, waving her into the driveway.

They sat in the kitchen while Grace moved around behind them, starting her family's evening meal.

"Ruth came down for butter," he said. "She told me you were out walking the boundaries. You aren't going to get all that in a day, woman."

"Yeah, that wasn't exactly what I was doing," said Katie.

"I thought not," he said. "I made you a map to help your memory." It was a nice way of saying if you don't know.

Raymond produced a piece of notebook paper covered with a labeled drawing. "This is the Parentville-Charlotte Road," he pointed out, "coming from the village. This is where Stacey brook crosses before it dumps into LaPlatte brook. That's your easternmost border. Then the line runs up along Fire Lane 61 between our farms all the way up to the top of the mountain. On your side, there's the house and barn, pond meadow, high meadow, and woodlot before it all turns to shale. Got that?"

"Yes, I've been over the mountain, years ago with Poppa."

"Okay so, this isn't an accurate showing of distance, but the line runs along the ridge, comes down over here back into the woodlot, and against LaPlatte running east back to Stacey. This area between the meadows and LaPlatte, including behind the orchard and burial plot, all used to be grazing land. The herd was sold after Fred passed away, so it's overgrown now. The last meadow is the one below the rise that the house sits on. We rent all three meadows, harvest them, and keep the edges cut back, that's it."

Katie studied the map.

"Did you know?" Grace broke into Katie's thoughts, "The lane used to be called Lover's Lane?"

"You mean people used to drive out there to go parking, necking and whatever?"

Raymond laughed, embarrassed at Katie's shocked expression.

"No." Grace handed Katie another plastic-wrapped plate with two pieces of strawberry pie on it. "There were only two lovers. On this side, the property belonged to the Moore family, and on the other side of the ridge, the property belonged to the Roser family. Your grandparents traveled that route when they were courting. For a whole year, Fred kept it cut clean and plowed using horses. He told me one time he married Irma to cut back on the amount of work he had to do."

Katie smiled, unable to open her mouth to answer for fear tears would fall. Grace went to the door ringing the bell that hung on the porch calling her family to supper.

Folding the paper, Katie offered her hand to Raymond.

"I appreciate you explaining the agreement to me. This will make it easier for me to know if I'm wandering around where I have a right to or not."

Concern flickered across his face. Katie hadn't said anything about the continuation of the agreement he had with Irma.

"What happened to your car?" Raymond asked.

"Roofing nail."

"I told her to park on the other side of the lot from where they're working," Grace said as she returned.

"I think she was worried I was the victim of foul play," said Katie.

Grace ducked her head.

"Ruth told me Irma's tires had been slashed, this was just a nail." There was silence for a moment, Katie stood to go, then turned to Raymond. "I heard one of your brothers was going into the maple sugaring business. I'd like to talk about that sometime."

"I'll tell Steven to give you a call," Raymond said. "Are you going to the town picnic on Sunday? He'll probably be there. Also, before I forget it, why have you been running the barn lights all night? That's got to be jumping your electric bill way up there."

"I haven't been running the lights. I didn't even know they were working."

"Well, they come on around ten o'clock and run straight through until around four in the morning. I see them when I get up. Even the haymow lights are on."

Shaking her head at another mystery, Katie walked up the road. Swallows crossed over her head, evening birds were just tuning up, and everywhere there was a sweet country smell she realized she'd been missing for a long time.

Once again Katie walked in the front door of her own farmhouse and out the kitchen door looking for Ruth. She could hear the cats calling already locked away in the cat room.

"Ruth," she called from the stoop.

"Down here," Ruth called back from the milking parlor.

Katie found Rick's A-frame signs whitewashed and standing in the sun. An arena of plank benches held buckets, tools, kitchen items the weather wouldn't bother, and even a blue Schwinn bicycle.

"Wow," said Katie. "What happened to working down at Deans?"

"I did that too. I did most of this in the afternoon when I got back and I found some black paint for the lettering. It's really not all that much. I had to lock the cats up while I did the whitewashing because they were playing in it."

"Ah. Well come up and I'll make supper." Katie shortened her stride to match the slower one of the sixty-plus-year-old woman. "I think you might have overdone it today."

"Well, I'll sleep good tonight." Ruth bathed while Katie fried ham and made a pot of sliced potatoes and vegetables. In the dish drainer were more freshly washed pint and quart jars.

"Quarts?" she asked Ruth, who once bathed and fed stretched out on the sofa.

"Tomatoes," yawned Ruth settling on the couch. Freed from the cat room when the women returned, but still limited to inside the house, several furry bodies curled around their old friend and snoozed with her. Ruth told Katie that when the television quit, Irma hauled it off. The radio played the same sixties music Katie heard when she first arrived and she thumbed through the Sears and Roebuck catalog, checking the price of work jeans. She'd get her first paycheck at the end of the week. Maybe she'd have something decent to wear if she went with Ruth to the town picnic.

Chapter Thirteen

It felt weird to be working at the feed store the next day after Rick left for his afternoon off.

"You're in charge," he said, waving goodbye at eleven o'clock.

"Yeah, like that's true." Katie laughed. Once he left, she stood in the open space looking around. Suddenly she realized she was looking for him, even though she had just watched him drive out of the lot. It didn't feel right to be there with only the young guy Stan had sent out to fill the old man's place.

She worked through her lunch to avoid having to chat with the younger guy she didn't really know. It was a relief to be in her own car driving away at one-thirty.

I'd better grow up and get over these abandonment issues if I'm going to be able to work without a babysitter, she thought.

Returning to the barn Katie went back to moving the stanchion pieces. The pile outside grew steadily. Ruth came down to say she was leaving to help in the garden.

"The beans are growing hog wild," she said. "We're trying to get ahead of them."

"There's a lot more here than I thought," said Katie, wiping her brow. "I wonder how much Rick will want to take?"

"Well, it's not as if the weather will hurt any of this stuff if you have to leave it laying out here," Ruth pointed out.

Katie finished getting everything beside the barn lane before Rick arrived. Wiping sweat and dust from her face, she went back into the barn. Turning the spigot and getting nothing, she remembered the water had been shut off long before. Then she remembered what Raymond had said about the lights. There were switches on the wall in the milking parlor. On the outside of the building, there was a wooden cabinet that housed the electrical panel for the whole building. Several of the fuses were missing. Most of the connections were identifiable by words written in ink on the bare wood. The fuses still in place were labeled lights. Each connection had a small black plastic box connected to it that looked much more modern than the fuse box.

Katie closed the door and went back up to the house to wash and wait for Rick.

While hauling everything outside Katie had divided the large box of small parts into three milk pails, which though only half full were still heavy. While they loaded his pickup, Katie told Rick about the barn lights that came on by themselves and burned all night.

"And Ruth didn't turn them on, right?" he asked.

"I asked her, she said no. I wanted to pull the fuses, but there's some connection thing in there I don't know about. I don't want to give myself a permanent perm disconnecting them."

Pulling the last tie-down taut, Rick wrapped the end into the knot before answering.

"Let's check it out," he said. It took him only a moment to evaluate the inside of the fuse box. "These are some kind of timers."

"Why would there be timers?" Katie scoffed.

"Well off-hand, I'd say it's another dirty trick." Rick used his pocket knife to loosen screws while he spoke. "If the lights are coming on late and going off early, most people wouldn't know they were running. Both Ruth and your bedrooms are on the opposite side of the house. What we're going to do is take all these fuses and timers out of here. We'll fix it so no one can open this door and screw with this again. It'll mean there's no power at all in the barn, but that's how it's going to have to be."

While Katie found a box in the barn, Rick got a hammer and spike out of his truck. Katie took the box of fuses and timers up to the house and after nailing the fuse door shut, Rick picked her up.

"It's just one nail and you know where it is. Anyone else will have to spend time figuring out what we did, then replace all we took."

"Should we tell the sheriff?" Katie asked.

"You and him suddenly on good terms?"

It seemed serendipitous to Katie that no sooner had they left Fire Lane 61; they should meet the sheriff's cruiser traveling in the opposite direction. Lewis' eyes scanned the cab of Rick's truck. As soon as she recognized the cruiser, Katie became very interested in the ditch side scenery beyond her window.

"Is he turning around?" she asked.

"Of course not," said Rick.

"Aren't you worried about being seen with me?" Katie asked.

At the negative shake of Rick's head, she asked, "Why not?"

"I know something his wife would like to know." Rick looked at Katie with a gleam in his eye.

She couldn't help laughing. No one in town gave the truck piled high with junk a second look.

"You know, if we were in Chicago people would be stopping to stare."

"Good thing we're here then, ain't it?"

On the Monkton Road, they passed the dump where Katie could see Chet rummaging around his truck. A quarter of a mile further on was the furniture factory where Irma had worked for years.

"Wait!" Katie cried. The truck jerked to a halt. Beyond the ditch was a long, run-down wood building. The red paint was faded or flaked away, and around the yard were piles of rotting sawdust and discarded lumber. The surface of the dirt drive and parking lot was a minefield of enormous potholes. On the sawmill end of the building, boards had been haphazardly nailed up to replace the original walls.

"What happened?" Katie demanded.

"Out-of-state owners came in," said Rick, putting the truck back into drive. "Work went away. There are only about fifteen guys working there now. The sawmill is shutting down. That's why Steven Dean got his own mill up and running. He used to be the head sawyer here."

Katie's shoulders slumped. She had considered going to the furniture factory for a job. From the resignation in Rick's voice, there wouldn't be anything available.

Just before they arrived at the metal works, Katie remarked on the number of small ranch houses lining both sides of the road. Rick nodded, silent, his mouth a thin line. He turned down a straight dirt road that ran beyond a tall cedar hedgerow emptying into what was obviously a dump dedicated to all things metal. Rick pulled up to the guard shack.

"Hi ya." A man in coveralls emerged from the shack with a clipboard in hand. He walked around the pickup scanning the load, then directed Rick onto the flatbed scales.

"When you come off," he said, "pull over there to unload the steel, then back around here."

After the employee weighed the truck again, Katie and Rick off-loaded the aluminum. The pickup was weighed again on the big scales. Then Rick and Katie hauled the box of brass over to a set of barn scales.

This sure seems like a lot of work for maybe a couple of dollars, thought Katie, swiping her hand over her forehead.

While waiting in the office for the tally and check, she asked about rates and was given a mimeographed sheet of current prices. She was also told how to separate if she was coming back again.

"It'll just make it easier for you." The man handed her a check and receipt. Katie got back in the truck with a stupefied look on her face.

"Holy Hannah, Rick," she said. "It isn't all that much, but I have to tell you, I was expecting maybe only fifteen dollars. And those guys were really nice."

"Stanchions are older, higher grade metal." He started the truck and in an exaggerated western accent said, "Did you get enough to save the farm, little missy?"

"Nope," Katie responded in kind. "But I'll be able to register Gram's truck and maybe buy toilet paper."

"Gee-haw," Rick yelled. At the end of the dirt road, he turned in the opposite direction of Parentville.

"Where are we going?" asked Katie.

"We're going to take a little ride around the horn," said Rick. "There's stuff

I want to show you."

Their ride circled to the east of town, closer to where Interstate 89 had gone in bringing the city to the country much quicker than ten years before. With the heavy load of metal gone, they traveled faster. They road in silence, each in their own thoughts. Just before they crossed the Monkton line, Rick turned down a side road. Though the road was paved, it was so narrow each time they met another vehicle, Katie was sure her side of the truck would be wallowing in the ditch. Rick slowed down as they passed an old and small mobile home.

"Take a good look," Rick said.

The trailer was back from the road with the area between a carpet of long matted grass, littered with discarded appliances, and junk cars.

"Are you trying to scare me?" Katie asked. "Is this a *Christmas Carol* intervention about where I'm going to end up?"

"No, this, sweetheart, is the home and hearth of Al Lewis. Dear old dad to Sheriff Martin Lewis." Rick pulled into the next driveway to turn around. "I brought you out here so that you know where the long arm of the law comes from. The next time the little prick gets on his soapbox making you feel bad, you can visualize his roots. Maybe it'll help keep him from getting under your skin."

Katie sighed, "I don't know how well that will work, but I'll try anything." She still held the check in her hand, and her mind drifted. *I have to agree I hate to worry about Lewis being in my face, but the Subaru is registered until November. I'm going to need the truck. I'll just start with getting a Vermont driver's license and hope for the best.*

"Look at these houses, Katie." Rick cut into her thoughts.

They had pulled into a little cul-de-sac which contained a half dozen identical houses, two blue ones, two green, and two beige.

"Oh look," said Katie. "This guy only knew how to build one kind."

"Actually, because they're working on multiple houses at a time, it's easier to stay with one design." Rick pulled back onto the main road. From that point, Katie was more aware of the houses and appalled at the number of small developments they passed.

"These people all mostly work in the city, they're young families," Rick explained. "We collect their taxes, they go to our bigger and better schools, and they pollute the landscape. It's a fifty-fifty deal. They want what we have, we want the income. We're learning to share." They drove past CVU High School and when they arrived at the Williston Road intersection, Rick once more turned away from town.

"I want to show you where I live," he said. "If you can't get hold of me and you need to be somewhere else, you can go there."

They turned right on the Hinesburg Road and drove another three miles. On the right was a sign advertising Tandy Motor Court. It was a trailer park where the diagonally parked trailers were separated only by the width of the driveway. Many of the trailers still had the hitch on the front which obscured the four-foot by four-foot lawn. A similar patch on the backside was the designated yard. The crooked roads were narrow and rough. There was no green space and as far as Katie could tell, no hope for privacy.

"You live here?" she asked in disbelief.

"Yup, couldn't afford a house, got the trailer as a deal, someone ordered it special and then couldn't come up with the money. I've been saving for land to move it to." Rick pulled into the drive of a larger, newer model. "If you lift the lid to the porch light, there's a key taped there. If I'm not home, just go in." He backed out and followed the crooked road back to the tar. "Depressing isn't it."

She nodded, unable to answer.

At the intersection for the turn to CVU, they turned right on the Shelbourne Road.

"Let me guess," Katie said. "We're taking another detour because you want to show me what?"

"We're only going a little way this time," said Rick. Once they were over the next rise, they came to a place where there were developments of five or six houses, one right after the other.

"This whole farm sold out," Rick said. "A developer bought it when they went under and cut it into little chunks." He pulled over to the side of the road and pointed toward the houses. "Back there is LaPlatte Brook, after

99

that your place."

"I was down in the pasture and saw where they were building beyond the windbreak," she said.

"Yeah, one development behind the other. Lot of locals are working the jobs, lot of outsiders too." He turned around on one of the side roads. "Banks still open," he said. "Want to cash your big check?"

Chapter Fourteen

E ven with the check for the metal and her paycheck the next day, jeans would have to wait. The telephone company demanded payment and Sheriff Lewis stopped in at the feed store again regarding her car registration. Rick's suggestion didn't work as well as he'd predicted it would. Though Katie got a chuckle as Lewis sauntered away. She had decided during the previous evening to register Irma's pickup. It would be handier than the Subaru. After Lewis left, Katie headed over to the town hall on an early lunch.

There was a different woman behind the desk who confessed she wasn't as knowledgeable. Getting Irma's truck registered took longer than Katie had planned.

"I can't seem to find the paperwork you said you turned in. I'm not sure how all this works, but we'll go with what we've got done here. Someone from the town will be in touch if there's something else that needs to be done," the woman said.

You mean if you got it wrong. Katie nodded, deciding to cut through the sheriff's office on her way out. Maybe she'd run into Lewis and tell him it was taking time for her to do as he had directed, take some starch out of his shirt.

The woman sitting at the desk in the sheriff's office wore a khaki uniform. Seeing her surprised Katie who figured Lewis was a card-holding member of the good old boys' club.

"Hi," Katie said, and then without thinking, "are you a deputy?"

The woman blushed bright red right up to the roots of her hair.

101

"I'd like to refer to myself as such," she admitted. "The sheriff, however, considers me more of a dispatcher."

"Oh," said Katie. Reaching across the desk, she said. "Katie Took."

The woman, short, buxom, and wearing her hair in a low bun, rose and extended her hand as well. Katie had a firm handshake, so had a good grip on the woman's hand as a tingling ran through her senses. From the widening of the other woman's eyes, Katie knew she had felt it too.

"Marlene Foster." The woman dropped back into her seat, fingers tugging free of Katie.

Suddenly embarrassed at the amount of time she had held on, Katie backed away.

"Ah, great, well thank you, Marlene," Katie said, hurrying out the door, andtotally forgetting her desire to ding Lewis.

"Marlie," a voice whispered as the door closed.

Chapter Fifteen

"Guess what?" said Ruth. "We're short another cat."

Amazed at the joviality in Ruth's voice at the news one of the beloved felines had died, Katie's head jerked up. Ruth, who was removing jars from the canner, didn't notice Katie's reaction.

"Father Messier from St. Jude's church down in the village came out this afternoon to borrow one." Ruth laid another jar on the thick padding of towels covering the counter. "Seems they're having a little rodent problem in the vestibule and trapping hasn't worked. I gave him Boots, she's a good mouser, and he wanted an older cat who would stay inside. She doesn't like to get her feet dirty so she'll stay indoors.

"Maybe." Ruth turned to smile at Katie. "He'll like her and she'll get to stay. If not, I told him rent was two bags of cat chow."

Katie laughed. "You're a bad girl, Ruth."

"Hey, I didn't ask for money, just a little help with the mess of them. I put a notice down on the barn for people to see if they stopped. I already showed the kittens to one customer."

"So now, we have one cat who is gainfully employed," said Katie. She went back to tinkering with the broken lamp switch. It would be nice to have a lamp in her room instead of just the overhead lights. The lamp had come out of the barn collection.

"How do you know how to do so much, Katie?" Ruth asked.

"I don't know all that much," said Katie. She plugged in the lamp, pushed the switch and sixty watts of glow lit the room. "Viola."

"See, that's just what I mean."

"I guess I owe it to Poppa, he taught me a little." Katie picked up her tools. "He also taught me to look at something and see more than the picture, you know, like what's inside. I have a good memory, I'm nosy." She laughed. "I guess I want to know, so I remember."

"I admire that," said Ruth.

"You know admiration can be a two-way street," Katie said. "The day those kittens came in you knew exactly what they needed and were quick to get it." She paused, gazing out the window as she rinsed her hands in the kitchen sink. The horizon was dark, rain was in the forecast for the next couple of days. "I knew they were going to die. Trying to keep them alive was a futile effort. Now, look. Not only are they alive, but you have homes for them. It makes me proud to see you do that." Katie's eyes snapped open. Once again, she was talking as though the two women had a rapport, not what she was looking to do.

Katie reached over the sink pulling the window closed and ended up tipping Irma's china ring bowl off the sill and into the sink. The china broke into several pieces, but Katie's eyes were held by what had been laying in the bowl. Several roofing nails lay in the sink surrounded by the glass chips.

"Where did these nails come from Ruth," she asked, turning to Ruth who was on her way into the living room with Shade in her arms and three more buddies following.

"Are those the ones from the ring bowl?" asked Ruth. "Irma kept them, she found them spread around in the driveway."

It was a cinch; they had come from somewhere else because Katie had pulled out a ladder to check the rust-colored metal roof on the farmhouse. No one had worked up there in years. Fortunately, everything still looked securely fastened down, and she climbed down, sweaty hands tight around the ladder's side while telling herself there was no need to go up again. Ever.

"When?"

"I don't know." Ruth stopped to face Katie. "Maybe sometime around the Fourth?"

Katie carried the nails upstairs, putting them with the one she had carelessly discarded from her pocket.

"What else?" she asked herself. "What else did they do to harass you, Gram? Show me, give me a clue who wanted to hurt you."

Chapter Sixteen

The feed store closed at noon on Saturdays. Katie was pulling the doors of the storage building shut, padlock in hand when the roofers pulled in. Stan had said the men would be there on Saturday and work through Sunday to finish the area directly abutting the delivery bays.

"Hey," said Katie, walking up to the single man wearing a white hardhat. "You must be the job boss?"

The man nodded.

"I just wanted to let you know," Katie said. "I picked up a roofing nail in one of my tires a few days ago. Ended up with a flat."

"Really?" The man got huffy. "What day was this?"

Katie held up her hand. "Take it easy, man. I'm just letting you know." Her skin prickled. Stan and most of the guys had left for the day. There was no one else around where she was talking to the roofer other than his own guy, and even he wasn't standing nearby.

"Sorry, didn't mean to sound so rough. We put up the sawhorses so people can't drive under where we're working. I wanted to know what day it was, so I could talk to the guy handling the rake."

At Katie's confused look, the man waved her towards the back of his truck. Pulling out a four-foot metal bar attached in the middle to a rope, he pulled a few nails from his pocket and threw them on the ground. Tossing the bar, he pulled it back towards him over the nails. With a sharp ping, each nail attached itself.

"We call this the rake," he explained. "It's a magnet and several times a day we pull it over where we're working. Each day a different guy is responsible for it. I got tired of paying for flat tires. Were you parked inside the sawhorses?"

"No, I parked over there." Katie pointed across the lot.

"I'm sorry, ma'am," the worker said. "that's way too far for us to have dropped a nail. I'd need a slingshot."

Katie nodded her thanks as he walked away.

* * *

A telephone call from the sheriff just before supper surprised Katie. Especially when he didn't tell her he was coming out with the air national guard and handcuffs.

"Irma was our animal control officer," said Lewis. "The town paid her to handle the problem on an on-call basis. You know, when we needed help with an issue involving a domestic animal, or sometimes a wild critter if Fish and Game wasn't available. I want to know if you're willing to do the job until the next election?"

"Ah, what does it entail?" Katie asked. Ruth was listening to the conversation.

"Rogue skunks, loose dogs, that sort of stuff."

"No bears, or rabid foxes, or herds of rampaging deer?" asked Katie.

"What?" demand Lewis. "No. What kind of foolishness is that?"

"I just never considered what that type of job would cover." She wiggled her eyebrows at Ruth, who giggled behind her hand. "What does it pay?"

"Twenty dollars for a pick up if it's alive, ten dollars for roadkill," Lewis said.

"Huh, yeah, I'll do that." It sounded like an easy twenty dollars to Katie.

"Okay," Lewis said. "Get down to my office, someone left a critter here this afternoon while no one was paying attention."

"Sure," she said. "I'll be right there."

"Wow," said Ruth after Katie hung up.

"What did Gram take to go out on a call?" Katie asked.

"Small animal carrier, maybe a larger crate if needed, snare for snagging at a distance, pepper spray, and her heavy leather gloves. Oh, and you might want to wear her knee-high barn boots. Doesn't sound like you're going to need a live trap."

"Sounds like a lot for a critter left at the sheriff's office, but okay."

They loaded everything into the back of the Subaru and Katie headed into town. Supper would have to wait.

When she arrived, the lights were still on in the town office. It was the last day to pay taxes, and the office offered extended hours. Katie went there first to pick up the voucher she'd needed to be paid for animal removal.

"All the vouchers get paid at the end of the month," the friendly clerk told her, handing over a half dozen blank pages. "I get the white one, you keep the carbon."

"Monthly's better than quarterly, right?" grinned Katie.

She entered the sheriff's office through the inner door and found herself facing his back.

"Hi, Sheriff Lewis," she said.

He spun around, eyes wide. "That door is only for employees," he snapped.

"Sorry, I didn't know." Looking around the office, she saw nothing that looked like a deserted cat. "So, where's this critter you need hauling off?"

"Outside." His sour look changed to a grin. "My deputy will help you load it."

There was a glint in his eye Katie didn't like. For the first time, she considered the wisdom of taking the job sight unseen. She exited the parking lot door ahead of Lewis and initially saw nothing more than a male deputy and Marlie. Then there was a movement behind them, and Katie saw the thirty-pound pig tied to the bumper of one of the cruisers. Her mouth dropped as she spun around toward Lewis. He spoke before she had a chance, thrusting a ripped piece of paper at her.

"There was a note attached to the railing." Lewis smiled, showing uneven teeth across his bottom jaw. "Seems it's a pet and her name is Bonnie." Over her head, he said to his employees. "Load her up."

Katie whipped back toward the people surrounding the pig. "Wait!" She called out, holding her hand up as a sign to stop. Behind her, the door closed firmly. Before she could run across the lot, the two deputies wrestled the pig off its feet and between them got her to Katie's car. She was still imploring them to stop when the man freed one hand, yanked the back door of the Subaru open, and shoved the pig in.

The deputy walked away with a disgusted look on his face while brushing the front of his uniform off. Marlie followed more slowly.

"Sorry, Katie," she whispered.

Refusing to allow Lewis to see how horrified she was, Katie got into the car. She was burning with rage. Pulling out of the lot with a squeal of bald tires on pavement, she said, "Buckle up, babycakes. You're in for a rough ride."

The pig rode quietly in the backseat, making a huffing noise as they drove through town. Everything was going fine until Katie slowed down for a milk tanker pulling out of the creamery and someone on the side of the road yelled, "Hey, look, there's a pig in the backseat of that car." Katie could feel her neck getting shorter as her ears burned the rest of the ride home.

Ruth was standing in the driveway, waiting for Katie's return. When the Subaru went past the drive and pulled onto the side yard, Ruth hurried around getting there just in time to see Katie yank the door open and the pig scramble out. Ignoring the pig who ran, skipped, and played on the grass, glad to be free of the mechanical crate, Katie opened all the doors and retrieved the hose.

"The sheriff wanted you to pick up a *pig?*" Ruth looked as surprised as Katie had felt earlier.

"Yes, he did." Katie turned the water on full force and sprayed the inside of the Subaru.

"What are we going to do with a pig?" asked Ruth.

"Eat it," said Katie as she continued to fill the back seat of her car with water.

"Katie, the note says it's a pet." Ruth had rescued the note from the front seat of the car. "If someone made a pet of this animal, you can't eat it."

"Watch me." Shutting off the hose, Katie made to slam the door, then decided with the amount of water still running out she should let it dry. The pig tired of frolicking walked up to a puddle for a long slurping drink. All the time Bonnie sucked water; her tail wagged happily. When she was full, she went over to where the women were standing and dropped to the ground ready for a nap.

"Should we tie her up?" Ruth asked.

"Leave it, maybe it'll wander away and a bear will get it."

"Katie!" said Ruth. Just like Katie, Ruth was at a loss. Irma had brought home cats regularly, the occasional dog, and periodically a wild animal they would take to the rehabilitation center in Vergennes. The pig was different. It wasn't quite a farm animal or a household pet either and it was obvious Katie was looking to dispose of it any way she could.

But Katie had walked away. Once inside the house, she changed clothes and began putting their evening meal together. Outside, Ruth considered their options. The half-grown pig couldn't be left wandering free outside overnight. After rolling down the windows of the Subaru and closing the doors, she took a hank of old clothesline and tied it around the pig's rear ankle. Calling it to her, Ruth waited. The pig ignored her. She went to the hen-house returning with a hand full of cracked corn which she offered the pig. Once Bonnie was on her feet, Ruth walked in front of her calling and periodically tugging the rope when the pig stopped. It didn't take long for Bonnie to realize the way to avoid the uncomfortable pulling on her rear leg was to follow the woman.

In the barn were free stalls. Small rooms meant to hold animals that couldn't be held in the stanchions. Ruth locked Bonnie in a free stall, returning with a pan of water and the last of the hen's corn.

"This is the best we've got for tonight," Ruth said. "Goodnight."

Bonnie gobbled up the corn, then rooted around in the old hay until she had a comfortable spot. With a sigh, she laid down.

Ruth found Katie still seething about the sheriff's trick. Dinner was a tense affair. While Katie bathed, Ruth called down to the Dean farm.

Katie exited the bathroom at the same time Raymond and Davy knocked at the kitchen door.

"Hey Katie," said Raymond. "I hear you've got yourself another boarder." He had a wide smile on his face. Even though Katie was still angry, she couldn't help grinning back.

"Yeah, and this one is a real oinker," she said.

"Let's go check it out," he said. Down in the barn, he threw the light switch that should have turned the overhead lights in the main aisle of the barn on. When the area remained shadowed, he turned to Katie and found her holding out the flashlight she had grabbed on her way out of the kitchen. Nodding his understanding, he followed her to the free stall. Raymond, Katie, and Davy stood in the doorway watching Bonnie sleep in the hay. Ruth stood behind them, wringing her hands.

"Pretty small for this time of year, must have been a summer litter instead of spring," said Raymond. "Shoat."

"What?" asked Katie.

"Half-grown pig, like a teenager? It's called a shoat."

"What's its name?" asked Davy.

"Bonnie," Ruth chimed in.

"We're not calling it anything," said Katie closing the door, "except maybe lunch."

"Easy there, Katie," Raymond cautioned. "There's some legal deal with critters the dog catcher picks up."

"What are you talking about?" Katie demanded, hanging the padlock on the hasp of the milk parlor door as they followed Ruth and Davy back up to the house.

"Ruth said the town is paying you to pick up the pig, like a stray dog or something. I don't know the rules exactly, but there's some stipulation about holding strays for a specific amount of time while you search for the owner."

"Are you serious?" Katie stopped walking.

"Yes, I am actually. Irma used the free stalls for dogs, feral cats, whatever. Ask Ruth or the vet about it. Tomorrow you better pick up a copy of the agreement Irma had with the town."

"What if the town hasn't paid me yet? Or the fact somebody tied the pig to the sheriff's bumper and abandoned it."

Raymond shrugged his shoulders. "Don't know. Though I find it very appropriate that a pig was tied to Lewis' car."

Davy came running up, "I think you should call your pig Oreo because she's black on both ends and white in the middle."

"She's not my pig," said Katie.

"Good luck with that." Raymond waved as he got in his truck. "I'll have the boys cut some corn out of the field tomorrow for you to feed her."

Soft summer rain fell on Katie's shoulders as she stood in the yard after Raymond left. Ruth was calling in the last of the cats that had sneaked out while the people were going back and forth. Katie walked over to button the chickens in for the night. She closed the two western-facing windows but left the others open.

"It'll be too hot in there if I close everything," she explained to the softly clucking biddies already in their nesting boxes.

"Great," she cussed, walking away. "I was trying to get out of this hick town, now I'm talking to chickens and babysitting a pig."

Chapter Seventeen

To avoid having Ruth get attached to the pig, Katie went down to the barn the next morning with a bucket of water and the leftover oatmeal Ruth had made for breakfast. Katie hadn't worked up the nerve to tell Ruth, she didn't like oatmeal, which was why she never ate more than a few bites. The chickens however seemed to like it. Maybe the pig would, too.

Bonnie was awake and as soon as the door cracked open, she made a dash for the outside. Katie jumped out of the way, stumbling on a pile of yard tools.

"Come back here," Katie screamed, furious the animal had escaped into the rain.

Bonnie high-tailed it out of the barn and into the weed patch that surrounded the lower end close to the lumber pile.

"Good riddance to you," yelled Katie. She left the oatmeal bowl on the floor in the stall before going back to where Irma had been dismantling the stanchions. Now that she knew where to take them, Katie wanted to dismantle more. She needed to look at what the job would entail and perhaps start later in the afternoon. It would be a good job for a rainy day. To her dismay, not only were the nuts and bolts heavily rusted, but there were several coats of whitewash holding the metal solidly together. Moving the pieces, the day before proved they were heavier than she expected, causing her to sit and rest before she was through. There were also no tools lying around, which meant the job not only appeared more difficult than she would have liked, but that she needed to search in the shadowy barn for the tools to use.

Just as she was getting ready to leave, Katie heard a rustling sound in the open stall. When she peeked in, the pig who had been working on her nesting place looked up expectantly. The oatmeal was gone, but the pig woofed in anticipation.

"I have nothing for you," Katie said. Outside, the noise of a small engine she had heard earlier grew. Stepping through the milking parlor door, Katie found Davy and Billy pulling in on a four-wheeled contraption hauling a small trailer.

"Dad said not to give her all the corn at one time," said Davy grabbing an armful, "or all the bedding hay either."

Katie explained the pig had gotten out earlier, then much to her surprise had come back.

"It's because she slept here. She probably thinks this is her new bedroom," said Billy, scratching Bonnie's ears. The boys unloaded the trailer. They opened a second stall; this one had several pieces of horse harness thrown inside. They left the extra corn and two-thirds of the hay bale there.

Katie watched the pig for a short time after the boys left. It was funny to watch Bonnie check out the groceries, snack a bit, then move to the bedding where she picked up the bale sections and tossed them into the air to break them apart. Leaving Bonnie to her housekeeping, Katie went back up to the house. The sun was breaking through the thinning rain clouds. Off to the east, the sky was a pale blue. The town picnic would start after church, and Ruth would ride into town with Rick. Katie had put together a food donation telling Ruth delivering it was the other woman's responsibility.

Kicking her boots off as she entered the kitchen, Katie spoke to Ruth. "Looks like the sun is going to shine after all so you won't drown at the picnic."

"You're coming, right?" asked Ruth.

"Ah, yeah, eventually," Katie spoke quickly, cutting Ruth off. "What happened to the tools Gram used to take apart the stanchions?"

"She probably put them back on the workbench. It's the only way she knew she'd be able to find them later. She spent as much time searching for what she needed sometimes as she did working." Ruth shook her head. "I have an umbrella, what about a raincoat?"

"Your guess is as good as mine," said Katie, pulling a roasting pan of baked beans out of the oven.

Chapter Eighteen

"Okay," said Katie, passing the big oval roasting pan to Rick who was stowing everything in the cab of his truck. "You have two mixed berry pies and a mess of beans. God knows that's probably what everyone else is bringing, but that's what we had to work with."

Ruth sat in the truck holding one pie in her lap and surrounded by the rest.

"You're coming along soon, right Katie?" she asked.

"Yup, checking on Bonnie, taking a shower, and you'll see me before you know it."

Rick caught Katie's eye. She was lying, and he knew it.

* * *

Even though the ground was still wet, the sun was warm and a light breeze kept the humidity at bay. Ruth and Rick wandered around the lot where the barbecue was set up. On one side was the portable pit, made from half a two-hundred-and-fifty-pound oil drum. There were trestle tables and chairs borrowed from the high school, and a ring of tables that would hold salads, desserts, and pitchers of lemonade. On the side where the couple strolled a few craft vendors had set up booths along with civic and church groups hoping to earn money for their sponsor. There was a kissing booth, dunk tank, dart throwing, and in the circle, children racing around a makeshift oval.

When the bell rang signaling the chicken was ready, they got in line paper plate in hand, and walked down the line selecting their favorites.

"Katie's going to be sorry she missed this," fretted Ruth.

Rick nodded as they settled into their seats surrounded by friends, neighbors, and others from surrounding communities.

"You know, she's been kind of tense since I gave her that bag of Irma's things," said Ruth.

"What things?" asked Rick, holding up his cup for the server who circled the table pouring lemonade.

Ruth explained about the bag's contents and Katie's reaction. The server whose pitcher was now empty stood to the side, listening. There was no reason to get a plate and collect a meal because Ruth's words had destroyed any appetite. Perhaps it would be better to leave the event and drive out to the deserted farm.

* * *

The woman serving at the picnic had scouted around the farm several times. It was a walk to get up there from across the brook, but safer than driving past the Deans and taking a chance someone might be home at the farm. The couple of times Katie had almost caught her were a small price to pay in the long run. She'd even been inside the house with the foolish old cat lady to look at those nasty kittens. Like there was a chance one of those mangy barn cats would ever live in her house.

The only way she would ever be at a place where she could dump the rube she had married, and live better, like her sister, was to get hold of the land Larry wanted. He'd mentioned it several times. Her boys would be happy if they got to have something better. Her oldest son was on board. He might need a little guidance in keeping his mouth shut about things that had happened, but she could manage it. After all, he was her son. Scaring the other old lady hadn't worked. It was too bad the old bag had died, but it was just one of those oh-well things. The deed was done, there was no reason to wallow in guilt, better to get everything done and move ahead. Having that granddaughter show up had been a surprise, and who would have ever thought she'd stick around. Katie's appearance made little sense. If you were young with no kids and good-looking, why would you leave the city for the sticks?

Another accident would be suspicious. If that old man doctor hadn't owed her, the sick old pervert, the Roser woman's death would have gotten a lot more publicity and there surely would have been an investigation.

Chapter Nineteen

Instead of heading for the barn, Katie went back inside the house. On the second floor, she pulled down the ladder to the attic. Way back, Ruth had said there was more of Irma's collection of papers stored there. Though the entire area was packed to the rafters, Katie only found seven cardboard boxes. Most of which were filled with photo albums and scrapbooks. One by one she carried them down the ladder, then down again to the living room. On her last trip, she spied a large box with WINTER CLOTHES scrawled on the side. Unfolding the top, she found Irma's winter outerwear packed for the off-season with at least one box of mothballs mixed in.

"Phew," she said, "this is all going to have to air outdoors for a week." Katie was glad to leave the box and tear-producing mothballs behind.

The boxes she'd carried downstairs proved to hold framed pictures that had at one time hung in the living room. There was an old black and white tin-type of Poppa's parents, a slightly newer photo of an elderly couple Katie knew to be Irma's folks. They were sitting on the bumper of an open body pickup and smiling like they'd just come from the fair. She found a triple frame with three baby girls, her grandmother, mother, and herself. On the very bottom was her grandparents' wedding picture. Katie spread them around on the living room floor, studying her heritage. One picture at a time went back up on the walls. The nails had been waiting, and Katie was happy to oblige. She also spent a few minutes studying the pieces still hanging on the walls and found that most of them were pieces she had painted in art class or, as in her grandmother's room, framed awards Katie had received.

Two boxes held items that must have come from her childhood home. Katie had been too young to remember these items, but each piece was marked in Irma's small, tight script. The next box was marked with one word, *Katie.* She expected more items from her parents' home, but what she found was all the rest of the history of her life with Gram. School photographs, refrigerator artwork, and homework with 100%, gold stars, or my summer vacation scrawled on the top. Many of the pieces were brittle. Katie wanted to hug them to her, but crushing them wouldn't erase the pain in her chest. She didn't realize she was crying until a tear fell on her arm, leaving a small wet place as it rolled away. Tenderly she packed everything back in the box. Once again, she climbed the stairs, taking the last two boxes to her room. She didn't feel strong enough to go through any more of Irma's things.

"God," she moaned, "if I see one more thing to hurt me, I'm going to lay down and die."

The telephone shrilled in the kitchen, causing her to jump and yelp. Cats scurried into hiding.

"Cowards," she said. Lifting the receiver on the third ring, she belatedly hoped it wasn't Ruth.

"Hey, Katie," said Cindy, "Ruth wanted me to call and tell you to bring the pie server with you." There was a small hesitation. "You are coming, aren't you?"

"Well, yeah." Katie rubbed the back of her head. "I, ah, fell asleep, just dozed right off. I've got to tell you when the telephone rang, I almost jumped out of my skin."

Cindy laughed. "See you soon."

Chapter Twenty

Katie was still standing in the kitchen moments later with the receiver still pressed to her ear, thinking about these people who had so quickly become friends when she heard a faint cough and the clicking of a telephone being hung up.

Replacing the receiver, Katie walked across the room. Abreast of the table, she came to a hard stop, spinning to look at the black communicator. Growing up, the Moores had shared a party line with the Deans. Katie had learned that only when the telephone rang two shorts, not two longs was she allowed to answer the telephone. Gram had taught her it was a cardinal sin to listen in on somebody else's private conversation. She also knew the days of party lines were over. Gram had a private line and so did the Deans.

"So, how could someone else have been on the telephone?" she wondered aloud.

"Because they're in the barn!" she yelled, jumping over cats and racing for the kitchen door. There was a second black telephone hanging inside the main room of the barn. Poppa had taught her the trick of dialing their own number, letting the first ring getting halfway done, and hanging up. It was a signal for someone in the barn to lift the telephone and talk to someone in the house, but if someone called from outside, both telephones rang.

Racing across the lawn, down the short rise, and across the barn lane, Katie ran straight for the milking parlor door. The hasp was set with an unlocked padlock hanging in the hook. She ripped the lock off, threw the hasp, and yanked the door open. Across the room, she struggled with the stubborn sliding door. When it was open enough for her to slip through, she

121

was in the barn rushing toward the telephone. The receiver was hanging in place, just like its twin in the kitchen. The top of the telephone was covered with dust and grain chaff, but the receiver was free of any long-term dirt.

Looking down at her feet, Katie realized that besides her footprints there was a set that appeared to have spun in place. She knew it could have been Ruth, but just as surely, she knew it hadn't.

To the left, at the back of the barn, one of the plywood panels blocking the collapsing area was cockeyed. Nails hung that had been embedded in the surrounding wood frame were now pieces of crooked metal in the light. Katie skidded to a stop at the opening and without thinking ducked through. She came up short on the other side when the sharp sting of barbed wire jabbed her abdomen. Removed from the posts outlining the farmland, several messy rolls of rusted wire had been left just beyond the plywood wall. There was a narrow, cleared path along the plywood wall that led to the opening where Ruth removed boards. Ripping her shirt free from the barbs, Katie moved toward the outside.

Once she stood in the sun, Katie stopped looking for her prey. There was no one in sight. Panting, she scanned the surrounding grassland and orchard again.

"Come out!" she ordered. "Show yourself, slime ball." There was no movement nor the sound of someone running away. Katie drew a ragged breath.

"You killed my grandmother and scared my friends," she yelled. "As I live and breathe, I'll find you S.O.B. and you will pay." She stepped back into the shadows, waiting.

Not twenty feet away Katie's prey lay in the grass behind a small boulder, pressed as flat as possible onto the uneven ground with eyes focused on Katie. The stakes in this game had changed.

* * *

Katie waited until the sweat running down her back began to chill. There was no movement. She returned to the barn the same way she'd come out.

After yanking the plywood back in place, she searched through Poppa's old workbench until she found a claw hammer and a tobacco tin filled with nails. Replacing those nails sticking out in the air, bent when the plywood was kicked free of the supports, Katie banged in enough to deter anyone from entering. Only when she finished and leaned panting on the wall, did she become aware Bonnie was inside her stall woofing in an agitated manner.

"Did you get scared?" Katie asked when she opened the door. "Some jerk was running around in here, probably didn't even know you were here too, then I was yelling and hammering."

Bonnie snuffled at Katie's feet. The pig let out a little squeal and pushed.

"Okay, you can come out, but you'd better watch yourself. The coyotes aren't the only scavengers out there."

Katie climbed the rise to the house, unaware the pig was four steps behind her, and in the orchard, someone else skulked toward the brook.

Chapter Twenty-One

Holding the hose high, Katie dowsed herself with cold water, wetting her clothes and running water into the scrap marks on her stomach.

"Ye-ouch," yelped Katie.

Bonnie grunted and came around to see. Discovering the puddle at Katie's feet, the pig flopped down in the cool wet wiggling back and forth on her back.

"Oh nice, look at you," laughed Katie. "And I've ruined one of my t-shirts."

An hour later Katie sat on the stoop, showered, and having plied needle and thread to the small tears in her shirt. Under the big maple, Bonnie snoozed while Gertie and her friends caught grasshoppers. Rick's pickup pulled in, and Ruth, sunburned and smiling, climbed out.

"What happened to you?" she demanded.

"I fell asleep and woke up only after Cindy called. The nap felt so good, I thought I'd have another," said Katie.

Ruth looked skeptical.

"Then." Katie paused. "Because you all didn't pick up the sign out on the main road when you left, the barn sale had customers."

"Really?" beamed Ruth. She carried the two empty pie pans back into the kitchen. Rick, who was following with the roaster still half-filled with baked beans, followed.

"Liar," he said.

Ruth came right back out with her notebook and plopped down next to Katie.

"Did they buy anything?" she asked. "How much?"

"Ah, seven dollars and fifty cents. I'll get the money for you in a minute." Katie's mouth was dry. She was having a problem looking at Ruth.

"I'm so excited." Ruth jumped to her feet. "I'm going to go put more stuff out." As she turned toward the barn, Bonnie raised her head and woofed.

"Bonnie is out," Ruth said.

"It got hot in the barn," Katie said. Her stomach churned. In a few minutes, she'd be 'fessing up to all the little white lies she'd been spewing. She held her tongue tight against the roof of her mouth until Ruth was too far away to call back.

Ruth filled a bucket with water for the pig's dish and headed toward the milking parlor.

"You're a lousy liar, Katelyn," said Rick.

"You're not my father, or my grandfather either," she said.

"But I am your friend, so I think you might want to be honest with me."

"Well, if you want to know, let me get Ruth so I only have to go through this one time."

"I'll get her," said Rick.

As Katie picked up her sewing utensils, she could hear Rick coaxing Ruth back up to the house, telling her she would be overtired, and he wasn't strong enough to carry her. Laughing, Ruth came with him, agreeing her legs did feel like she'd hiked ten miles.

They sat in the living room with cool drinks, and Katie told them what had transpired after Cindy's call. Ruth covered her mouth with one hand, the other clutched tightly in her lap.

"For crying out loud," said Rick. "Why would someone eavesdrop?"

"I don't know," said Katie. It was clear in her voice the question irritated her.

Rick went into the kitchen with his empty glass, the kitchen door opened and closed, and the women heard him call Bonnie.

"Come on pig, it's time for you to go to bed. Here's an apple for you. That's a girl."

Ruth immediately clucked to the cats. As soon as they heard the top of the food bin open, they rushed toward the cat room. Left alone, Katie decided getting the chickens in the coop that evening would be her project. She got outside just in time to see Rick latching the small door. On the ground near his feet was the telephone from the barn.

He passed it to Katie as he went by.

"I'm sleeping on the sofa tonight," he said.

"Why?" she demanded.

"I had too many beers to drive home."

"How many did you have?" Fumbling with the filthy telephone, she followed him back inside the house.

"Two."

Rick was washing dishes from their cold supper of fresh vegetables and left-over baked beans when Stan and Cindy showed up.

"That's a nice look for you," laughed Stan. "Where's Katie?"

"Down looking at the stuff Ruth dragged out for their barn sale. Ruth was trying to figure out how to price it, so Katie went to see if she could help."

"A barn sale?" smiled Cindy already edging toward the barn. "I'll go get them."

"Might as well make coffee," Stan sighed.

Rick pointed to the half-full percolator left from supper.

When the five of them sat on the porch filling the hanging swing, rocker, and two kitchen chairs, Stan said. "Are you planning on selling the little farm, Katie?"

"Are you interested in buying?" Rick asked.

Stan held up his hand, still watching Katie.

"I don't know what I'm going to do," she said sadly. "It isn't worth anything."

"Once again," he said. "You're young. What you need is a business manager, or maybe a business consultant."

Katie fidgeted in her seat. Her look made it clear she didn't have any idea what he meant. Stan sat back, arms crossed. After a moment, he nodded toward Cindy.

"My degree," said Cindy, clearing her throat self-consciously, "is in real estate development. Stan told me what he saw there and asked me if I'd drive over and look at the property. I told him I wouldn't go out there without your permission."

"You want me to sell it?"

Ruth gave a soft sob. Without another word, she got up and went inside. Rick made a move as if to follow her, then sat back down.

"No actually, *I* don't." Cindy pulled two pages of notes from her pocket. "I'd like to go see it for myself, if it's all right with you. I put together some preliminary ideas you might want to consider. I watch this stuff in the paper all the time, I'm probably seeing opportunities you don't notice. Managing the property is what's going to help you out. Take your time and look over what I wrote out there. However, do not take your time in writing a letter to the Charlotte tax collector. Tell him you just inherited the property, you didn't know about the taxes, and ask for an extension while you gather information. Hand deliver it, talk to him if he's available, but make sure you leave the hard copy."

"Ok-ay," said Katie. "Is that going to do any good?"

Rick looked hopeful.

"It works for other people. If this guy is decent at all, he'll at least consider it. It also puts the town on notice that no matter what, you're trying. If he refuses you, your next step is the board of selectmen."

"You have my permission to go out there, but wear boots because it's sort of wet out back where the pines are growing. I'll write the letter tonight."

Cindy and Stan stood up, ready to leave.

"Office opens at eight," said Stan, "you can go there before work. Also, the guy you're replacing just let me know he's not coming back. At least not soon. He's going to Florida for the winter. I wanted to offer you his full-time job, but you probably don't want to deal with that right now."

"I'll take it," said Katie without hesitation. "Do I get a raise?"

Stan laughed. "You're so funny. Starts tomorrow."

"Great my first day, and I'm going to be late," said Katie. She was standing in front of Cindy's Ralley STX van. "Did you hit a deer?" she asked.

Right in the middle of the bumper and grill was a vertical indentation that seemed to be perfectly rounded.

"No," Cindy laughed. "Right after I got the van in March, I pulled into the parking lot and it was a sheet of ice. I braked, slowed down, and slid gently into the telephone pole near the office door. I barely tapped it and yet, look at the damage."

"Seriously, that was it?" asked Katie.

"Yup, and I'm not getting it fixed because if I do, I'll be asking for another ding."

"She's the queen of dings," said Stan. He patted his wife on the head before climbing into the driver's seat.

It wasn't until after Ruth went to bed leaving her in peace that Katie got the letter for the tax collector written to her satisfaction, wondering all the while why she was bothering to do it. She wrote out a copy for her file drawer and went upstairs. Ruth had left the door to her bedroom cracked open. When she paused, Katie could see the silhouette of several cats laying on Ruth's bed.

Not for me, she thought. Katie always closed the door to her room to keep the cats, with the exception of LG, out. Ruth had told her the sleek tiger was an anomaly in their household because she was a youngster, less than three years old. However, her propensity to bite kept most people away. Katie gave the cat her space. Yet, LG had her own ideas about where she should be.

Katie put her hand on the doorknob and LG scooted around pressing her nose against the door ready to dart inside. Like most nights, LG sat on the chair waiting for Katie to get settled for the night, then when the tossing and turning stopped, the cat circled to the foot of the bed and jumped onto the covers. Tonight, the pattern changed. LG walked up to the pillow and burrowed under the quilt until she found a place in the crook of Katie's knees. Curling into a tight ball, she shut her eyes. The cat was soft and very warm against Katie's skin, like a hug with a built-in purr.

Scrubbed and meek the next morning, Katie arrived in Charlotte and was able to speak with the tax collector directly. The man listened to what she had to say, promising to check on the regulations and get back to her. He also offered to mail her a copy of the last five years' tax bills and payment receipts.

"Before you leave," he said, "you might want to pop into the town planner's office get a copy of the site map. The town had that area surveyed a few years back. There might be information on it you could use. The zoning status will be printed in the legend."

The tax collector's office was in a large common room with three other desks. The zoning officer rated her own closet-size office. Though the space was small, there was a beautiful old twelve-pane window.

While Katie had been talking with the tax collector, other people had been doing business. Among those waiting was an individual seated in one of the vintage oak chairs lined up near the front door. The seated individual was intent on the local paper, which she held high and close. When Katie, with Ruth in tow, went into the zoning officer's office, the individual moved down the line of seats to the empty one outside the small office door.

Following the tax collector's suggestion, Katie was given several more pages. As an added tidbit, the planning officer told Katie, Irma had paid the extra fee to have the Roser survey sealed in Mylar. Therefore, according to the law, it was a certified copy with grandfathered rights newer developments didn't receive.

While working, Ms. Deyak remarked, "There was someone in here a while ago asking about property on the Kitteridge Road."

"Huh?" said Katie.

"Yeah, I think they were talking about a house lot to move a modular to. Anyway, I believe this is all you need. You can contact the state for a booklet on state rules that might be different from the county regulations, but usually, ours are stricter."

"Thank you," said Katie, rising. She shook Ms. Deyak's hand and exited the office. The row of oak chairs was empty.

They exited the building just as a suited gentleman crossed the lot and climbed into a new white Cadillac parked at the far end of the row in front of the town office.

Ruth waved energetically at the woman sitting in the Cadillac. Even though the woman faced them, she didn't appear to see Ruth.

Checking for traffic on either side of the stop sign, Katie noticed Ruth's frown.

"What's the matter, Ruth? Was that someone you thought you knew?"

"I know who she is, just not her name," Ruth answered. "She's our best customer at the barn sale."

"Is that so?" Katie's mind was on the information she had just received from the Charlotte clerk.

"Yes, she comes in two or three times a week. I recognize her car and her plate says MISSUS, like either Mrs. or did you miss us? It's funny, don't you think?"

"Ah-huh," said Katie.

"She's very friendly, always has time for a chat." Ruth sighed. "I guess she just didn't recognize me."

Back in the lot, the woman reached into her handbag for the crumbled Marlboro pack.

Chapter Twenty-Two

Cindy was in the feed store office wearing jeans and boots when Katie arrived after dropping Ruth off.

"This is great!" She beamed at Katie. "I'm going over later this morning. Ruth said she would watch the kids while I'm gone."

"Is that okay?" asked Katie.

"Yes, she'll be fine. They love hanging with her. She told them they could all go to the churn house, so Grace will be around. This should only take about three hours."

That morning Rick had been gone before Katie was downstairs. The blankets and sheets he'd used the night before lay folded on the arm of the sofa.

"Rick left a while ago," Ruth had explained while stirring the inevitable oatmeal. "He said he needed to get some work clothes, though to tell you the truth, all his clothes look the same to me."

"Kind of like mine," Katie pointed out.

Now she spied him walking across the lot. "Hey," Katie yelled. "You left before breakfast this morning and I wanted to talk to you."

Several people in the lot jerked to a stop, heads turning from the young woman to the old man. Katie immediately realized what her statement had implied. She held up her hands.

"No, no, it's not like that," she said to those assembled. "He had too many beers and slept on the sofa."

Someone let out a wolf whistle.

"Be quiet, Katie," growled Rick, moving toward the office door. "You're

131

only making it worse."

Running to catch up, she pinched his shirt sleeve. "I was only trying to explain," she said.

"Yeah, well, I think you said enough." Rick turned to a group of sniggering co-workers and flipped them off.

During the rest of the morning, Rick avoided being alone with Katie. Frustrated with her inability to get him to listen to her, she sat near him at lunch, speaking in whispers.

"I'm worried that whoever is hanging around the house might do something dangerous; you know like bad enough to hurt either Ruth or myself. I'm wondering about filing for some kind of protection order."

"What good is a protection order going to do you, if there is no one to serve it on? Who's going to know they have to leave you alone if they haven't been told?"

Though to anyone else the conversation sounded convoluted, Katie got it.

"Then why did you insist on sleeping on the couch?" She leaned back on a hay bale, shaking her bangs out of her face.

"Seemed like a good idea at the time. You need a haircut. You're starting to look like a sheep."

Katie bit back a sharp retort. She'd embarrassed him. She knew he needed some time to get over it.

Moments later, the PA called Katie to the telephone.

"It's the town," said Stan. "If it's a work call, make sure you get directions."

Katie's eyebrows shot up.

"You took the dog catcher job, it's like being a fireman, the call comes, you go. If you know exactly where you're going, you'll be faster."

Sure enough, the call was for an older dog dragging a rope behind him and trying to get into a stranger's house. Katie arrived, and the distressed Basset Hound willingly allowed Katie to heft him into the Subaru. He was wearing a license, so Katie went right to the town hall.

"This is the book you use if they have a license." The clerk handed her an old ledger. "Year, then number. Here's a voucher."

"I have vouchers but all I did was pick him up and I'm going to take him home."

"Doesn't matter honey, you went on the call so you get paid."

Katie took the dog back to his home, tied a knot in his rope, got him water, and left the owner a note. Later she went out on another call where a woman in high heels and skin-tight jeans pointed toward a dead sparrow on the lawn. The jangling of several bangles was distracting, but eventually, Katie realized the poor bird had slammed into the picture window.

"People hang sun-catchers and things in the windows so the birds understand they can't just fly through," Katie told the woman who covered her eyes so she couldn't see the bird Katie had wrapped in a glove. "I'll take him home, bury him. I have to tell you though, you reported a game bird and this is a sparrow. Can you sign this voucher for me?"

"You should have seen her," Katie told Ruth. "She was hysterical."

"It's a shame people don't realize what they create wreaks havoc with nature's babies." Ruth took the bird and a shovel to the orchard.

Katie's first day full-time had proven to be fewer hours than part-time. She sat down with a copy of Irma's contract with the town in hand. She was of two minds about keeping the town job.

"If I keep getting called away, Stan might let me go," she explained to LG. "On the other hand, if I'm leaving anyway…"

Are you? Asked the voice in her mind.

Chapter Twenty-Three

Night had once again proven to be a magician changing the weather, not caring about residue damp or humidity or the plans of mice and men. Outside, the woods on the other side of the lawn faded in and out of a cloying fog.

"I can't tell if I'll get soaked today or sweat bullets until I'm a shriveled-up stalk," said Katie.

"I know," said Ruth, pulling her sweater nearer. "My friend Arthur Itis was complaining last night."

Katie shook her head. "You've got some mighty strange friends, Ruth. I'll feed Bonnie before I go."

"I'll get her," said Ruth. "She's going to want to be out for a little while. I think she likes to play in the puddles left by the rain."

Hoping Rick would be in a better mood than the day before, Katie stopped and bought him a lemon-filled raised doughnut. She left the peace offering next to his thermos and retrieved her first order receipt. As she moved away to collect the order, she heard him say:

"Yep, this will go great with the rest of my breakfast. Nothing like a cold chicken leg and a mushy doughnut."

Katie turned toward Rick; a retort sharp on her tongue. But Rick was looking beyond Katie, and she swung around.

Ruth stood in the entrance to the feed store storage barn. She had changed into a cotton dress since Katie had seen her earlier. The older woman looked sweaty and wan.

"It's a good thing I've got strong legs," she said.

Both Katie and Rick gaped, surprise on both faces.

"What are you doing here?" Katie asked.

"Why didn't you call if you needed a ride?" asked Rick.

"I can get around all by myself, thank you very much. I rode in as far as the creamery with Grace," Ruth said to Rick. Turning to Katie, she said. "A woman called from the feed store and told me you wanted me to come down. So, I came."

Katie walked over to Ruth, pointing to a bale of hay for the woman to sit on.

"I didn't ask anyone to call you, Ruth. I wouldn't make you walk into town, especially not in this humidity."

"Was it Cindy who called?" asked Rick. "She's the only other woman than Katie that works here."

"It wasn't Cindy. This woman had a funny sort of accent," said Ruth.

Katie and Rick looked at each other, both worried this was a troubling manifestation of Ruth's confusion. Ruth watched them both. With the return of her medications, her mind was clearer, and she knew it. It was obvious what the other two thought, and though it was on the tip of her tongue to argue with them; she kept silent. Arguing with the police and lawyer when George died almost got her arrested. When Irma had been lying dead in the meadow, Ruth had demanded answers and the town doctor gave her a shot that knocked her out. Neither incident had worked well for Ruth and at that moment there didn't seem to be a good reason to bother ruffling up Rick and Katie.

Ruth had used notebook paper to create notices about the cats and the barn sale. She had carried them with her in her tote. Now she pulled them out to make sure they weren't crushed.

"I made these to hang up," she said. "I'll get that taken care of now and then go home. Grace is probably still at the creamery."

"I have a doc...an appointment this afternoon," said Katie. "If Grace already left you can walk around town and hang up the notices. Then I'll take you home when I get done." She read the page Ruth offered. "Good job."

Ruth smiled. Rick who knew where Katie was going relaxed. He was sure telling Ruth that Katie's appointment was with the doctor Ruth no longer trusted would have caused difficulties.

After explaining to Stan, she had to leave early to see the doctor, Katie drove over to the library parking lot. Her plan was to leave the car there in the event Ruth finished before she did. Once Ruth and the first of her notices were safely inside the building, Katie crossed the street to the gray single-family dwelling the doctor now both lived in and worked out of.

"Well, hello, Katie," said the doctor walking into the exam room. "I hear you've suffered a sprain that's not healing. You must be new here I don't remember seeing you before."

"Actually," said Katie, sitting on the exam table swinging her legs back and forth, having totally ignored the gown the nurse left for her. "I believe you do know me."

"Is that so?" The doctor smiled, closing the door behind him.

"Yeah," said Katie. Getting to her feet, she walked around the doctor to lean on the closed door.

A brief flash of doubt furrowed his brow.

"Actually, you probably know my grandmother better."

"What's your game young lady?" His smile disappeared. Now he was the professional whose demeanor demanded she step down.

"Chill out," said Katie. "I have some questions."

"About?"

"Irma Moore. Remember, I said my grandmother?"

If there was a chance the old man would wet himself, that was it, and for a second Katie thought it was a possibility. The doctor staggered, his left hand catching the side of the exam table Katie had just vacated, steadying himself.

"What? Who?" he croaked.

"I told you who. Now I want you to tell me what." Katie straightened up, pulling her five feet nine inches as tall as possible. "You said she had a heart attack. That's a crock of bull pucky, and you know it. You signed your name on a death certificate. Are you ready to recant, tell me what actually happened?"

"Get. Out." The doctor's arms shot up pointing to the door. In the small room, Katie almost jumped away from what could have been him slapping at her. Instead, she held her ground. Spittle appeared at the corner of his mouth. He swiped at it with a trembling hand and fingers that wouldn't straighten to work correctly. "You, you get out of here right now before I call the police."

"Sure," she said, sighing but still with a small smile. "You can call the sheriff. But before I go, I have one other question. Did you know that two days prior to my grandmother's death, she'd had a full physical by a doctor at Mary Fletcher Hospital in Burlington? Yeah, and that doctor is willing to give me a sworn statement that there was no way Gram could have had a heart attack. So, sayonara sucker. My lawyer's name is Wilkins. You'll be hearing from him." She stepped out, slamming the door as she went.

"Miss," called the receptionist, "payment is due at the time of service."

"There won't be any charge," said Katie without turning around. She returned to her car and though it was drizzling again, it was sweat that soaked through her clothing. She waited for Ruth, expecting to hear sirens any moment.

"How did it go?" asked Ruth, climbing into the car.

"Like throwing gas on a fire," Katie said. Sitting there with her hand on the key, Katie decided to tell Ruth about visiting the doctor. There was a chance the old man was going to make a call, and Sheriff Lewis would show up at the house. Ruth needed to be prepared.

"What?" Ruth's mouth dropped open.

"Yeah, I went to visit the doctor. I had questions, though I did forget to ask him about the autopsy results. I just threw a bald-faced lie at him which is going to make him panic. He's probably going to call whoever else is involved."

Ruth sucked air through barely parted lips. "There wasn't an autopsy," she said.

"You know that for a fact?" Katie turned the ignition key while watching Ruth.

"When I asked him how they could have cremated Irma so quickly, I specifically remember him saying there was no reason to wait. He said they didn't have to do an autopsy because the reason for death was so obvious. Heart attack."

"Okay, well, it's a good thing I told Stan I probably wouldn't be back today because we're going to make another stop on the way home," said Katie.

At Ruth's questioning look, Katie added. "We're going to Williston and visit the state police."

The desk sergeant was very clear that for most county calls, the sheriff ranked higher than the Staties. Katie's mouth gaped open.

"I believe it's possible my grandmother was murdered. I need to see some kind of accident report. There is also the issue with her being cremated before anyone in the family was notified."

The sergeant summoned a lieutenant who took the two women to an inner office. Katie repeated her demands while the man took notes.

"Were there any witnesses? Did you see anything that would raise suspicion?"

"I wasn't here," Katie said. "Ruth found Gram about dusk."

"So, the deceased was an elderly person, and you," he nodded toward Ruth, "who are also of advanced years went out in near darkness looking for your friend? Did you have a flashlight?"

"I am neither senile nor blind," spat Ruth. Her lower lip trembled. Both Katie and the lieutenant noticed.

"Point taken. No matter the cause, every time an officer of the law goes on a call, an incident report needs to be generated. I'm going to contact Sheriff Lewis and ask to see the report. You," he nodded at Katie, "have the right to see both that report and the coroner's report. There are forms they will probably demand you fill out if they are not forthcoming. After I see both reports, I will contact you with my findings. As far as the cremation, if the decedent had left written instructions, the doctor wasn't in error. Why he didn't wait until after you were notified, I'm unsure. That's a question I will ask him. You should also be able to read the statement Ms. Beauregard gave the investigating officer."

There was a moment's silence and Ruth said. "No one took my statement."

Both the Lieutenant and Katie looked at Ruth. Katie's jaw dropped; she couldn't believe she hadn't asked Ruth this before.

"No one asked you any questions, not one? Or take notes?" asked the lieutenant. "You didn't sign a document about what you saw or said, or maybe he read it back to you and you agreed?"

"No," said Ruth, "and I'm sure of it." She sat back, glaring at the others.

Katie left the state police office feeling exhausted. In her seat, Ruth slumped against the door. Concerned she might have pushed Ruth too far, Katie asked if the older woman wanted to get something to eat.

Ruth gave a harsh laugh. "Neither you nor I have two nickels to rub together," she said.

Katie's concern was not assuaged. Pulling into the next mini-mart, she came back with a black coffee, a highly sweetened tea, and a package of cheese and crackers. "Sometimes, the best way to help yourself is to treat yourself," she said.

"Is that a commandment?" asked Ruth, slurping from the hot cup.

"Yeah, number fifteen I think."

Taking a chance there would still be someone at the sheriff's office, Katie stopped there next. It was a relief to find Marlie seated at the desk. The other deputy who had helped with the pig wrangling sat in Sheriff Lewis's office.

Katie stood to the side and kept her voice low. "Hey, Marlie, it seems I need a little help here. Sheriff Lewis has some information I need."

Marlie walked over to the office door and pushed it shut. "What kind of information?"

"I need to get an incident report for the day my grandmother died and a copy of the coroner's report. Is there a chance Sheriff Lewis would have that too?"

"These are the same reports the state troopers just called about?" asked Marlie.

"They already called, huh?" Katie's hopes were flagging.

"That's what Boyd is doing," said Marlie.

"I hear there are forms to fill out," Katie said.

"Sometimes," said Marlie.

At Katie's questioning look, the deputy continued. "Anytime you're going to use the information for any type of legal action, you need to establish the transfer with a paper trail. Lots of times no one wants a copy, but if they do, want to hold it and make a bad situation real in their minds, the sheriff just gives it to them. I'd have to check and see what he wants to do this time."

"O-kay," said Katie. Her submissive demeanor was quickly changing to anger.

Marlie was aware of the change.

"How about if I give you a call in a little while?" she said.

Katie nodded and left.

* * *

Supper and cleanup were through when a knock sounded at the door. Katie found Marlie standing outside. When Katie invited Marlie in, the deputy hesitated.

"Yes?" asked Katie. Unsure why Marlie looked so nervous, Katie stood to the side waiting, in the event the issue Marlie was wrestling with would be solved, and she would come inside.

"Did you know I grew up in this town, that I was in the same grade you were?" asked Marlie.

Katie blinked.

"No, I can see you didn't. But you were one of those kids. The ones we were all warned about. One foot in a dark place looking for trouble, the other in line getting awards for stellar grades. Me, I was one of the poor kids who couldn't afford hot lunch. Lived with my drunken mom in shantytown. My dad was a loser who only came around for a week or so every couple of years. Then he'd leave again, and I'd get a new brother or sister. If I hadn't felt responsible to make sure the kids had something to eat, I'd have been doing drugs or knocked up myself. I was on the verge of dropping out of high school when CETA came along. It was a federal program that paid us to go to school, found us jobs where we could get some training and work after we graduated or got our GED."

"I was working at Green Mountain Glovers the last time the cops hauled my mother away. They took the little kids into state custody and left me alone. I remember standing in the doorway watching them go, it was a day like today with the rain falling down. This one cop turned around to look at me. She didn't say anything, but sort of smiled like she knew how hurt I was, but I was going to be okay. I don't think she knew how to help me. She was the only woman cop I'd ever seen. I didn't even know women could be cops."

"I worked hard to get to where I am, Katie Took. I don't want to lose it."

"I respect that," said Katie. "I would never do anything to jeopardize your career. I can take no for an answer."

Marlie stepped over the door-sill into the living room.

"That said, I firmly believe," said Marlie, "that if the state police are allowed to receive information with no more than a telephone call, we should allow the family the same rights." She held out a manila envelope to Katie.

"Cup of tea, Deputy?" Ruth, who had been standing in the kitchen doorway, offered.

"No thank you, ma'am, I'm on my way out."

After Marlie left, Katie sat in the rocker carefully reading every word. Ruth made tea for them, put another piece of wood into the stove, and taking up her knitting waited for Katie to speak.

"It seems," said Katie, "Sheriff Lewis' report reads exactly as he said. He received a call regarding a death, found an elderly woman lying in a field, county doctor said heart attack. No next of kin to contact. Hm."

"There's also a copy of the coroner's report, which would be the local doctor. Pretty much the same. He writes that death was evident, no family for consultation. Written request found in the home indicated party wished to be cremated with no other arrangements. He also added a note that he contacted the crematorium in Saint Johnsbury and they replied they could process the remains immediately. They sent transport."

"Does that mean this is the end of it?" asked Ruth in a small voice.

"There's a big difference between what people knew and what they wrote," said Katie. "If this is their story and they want to stick by it, so be it. Me? I'm stepping up the game." Katie looked at Ruth wrapped in a throw, surrounded by cats, and looking frail in the lamplight.

"I think we should take Rick up on his offer and you should stay there for a while. I'm stepping out of the shadows, Ruth. I don't want to take a chance of you getting hurt."

Ruth laughed. "You really must think I'm a candy butt. I'm not going anywhere. Who do you think shot the deer in the freezer? I'm perfectly capable." After neatly folding the throw, putting away her knitting, and rinsing out the teacups, Ruth retired.

"What I'm worried about," Katie said to LG, "is that if I can watch her behavior and predict what she's about to do, so can someone else." She shut off the lamp and sat in the darkness with the muted radio playing as she considered what to do next.

Chapter Twenty-Four

E ven though the rain had stopped and the suffocating late summer heat returned from the day before, there were still muddy puddles in the parking lot. Katie could see the shimmer of vapor from where she stood on the edge of the concrete loading dock. Behind her, Rick was enjoying a cool drink of water from his thermos jug.

"You know, Raymond said a truck or trucks with wide tires made the tracks in the hayfield. Even these tires," Katie pointed to the delivery truck parked below her, "aren't all that much wider than a car's, but if you were going to la Bamba up a truck, you'd buy something that all your macho friends wouldn't miss."

"La Bamba?" asked Rick, eyebrow rising.

"It's a term from out west. It means jacking a truck up, or making it more macho, you know what I mean? It's a male hormone thing."

Both of Rick's eyebrows shot up.

"For crying out loud, Rick. Eighteen-year-old males, remember those days?" Exasperated, Katie threw her hands up.

"I know exactly what you mean," said Rick. "Now tell me what this has to do with unloading oats."

"You've seen the dent in Cindy's van?"

Rick nodded.

"She said she was barely moving and yet ended up with all that damage. How much damage would you do if you were racing across a hayfield and hit a hundred-and fifty-pound woman?"

Rick exhaled, parking his haunches on the oat sacks.

"I'm thinking," Katie continued, "a lot more. Enough so you'd have to get repairs. Maybe enough so you'd turn to your insurance company to cover the bill. And where in this town would you go for those repairs, or even for an estimate?"

"Son of a…" Rick began.

Suddenly Katie became aware customers had come up the steps and were walking toward them. She held her hand up to stop Rick, then moved out the way so the man and the woman could give Rick their receipt. While Rick scanned the paper, the customers eyed Katie, who stood with her back to them. Both people speculated on whether she was waiting for help or supposed to be waiting on them. At the end of her shift, Katie pulled out of the employee parking area, bypassing the turnoff to the Parentville-Charlotte Road as she drove north. In the store parking lot across from the intersection, a cigarette butt flipped out of the driver's window as they shifted the vehicle into drive following the Subaru.

When Katie pulled into the entrance for Phil's Automotive, the other vehicle continued past.

"Hey Philip," Katie called out. "Are you still in here?"

From beneath the front end of an older Chevy pickup, a voice answered. "Over here."

Katie found a pair of legs wrapped in oily coveralls sticking out from beneath the truck. The rest of the body laid atop a creeper out of sight. "Do you have a couple minutes?"

"What can I do for you?" The legs jiggled as Phil worked, but he remained beneath the chassis.

"Have you done any repairs, or maybe estimates on a vehicle that hit a… deer, since the first of July?" Katie held her breath.

"A deer you say?"

"Well, anything bigger than maybe a raccoon."

"Yeah, I've done some. Why?"

"Do you have any sort of records?"

"Sure, I do. I get a receipt for every job, except maybe fixing a flat." Philip laughed. "In the office, hanging on the wall is my clipboard. Knock yourself out." Metal clanged on metal.

Katie turned away, then stopped. What office? Other than a restroom she might want to avoid, there wasn't another room. Then she noticed the tall stool in front of the workbench.

"I guess," she murmured, "your office space is all in your own perspective." Over the workbench was a cork pinboard, a calendar of questionable subject matter, and the clipboard. Taking it down, Katie started flipping backwards through it. She got all the way to March before she found a vehicle with a deer collision note.

"Nothing," she said.

"What exactly are you looking for?" said a voice directly behind her.

Katie screamed, jumped sideways, and slammed into the workbench.

"That's going to leave a mark," said Philip, wiping grease from his hands with an already blackened rag.

Rubbing her hip, Katie glared at him.

"I'm looking for some young hotrod's pickup truck that sustained front end damage," she said.

"Which hotrodder's?"

"One with extra wide tires."

"Yeah, like that's not all of them." Philip threw the rag on the workbench. Reaching around Katie for his lunchbox, he said. "If this kid did anything less than serious structural damage, he could have fixed it at school. CVU has a mechanic's course. They fix cars, tractors, stuff like that at cost. It's cheap and is part of the hands-on vocational training. Also consider, if you contact your insurance company, they might send you to a repairman they contracted with."

After locking the door, he said, "I'll check around. I don't need to be involved, but sometimes deer are dear."

Katie was back in traffic before it occurred to her that as Grace's brother, Philip probably had a fair idea why she was fishing for information. She chided herself, unaware that the vehicle which had followed her earlier was once more behind her. When she turned on Fire Lane 61, the other car continued without slowing down.

Once in the kitchen, Katie crossed her fingers and dialed the telephone.

"Chittenden County Sheriff Department, Parentville office," said a female voice.

"Hi, Deputy Marlie?" Katie reddened, unable to remember Marlie's last name.

"Foster," Marlie answered. "Can I help you?"

"Whew, Marlie, this is Katie Took. Can you tell me what the law is regarding the filing of a police accident report if you have to file an insurance claim?"

"Of course." Marlie's voice warmed. "In regards to a motor vehicle accident, if there is over five hundred dollars damage or an injury, you need to have a police report. Other than that, you just call your insurance agent. Out here, if the accident happens on their own property, most people don't bother with us unless there's going to be an insurance claim. Is that what you need?"

"Perfect," said Katie. After a two-breath pause, she added, "Have a good day."

Katie hadn't found Ruth in the house, and with the kitchen door unlocked, the other woman had to be somewhere on the property. After checking the chicken coop, Katie headed down to the barn where she found Bonnie rolling in a puddle only slightly larger than she was.

"Are you getting bigger?" Katie asked. "I really need to find someone to adopt you."

Katie stepped into the milking parlor and looked around in astonishment. The windows, once filmed with years of dust, sparkled. Every spider web was wiped away and a coat of whitewash had been applied over the many years' collection of fly scat. Smaller pieces of furniture were gathered to one side and more plank shelves had appeared. These shelves, unlike the single-layer ones outside, were three high holding glassware, decorative items, and a basket of knitted cat toys. Ruth was organizing vases against the far wall.

"Better close your mouth, Katie," said Ruth, "before a fly pops in."

"Holy cow," Katie said. "Look at all the space." Then she realized what was

146

missing.

"Where's the milk cooler?" Katie had assumed the cooler was merely hidden from sight before by all the stacked clutter. For years the large metal container filled with cold water had taken up half the space. The heavy metal milk cans would sit in the water which was pumped in directly from the well. Then the water moved through the vat before flowing into the barn to the cattle water stations and other piping systems before flowing back out a pipe that hung above the orchard stream. As a child, she and the Deans had played in the spout of icy water throughout the hot summer days.

"The man that bought the tractor took that also," said Ruth.

Katie spun around, astonished.

"The tractor isn't in the barn!" she stammered. Right along she had believed the Massey-Ferguson dinosaur was also hidden from view in the clutter.

Aware Katie couldn't know all that Irma had done to keep the property; Ruth stopped sorting through the box in front of her.

"Listen, Katie, don't get mad at Irma." There was a clearness in Ruth's eyes Katie hadn't seen before. "When she got too old to do the heavy work at the factory anymore, and machinery was brought in replacing a lot of the people, money got tight. She got cut back to part-time, but refused to sell the land. She did what she had to. The tractor wasn't running. Some guy from Bristol answered her ad. He took the tractor, the manure spreader, and the cooling tank. She sold milk cans to tourists at the farmer's market. You know the herd was sold after your grandfather died. The single milk cow she kept in the orchard finally got so old, she had to go too. Every time she had to sell something, it broke Irma's heart. If she'd had to sell the farm too, I believe she'd have just laid down and died."

Katie nodded in agreement. "It's okay Ruth, Gram was so tight, I'm sure she wouldn't give anything away. She did what she had to do. I know that. It just, well, took me by surprise. I spent a lot of hours working on that old pile of junk. I mean, it didn't bother me at all when the John Deere tractor was sold after the cows were. I guess somehow I just got attached to the Massey." Shrugging, she continued examining the items Ruth had put out, picking up a wheat pattern plate from a stacked set. "I don't remember any of this stuff."

Ruth looked over the goods ready to be sold in the same way Katie did. She didn't remember ever seeing most of the pieces either, but all that mattered now was that they were out where prospective customers could see them.

"Tomorrow," said Ruth, "put the sign out at the end of the road. I can manage the one for the end of the barn lane. I'll watch for cars. I used masking tape as price tags. The things I didn't tag I'll just have to tell people."

"Tomorrow's not Saturday." Katie pointed out.

"One customer on a weekday is better than none on Saturday," Ruth replied. "I'll just listen for cars. I can put a note up telling them to blow the horn."

Back in the house, Ruth showed Katie an old vinyl bank bag she had found to use as a cash drawer. "I'll lock the house if I leave and put a cash tin down at the barn in case I don't hear someone pull in."

"Yeah, you could get old and gray waiting for someone to find us here," said Katie.

Ruth had left the mail laying on the counter; Katie took it with her, along with a cup of coffee. Among the bills and flyers were two envelopes from the town of Charlotte. One was from Ms. Deyak informing her the Roser property was zoned Agricultural/Commercial and grandfathered for multiple development platforms. The second letter was from the planning board addressed on the inside to Mr. Took, explaining these were the forms needed to proceed with the request for development.

Katie flipped back to the envelope and found it was addressed to Mr. and Mrs. K. Took.

"Who told them I had a husband?" she said. "Then again, what do they think I'm developing?" Putting the letters aside to show to Cindy, she went back outside to take the laundry off the line. Out of sight was out of mind, as she immediately forgot the letters now stored on top of the refrigerator.

Chapter Twenty-Five

"Katie, report to the office," said a female voice over the PA.

"Whoa," said Katie, straightening up. "Just like high school."

"Better go see what she wants, I'll finish getting that order together," said Rick.

Rigid with trepidation, Katie rapped on the office door, fearful her challenge to the doctor or some other place she'd been snooping around had come back to kick her in the butt.

"Come on in, Katie." Cindy smiled. Without waiting for Katie to close the door or sit down, Cindy continued.

"I wanted to talk to you somewhere there wouldn't be a lot of ears tuned in to our conversation," she explained. "I went out to the property and walked around. It went well except for the couple of minutes after I stepped on a grass snake. It's a good thing I was alone because there was a whole lot of cussing going on." Cindy laughed and Katie smiled in return.

"Anyway, I told you my education was in real estate development and consequently use of land or natural resources. I made a list of ideas for you to consider. The first and maybe the fastest would be the sandpit. Someone dropped trees across the entrance years ago to stop excavation, that's an easy fix. There's a lot of development around here right now. Contractors are hauling fill from all over. The sandpit on the Roser property covers a wide area. I think it might go all the way back to the mountain. If you go that route, you need to find out about permit requirements through the town of Charlotte. Then get a list of contractors. Each town has to license them or provide permits, it's a good place to start getting names. After that, you just send out a form letter, see who bites and what they offer."

Katie nodded.

"I could draft a generic letter you could mimeograph and mail out," volunteered Cindy.

Katie nodded.

"Ah, let's see." Cindy looked back at the paper in her hand. "There's soft wood that could be harvested, lots of old stuff in the sheds for your barn sale, and maybe you could check into the septic system and well where the house was. If you cleaned it up, maybe you could rent the spot for a mobile home?" She sat back and looked expectantly at Katie, who stared back, fascinated by everything Cindy had found. "Is there something wrong?" Cindy asked.

"No." Katie swallowed. "I thought that was just old farmland, not worth much of anything and yet you've found all this potential."

"Oh, don't get me started. I even considered a Christmas tree farm, but that's going to require clearing the fields, lots of work, and money. So, that would be considered a long-range, like a ten-year project. But thank you anyway," Cindy's cheeks pinked. "It was fun, except for the snake part. I may have found myself new employment."

Katie went back to work with the folded paper in her pocket and a new list of things to do growing in her mind. For the next little while, Katie slid into a daydream where she evolved into a billionaire land entrepreneur. She laughed as her cartoon skit had her wearing three-piece suits and passing out imported cigars.

"What's so funny?" Rick asked.

Katie stopped short. "The idea that I could fly in like superman and actually salvage something from all the mess at the farm." Her spoken words threw cold water reality on the pipe dream causing it to evaporate like steam from the teakettle and clearing the air for worry to move back in.

Unaware Katie's mood had taken a sharp dive, Rick said. "Well, I've heard truth is stranger than fiction and time is the great equalizer." He turned; his face as serious as hers when he added. "Which piece of the puzzle are you going to put down first? I'm betting from the grin on Cindy's face, she already gave you her two cents worth. What did she have to say?"

"What?" Confusion skewered Katie's face.

A truck horn beeped as a customer backed in.

"Like you said yourself, Rick, work at work. We can talk about all the rest later."

Being Saturday and the first day of the county fair in Essex, work slowed down by mid-afternoon.

"Going to the fair, Katie?" Rick asked.

"Doubt it," she said.

"You seem to have gotten a little on the subdued side. What happened to all that giggle earlier?" asked Rick. "Something stuck in your craw?"

Katie straightened up. Turning, she dropped all pretense and said, "I'm frustrated beyond belief, Rick. I'm not getting anywhere finding out what happened to my Gram. At this rate, I'm still going to lose the Roser farm. I've never amounted to much of anything, and since I've been back, I'm losing ground. When I first got here, I just wanted to get out, to be honest right now I'm not sure what I want."

Rick stared back at her, sucking his teeth. "So, you done bawling like a baby?"

"I am," said Katie. She felt an unreasonable amount of relief at giving words to her inner turmoil. "From now on, if somebody asks me who I am, I'm gonna tell them. If they tell me they knew my grandmother, I'm going to ask them how well. I'm thinking of going to see the lawyer and seeing what he has to offer for ideas."

"I see," Rick turned back to the job at hand. "What about what Cindy turned up, was it not worth her time?"

Katie blinked; she had been so busy chasing her problem around in her head; she had forgotten about Cindy's list. Suddenly, she laughed aloud. "Read this," she said, passing him the folded paper. When Rick finished, Katie said, "Tuesday was supposed to be my day off, so I thought I'd go then, but Stan said there's some huge fall order coming in and I need to be here. Which is good, I guess; cause I'm going to need to do more than pay the minimum on that stack of bills on the refrigerator. I'm not going to have time to get over to Charlotte."

"Call them on the telephone Monday," said Rick. "I'm sure they'll give you the permit information, maybe send the forms over to you."

"They're not going to give me the list of contractors over the telephone."

Rick stopped what he was doing, walked over to Katie, put his forefinger against her forehead, and shoved backward."

"Duh," he said. "Take your lunch while the Parentville town office is still open. Get your list off their permit books. Anybody working in Charlotte is working in Parentville too."

She grinned up at her friend. "Duh, you are so right. I've already got the letter Cindy drew up for me. I'll bring it Monday and just pay for the copies."

"Too late to get stamps today, but you'll need them too."

Katie two-stepped along the deck way. "Ya, oh ya, oh ya."

Rick laughed at her and a voice from down on the ground asked, "You guys having a party, can anyone join in or maybe just get my feed?"

Chapter Twenty-Six

"**K**atie, telephone for you," Ruth called up the stairs.

"Who is it?" asked Katie. With her right hand gripping the cannonball on the bottom of the stair railing, she cornered sharp and fast stepped toward the kitchen.

"Sheriff," said Ruth, but Katie was far enough past at that point to miss her words.

"Hello, this is Katie."

"Hi Katie, this is Deputy Foster," said Marlie. There was apprehension in her voice, Katie felt her shoulders tighten. "Listen," Marlie continued. "Sheriff Lewis told me to call you." There was a soft cough. "It seems one of the Vermont County Bank employees called. They're having an issue with a problem skunk who moved in under the back steps of the bank. They want it removed this weekend. The Charlotte animal officer is on vacation and Sheriff Lewis volunteered you." The last few words came out in a rush.

"He wants me to go to Charlotte to trap a *skunk*?"

"Yes," said Marlie. "I heard him say you'd be out there tonight."

"Really?"

"Yes."

Katie could barely hear Marlie.

What a jerk, thought Katie of Lewis.

"Okay, Marlie," said Katie, exhaling through pursed lips. "You tell him...," she paused and her eyes flicked up to Ruth who was watching with concern. "I'm on it." Hanging up, Katie turned to Ruth. "What are the chances we have a live trap for a skunk?"

"Irma kept it in the garage," said Ruth. "You can't put a skunk in your car."

With the live trap, a piece of tarp, and a jar of peanut butter in the back of the pickup, Katie drove over to Charlotte. Other than the gas station/convenience store, most of the businesses on the main street were closed for the day. There was an alley between the bank and the Burns' Accounting office building. Katie backed in. The back steps to the bank were constructed of wood and ended with a small platform level with the door. Katie placed the trap in front of the opening under the platform, collected some cardboard boxes from a neighboring Dumpster to create a single exit from the platform, and baited the trap.

"I'll be back tomorrow morning," Katie promised as she got back in the truck. "I promise." On the way home, she stopped at the Dairy Whip and treated herself to a soft-serve ice cream cone. "After all," she said, "I'm showered, cleaned, and don't smell stinky. Yet."

She was up and out early while Ruth was still barely moving around in her room. Arriving while the only traffic in Charlotte was headed toward the church, Katie backed into the alley again. She approached the trap cautiously. There was a muted chittering noise, and the trap rattled when the occupant became aware of Katie, who came to an immediate halt. Inside the trap, a large, furry, black and white critter attempted a one-hundred-and-eighty-degree turn. Katie backed away.

Laying atop the platform on her belly, Katie reached down, adjusting the tarp until the whole contraption was covered. Once she was on the ground and sure the skunk couldn't see her and therefore react, she hefted the trap into the back of the truck. Once again, she made sure there was no sneaky way the skunk could spray her. With the tailgate securely closed, Katie gathered the cardboard and threw it back in the smallish Dumpster. The morning was crisp, clear, and so fresh Katie couldn't resist inhaling deeply. Even though she was no longer in the vicinity of the skunk, she was still standing within whiffing range of the dumpster.

"Oh, gag," Katie coughed. Moving away she stood hands on knees coughing the stink out while facing the fields behind the main street buildings. A deep trench ran between Katie and the meadows where birds dipped and fluttered and the occasional suicidal grasshopper jumped into the sun's rays.

At the edge of the trench, Katie could see discarded cardboard. "For crying out loud," she cussed clamoring over the side of the ditch. "The dumpster is right here."

The cardboard proved to be a box filled with dishes. A white pattern encircled with golden sheaves of wheat. Her eyes narrowed. She had seen this same pattern recently. Folding the flap of the box over, Katie found a familiar tatter of masking tape with $3.00 written in pencil. Ruth made her tags in the exact same manner. Peering into the trench, Katie spotted several more items she was sure she had seen before in her own barn. Skiing down the bank, glad to be wearing Irma's barn boots, she examined more of the items. Everyone she looked at had a bit of masking tape attached. There were enough items in the trench to have filled the small dumpster.

"Hence the ditch," she said, climbing out. Bypassing the truck, Katie walked out to the sidewalk. Besides the bank and accounting office, there was a real estate office, a hair salon, and a small restaurant all on the same side of the street. Each building had one or two upper floors which surely housed apartments. Who had shopped with Ruth and why had they discarded everything so wastefully?

"I'm sure it's nothing to me," Katie said, climbing into the truck. Shaking her head back and forth did nothing to release her clenched jaw.

After finding a place to release the skunk where it would not encounter the human population, Katie returned home. She was still laughing at the skunk's waddling retreat when she pulled into the yard. Rick's truck was parked where she had been earlier, and he was wheeling a barbecue grill toward the kitchen door.

"Hey, what's up?" she asked.

"We're going to church," said Ruth. "Then we're going for a ride. Want to come?"

Both Katie and Rick looked at the woman in surprise.

"No," Katie laughed, embarrassed that Ruth would invite her on what Rick had probably planned as a daytime date. "I'm going to make myself an omelet, we have eggs and lots of veggies. Then I think I'll drive out to the golf course."

Ruth cocked an eyebrow. "The golf course?"

"Yeah, I'm just nosy. I hear they have skunks out there to move too." She turned away from Ruth, waving behind her. "Go ahead, have a great time."

* * *

It took only a few moments of wandering around inside the golf course's white clapboard clubhouse to realize her appearance put her at a disadvantage. There was an overabundance of women in short white skirts, midi-tops, and up-sweeps reminiscent of The Gibson Girl. Though still upscale, most of the men were less picture-perfect. Katie stayed on the fringes, avoiding the dining room, but continuously moving around the main activity room and bar area. Eventually, she spotted the man who had been most prevalent in Irma's newspaper clippings. His foursome was just returning, and he headed directly into the bar where he scooped up the cocktail in front of one of the bar-flies, slurping loudly. The whole group gave forth a guffaw of slightly metallic-sounding laughter.

The bar-fly spun around and Katie realized her prey had been sitting there the whole time unnoticed among her similarly artificially colored friends. Katie found a place to stand and observe. Eventually, the woman deserted her seat headed for the restroom. Katie followed. Unfortunately, Katie wasn't the only person who had been watching.

In the restroom, Katie took a position at a sink, lathering, and scrubbing. The woman left a stall and stood at the neighboring basin.

"Darn this mud," Katie muttered.

"Yes." The woman agreed. "Don't get it on your clothes, it'll never come out. Good turnout today for the senator, don't you think?" Primping in front of the mirror, she never cast a glance in Katie's direction. Finished, she turned toward the door. Katie turned, unsure what to do next, but was cut off by a golf course employee.

"Excuse me," said the woman. "Are you a member?"

Startled, Katie scrambled for an excuse. "Ah, no, actually I was just dropping some stuff off for my boss. You know? Work and play." She laughed.

The woman's smile didn't rise to her eyes.

"Have a good day." Katie bee-lined out of the building to the parking lot. As she paused at the stop sign, she caught sight of the employee standing on the veranda watching Katie's exit.

"Crap," said Katie, who had gained nothing more than a close-up look at both Lawrence French and his wife. She was sure her visit had been cut short because she hadn't blended in with the crowd. A newcomer to the barflies group knew different, having notified the club manager there was a gate crasher wandering around annoying members. The return of Katie Took to Vermont had been a minor annoyance, but was growing to be a much larger complication. The newcomer gave Mrs. French a quick hug and accepted the offer for a drink.

With Ruth still gone, Katie decided to tackle the rotting boards along the western edge of the porch. More than once she had stepped up where the railing was missing and felt her feet dip dangerously. Releasing Bonnie from her stall, Katie rounded up saw, hammer, nails, and after poking around for a while in the barn; found boards that would work for her project. Each time she moved from house to barn to house a string of cats and the pig followed her. With the passing of time and a growing number of trips, her entourage had shrunk to LG and Bonnie.

After cutting the boards to the right size Katie knelt on them holding them steady and in place while she pounded nails in. Behind her, Bonnie snuffled and squeaked in a happy voice. Katie sat back on her heels and turned to look at the pig. What she saw made her drop the hammer and scream.

"BONNIE!"

The pig was head down, holding the cat in place with its snout. The cat laid belly up unmoving while the pig mouthed at it. At Katie's scream, Bonnie squealed and ran for the barn. LG jumped straight up in the air and whipped past Katie into the house. Katie followed the cat. In the cat room LG was deep into the crate with her name on the outside and when Katie tried to drag her out, responded with claws and teeth. Ignoring the sharp pain and the oozing of her own blood, Katie finally pulled the cat into the open and flipped her over, checking for wounds or bites. There was nothing on the cat but a lot of pig spit. Katie released LG, who ran back out into the main house.

With her guts still shaking, Katie poured herself a cup of cold coffee and dropped into a kitchen chair. Her fingers touching her face were ice cold.

"I'm going back to Illinois," she said. "I'll figure this out. Then I'm telling Wilkins to go with Gram's alternate plan." She rose and went back to finish the porch repairs. Outside another surprise waited. Bonnie was laying against the trunk of a young maple on the lawn. She had obviously recovered from the earlier fright caused by Katie's scream. LG was also on the lawn, rubbing against Bonnie's face, head bowed, back arched, and tail tip flipped downward. No fear, only friendship.

"Were you two *playing*?" Katie moved toward the animals, incredulous of what she was seeing. As one the feline and the swine sprang away, running toward the barn lane. Picking up her hammer, Katie called after them. "I'm going to have terror-induced diarrhea for a month."

It was late afternoon when Rick's truck pulled into the drive. Katie had finished fashioning burgers of the meat Rick had left in the fridge. She looked up to see a very tattered-looking Ruth in the doorway. Though her church shoes had been replaced by a short pair of boots, her dress was rumbled and dirty. A bit of lace along the neckline was hanging by a few broken threads.

"What happened?" Katie's eyes bulged.

"We went for a hike," said Ruth, rushing past and into the bathroom.

As soon as Ruth moved, Rick stepped through the doorway. He was similarly dirty. "I tried to stop her," he said. "I'm going to light the charcoal, then I'll wash up while it heats." He disappeared back outside.

The noise of running water stopped and Ruth exited the bathroom, circling the far side of the table. She didn't look at Katie, only saying she would be right back. Katie sliced vegetables for a green salad and waited. When Rick was first to re-enter the room, Katie said. "If it's none of my business, just say that. If not, tell me you weren't in an accident."

Rick picked up the bottle of dish detergent before heading back out into the yard. "We went for a walk," he said. "We just picked a place that was rougher than we thought. I tried to get her back to the truck, but she insisted she wanted to go." He stood at the end of the stoop using the hose to scrub at a long oil smear on his arm. "Then I started dubbing around with something I found and Ruth had to get into that too."

"Tada. All better." Ruth entered from the living room, having changed into one of her everyday dresses. She cast a worried look toward Rick before rushing over to help Katie. "Sorry we were gone so long,"

"Did you have fun?" Katie asked, sounding a trifle weak.

"Yes," Ruth said. "We did." She had a secretive smile and a few twigs still clung in her iron-gray curls.

"Well, let me tell you about my day," said Katie. Avoiding any mention of her trip to the golf course, Katie took them out to inspect her repairs and told them about Bonnie and LG's attempt at giving her a heart attack.

While they sat on the porch, finishing up their burgers, Katie asked about the dishes.

"You sold those dishes with the wheat pattern, didn't you Ruth?"

"Yes. Did you know we used to get those in boxes of laundry detergent?" Rick nodded in agreement.

"I was wondering if your great customer bought them, the woman in the big white car."

"She did." Ruth pinked; pleased Katie would remember what she'd said. "It isn't her car though. She said it belonged to her boss, and she only drove it when she was doing his errands. Most of the time she drives a pickup."

Katie thought about the neighborhood she had been looking over near the trench. She hadn't seen a white Cadillac, but it seemed there had been pickup trucks parked nearby.

"A red one?" Katie asked.

"No, maybe blue or green, I think." Ruth passed a bit of her burger to one of the cats. But Rick looked at Katie, questions burning in the bright blue of his eyes.

When Ruth picked up plates and silver and headed toward the kitchen,

Katie told Rick about the trench.

"You're sure?" he asked.

"You've seen the price tags Ruth is putting on stuff. Would you recognize them if you saw them somewhere else?"

Rick sat on the top step and leaned back against the railing post. "I think," he said, "I'll pick up one of those little throw-away cameras at Beauregard's on the way home, maybe swing over to Charlotte before work. If there's no one around, I'm going to have a little look-see."

"Keep your eye open for a white Caddie," said Katie. "I'd like to know who that woman is."

"Oh," he said. "Wednesday is my regular day off. Now you're all trained, I'm taking it this week. Seems Ruth and Joyce are going over to the doctor's. Grace's boys have to have their pre-football physicals. I thought I'd meet the mess of them over there at Whirly Gig soft-serve ice cream stand and we'd have lunch."

"How are you getting away with that?" Katie asked just as Ruth returned.

Rick's eyes flicked up as his smile returned. "Gotta friend there, I wanta check on and you never know who you just might run into," he drawled.

* * *

Katie spent the evening pacing, unable to find something to occupy her hands and her mind. Her fingers kept worrying the folded paper in her pocket, but there was nothing to do about it until the next day. Ruth wisely let Katie work it out by herself. With a small blanket wrapped around her legs, with knitting and cats in her lap, and tea on the end table, the older woman hummed along with the radio while watching Katie from beneath lowered lashes.

Once more upstairs, Katie turned in place. Her eyes landed on Irma's tiny jewelry box. It was lacquered black with gold cranes painted on the outside. The top opened to display a minute ballerina who hadn't twirled in years. There was also a small drawer underneath. Katie fingered the costume jewelry left in a jumble surrounding the dancer. When she opened the drawer, she found the center compartment empty except for two thin gold bands tied together with ribbon. Both the woman's and the man's golden bands were etched with the nicks and scratches of hard work.

Katie held the rings in her fingers. The precious metal warming with her touch. Her mind was empty, her heart overfull. Wrapping the rings in the death grip of her left hand, she dumped the contents of the box on her bed. Frantically she searched through the jumble until she found a tarnished silver chain that held a Saint Christopher's medal. Shaking the chain free, she threaded it through the rings and dropped the loop over her head. Katie replaced everything she had strewn across the quilt in the box except the rings now tucked under her shirt. She returned to the first floor and removed an armful of Irma's clippings from the file cabinet. Long after Ruth had retired, Katie sat at the kitchen table arranging, reading, and rereading what her grandmother had left behind, certain the clues were there.

Chapter Twenty-Seven

A t eleven o'clock Monday morning, Katie punched out for lunch. "I'll be back in half an hour," she told Rick. He nodded and kept throwing grain bags in the back of a waiting truck.

Katie lucked out at the town office. The friendly clerk, Janice, was working. Katie explained she wanted to look at the permit applications for contractors that were working on housing projects.

"Are you ever in luck." Janice smiled. "I have a master list."

At Katie's questioning look, Janice continued.

"I was getting really angry having to call all over the state for missing information every time one of these guys dropped off an application. So, I started my own file with everything including all the telephone numbers you can imagine. If something is missing now, I either have it or I have the contact information to get it right away. Cuts down on my stress."

"Awesome," said Katie. "Can I copy the names and addresses?"

"You're kidding, right?" Janice pulled the notebook out of her desk. "There's a mess of them, Katie."

"I only need the ones that will buy sand," Katie said.

"Yeah, well, I don't have that in my notes," said Janice.

Katie's cheeks blew out.

"I tell you what," said Janice. "I'll make copies of the top page of each one, I get twenty-five cents for copies people want. I can take it out of your vouchers. I'll do it in between other stuff and call you when I get it done. Maybe tomorrow or the next day."

"Deal," Katie said. When she got back to work, she asked Stan about making copies of Cindy's letter.

"Sure," he said. "First twenty are on me."

"I sure hope that will be more than I need."

Stan nodded in agreement.

In the early evening, Katie was at home going over the notes Cindy had given her again when there was a knock at the door. Marlie was standing on the other side of the screen, looking unsure.

Equally hesitant, Katie waited.

"So, it seems Janice down in the town hall had some forms she wanted to mail out to you. She was just finishing up when I went in to have copies made. I volunteered to drop them off on my way home." She held a thick envelope out toward the door.

Releasing the hook installed to keep the cats from letting themselves out, Katie pushed the door causing Marlie to step back.

"Thanks," said Katie, accepting the missive.

Moments passed while the women evaluated each other

"Ok then," said Marlie. "Bye."

Marlie stood on the top step before Katie spoke out.

"Would you like a glass of lemonade, Deputy? Or I could make coffee."

"Lemonade would be great." Marlie beamed.

Thirty minutes later, Marlie's car pulled out of the drive. Katie stood on the steps. Raising her hand in farewell, she smiled, sure they were going to be good friends.

Katie had barely shut the door when Rick's truck pulled into the driveway.

"I met the sheriff's deputy as I was coming in," he said. "What's wrong?" He stood inches away from her, tense with the whites of his eyes bright.

"Nothing," said Katie. She exhaled, only then considering her problems were spreading to others, and it frightened her. "Relax before you have a heart attack," she said. "It seems we might have an ally in the sheriff's camp."

Rick smiled. "Nice."

Katie silently watched him, and it took Rick a moment to realize it.

"Oh," he said. "I went grocery shopping. You haven't had supper yet, have you?"

"What? No," said Katie. She didn't want to owe him more than was necessary.

"Yeah," he said, "I was over in Charlotte and I wandered into the mini-mart, then over to that little I-*talian* restaurant. You know, chatting, getting a feel for the locals. Who's who, that sort of thing."

"And?" Katie smiled.

"I ended up with supper." Rick went back to his truck, returning with bags smelling prominently of salami and Italian dressing.

While Rick went down to the barn to get Ruth, who was re-arranging her selling display in the milking parlor, Katie spread the food out on the table. There was enough for at least two nights for all of them.

"Oh my god," sighed Katie, "this was so good. I'm stuffed." Her plate held the remnants of stuffed shells, marinated mushrooms, antipasto, and Greek salad.

"Save room for the cheesecake. I hear it's this lady's specialty!"

"I shouldn't," moaned Ruth. "I really shouldn't."

Rick laughed. Getting up to pour himself coffee, he looked over her head at Katie.

"I went out to check on that, ah, stuff, you were interested in. That's how I ended up with all the food. I figured there might be more people around if I went after work. I got pictures. Tomorrow I'll go over to the drugstore and drop the camera off. They send them out to get developed. That'll probably take a week anyway, but the pictures are mostly so there will be a record."

"The ladies at the bank were all getting ready to go, and no one knew anything. But a funny thing happened while I was standing at the top of the trench." Rick paused as Ruth rose, picking up dishes and food containers. When she was busy at the sink, he lowered his voice and leaning toward Katie said,

"This guy in a suit comes up to me and starts bawling me out for tossing stuff in there. I got hot fast. I told him I didn't do it, but once I saw it, I was wondering who to complain to about it. You know Keep Vermont Green and all that. He backpedaled quick. I said it's a real shame, looks like someone was cleaning out a house. Guy started complaining about itinerant renters.

Yak, yak, yak. He did say he was on some town renters board or some such. I asked his name, but he was so busy shaking his fist at the world, he didn't even hear me. Then he stormed off. I thought he would go over to the bank but he went into that other building beside the alley."

"The old storefront?" asked Katie. "Was he kind of short, round, had a bad comb-over?"

"Nope, this guy was almost my height, greasy looking. He was wearing a gold lapel pin with what looked like the outline of a house on it. Weird jewelry for any dude. Oh, and a big college ring."

Katie shook her head. Rick wasn't describing the accountant Burns she had met. Maybe there was a partner or an assistant?

"But I agree with you," said Rick, interrupting her thoughts. "That stuff came from here."

Rick left after coffee, leaving Katie and Ruth to go over the pages Janice had sent out. Katie had her stack of letters, a box of envelopes, and a book of stamps.

"I don't think these are going to be enough," she said. Ruth who was folding and stuffing envelopes nodded in agreement.

"You'd better let me address the envelopes," Ruth said to Katie. "The post office isn't going to be able to read your chicken scratch."

"What, are you saying?" laughed Katie.

"When you leave me notes, it takes a Philadelphia lawyer to read them. Just figure out which ones to do first, I'll get started as soon as the dishes are done." Ruth carried the coffee cups to the sink.

With one cat sleeping in her lap, and another mewling on the floor for attention, Katie turned back to the list.

Ruth returned wiping her hands, a pen tucked behind her ear. "You know Katie, there might be other people who could help spread the word. You should send a letter to the planning board in Parentville and Charlotte, maybe Monkton. Oh, and how about real estate offices, they're the ones who'll be selling the land, right?"

Katie marked the companies that would receive the first batch of letters. Sipping coffee, she watched Ruth get organized. The years the older woman had spent working in an office environment mixed with her OCD meant she was going to need another notebook.

When they went to bed that night, there was a neat stack of letters on the table waiting to go into the mailbox in the morning. Katie spent a long while sitting on the side of Irma's bed looking out over the hedge toward the high meadow. The desire to walk there at that moment was strong, but common sense told her to stay put. That, along with the line of cats following behind her as she moved around while Ruth snored, kept her inside the farmhouse.

* * *

Even after Rick had gone on his way from the edge of the trench, the man who had questioned him stomped around his office spouting off about his disgust at the mess. His wife, who worked with him, and two of his buddies sat back, sipping coffee, letting him go until he wound down.

"You over it?" said one of the other men. "Can we get back to planning this fishing trip?"

While the men bent over a map discussing pros and cons, the woman walked into the restroom. She stood behind the closed door, biting her nails embroiled in her own silent raving. The first time she'd thrown the barn sale purchases over the edge her husband had been leaving the building. It had been a quick response to avoid answering questions Then it had become a habit. She hadn't expended a second thought about what she was doing or how much she was tossing away. Even if he questioned all the tenants living on the main street, her husband would never discover she was guilty, but the man her husband had been talking to felt like a threat. Hadn't hubby said the guy seemed to know the stuff was there and wanted the town to do something about it? Was there any way any of that junk could be traced back to that old crow's barn sale in Parentville? What were the chances that same old crow could somehow be able to identify one shopper out of them all?

Her blood pressure rose, her face flushed, and sweat began gathering on her body. Rinsing her face with cold water, she stared at the woman in the mirror.

"It was just some nosy Joe," she said. "Chill out, for god's sake. Relax." Once again in control, she went out to pick up the litter left in the office and welcome the next customers.

Chapter Twenty-Eight

Even though the next day had been scheduled to be her second day off that week, Katie was working to cover employees who had kids with farm projects at the Champlain Valley Exposition. It was also the day the largest of the pre-winter season orders arrived at the feed store. Besides just the usual grain and animal products the feed store carried, they had a complete line of yard and seasonal products. Pallet after pallet was unloaded, from one tractor-trailer into the feed storage barn, and from a different trailer into the supplement barn that held tools, fertilizers, and literally hundreds of things Katie never thought about.

By late afternoon, even Rick was showing the strain.

"I'm looking forward to having tomorrow off and lunching at the soft-serve ice cream stand," he said.

"Idiot," said Katie. Her back hurt and her arms felt ready to fall off. She was carrying around a visual of the big bathtub filled with hot water and bubbles. It was all that kept her moving ahead.

Marlie was leaning against her car when she left, but Katie could barely smile.

"Looks like you had a tough day," said Marlie. "I think I'll wait and talk to you later, maybe tomorrow."

"Okay," said Katie. Her brain didn't register that Marlie was waiting at the feed store to talk. She could barely fold herself into her car. "I'm going to need a can opener to get out," she groaned.

Katie let herself in the front door which was still locked, evidence Ruth was still helping Grace make pickles. Katie smiled, then realized there were no cats lounging around the living room. Only Shadow curled up and sleeping gave evidence of occupancy.

That's weird, she thought. *Where's the welcoming committee?*

She was almost to the kitchen door when she heard a small crash and a door slammed. Suddenly cats were running at her, past her, and skidding to make the corner of the staircase headed up toward Ruth's room and safety.

"What the hell?" cried Katie. There was more noise, like footsteps on tile. Katie darted around the kitchen table, slamming into the closed door of the laundry room. It took a solid push to open the door which was held in place by an overturned cat tree. Laundry detergent was spread across the floor like snow, causing Katie to slide into the side of the dryer, barely catching herself before she went down. The cat room door was also closed but opened easily. Across the room beyond the litter boxes, one of which was flipped over with its contents strewn about, the door leading back out into the driveway was wide open. Katie leaped over the offending litter box and out the door. There was no one there, nor were there any cats. To her inquiring look, the hard-pack earth gave no clue. Darting to the edge of the building, Katie looked beyond the hollyhocks and dahlias. Nothing. She went further back along the side, off onto the sloping lawn, and circled around to the road before returning to the open door. It was clear someone had been in the house, but Katie was totally mystified as to how they had gotten away without being seen. She stood in the doorway, tapping her foot, then remembered the tall herb planter off to the side. Tilting it back, she looked for a key, even running her hand along the bottom, but found nothing.

Closing the door, Katie went back through the house searching, finally returning with a broom and dustpan. After cleaning the litter box mess and checking again that the door was securely locked, she went back into the laundry room. She stood up the cat tree before sweeping up the spilled detergent.

"Well," she said to the cats who watched from the safety of the kitchen, "it's soap and the floor is clean, so we'll save it and use it later, okay?"

There was no answer. Because her skin still crawled at the thought someone had invaded her home, she paused again, looking at the cats whose tails twitched nervously. Each one watched her with expectant eyes. Before sweeping, Katie had picked up all the items that had ended up on the floor and now began putting all to rights. When she was done, she realized there was an empty space on the top shelf where the bag holding Irma's clothes had been. Twisting from side to side, she verified she hadn't missed it. Her guts knotted. The bag was gone!

"Hello?" called Ruth from the front of the house. "I brought pickles."

Ruth's joy was short-lived when she and Katie stepped into the kitchen at the same time, and she saw the stricken look on Katie's face.

"What's wrong?" Ruth's voice was a hoarse whisper.

"When you left, were all the doors locked?" asked Katie.

Ruth nodded.

"You're sure?" Katie's arm wrapped around her middle, holding the nausea inside. When her fingers touched the spot where her hip had made contact with the dryer, she cringed. "Ruth, someone broke into the house. I don't know-how. I checked all the door frames. It doesn't look like one was jimmied, and we picked up all the keys, right?"

Ruth nodded, then stopped. With eyes as big as silver dollars, she rushed past Katie, fumbled with the lock on the door from the cat room to the outside, and yanked the door open.

"There's a key for this door too." She sounded dry, raspy.

"I don't know where it is," said Katie. "I looked but…" She stopped talking when Ruth knelt beside the herb pot and tipping it back, picked up the silver key laying beneath. Katie's fingers were shaking when she reached for the key. "I looked there." Katie straightened, eyes once more roving the yard and land beyond.

"I don't know how I forgot it. Maybe because we never used this door." Ruth's movements mirrored Katie's. "It's the last one, I'm sure of it."

"There's more," said Katie, drawing Ruth back into the building. Once the door was closed, she told Ruth about the bag. Ruth sat down hard on one of the galvanized trashcans used for storage.

"No," she said, hand creeping up to cover her mouth.

***

In the orchard, a furtive figure hunkered low, clutching a paper bag to its chest. Rather than run down the middle row, the figure zig-zagged between the gnarled trees. By the time it reached the far side, it was gasping breath.

When Katie had rushed through the cat room door, the figure had been laying among the hollyhocks on the ground and wedged in tight against the foundation. Though immediate inclination had been to flee as soon as Katie was back inside, the rattling of the herb pot presented a different idea. It took nerves to crawl around the edge of the building and replace the key, just as it took guts to leave the security of the hollyhocks running in the open toward the broken end of the barn. Once there even with knees crying out to collapse, the runner had continued on. Safety was across the meadow, through the brook, and a long drive away.

Chapter Twenty-Nine

With Ruth seated in the living room weeping, Katie called the sheriff's office. A voice she didn't recognize answered. It took a moment to come to her.

"Boyd," she demanded. "Is this Boyd?" Not waiting for an answer, she rushed on. "This is Katie Took, Irma Moore's granddaughter. Someone broke into my house. They were here when I got home. I need the sheriff now." Unaware, her voice was rising both in volume and octaves, Katie clutched the receiver, pressing it against her ear. "Hello? Can you hear me?"

"Easy Ms. Took," Boyd said. "Is the intruder gone? Are you safe?"

Katie nodded.

"Hello?"

"Yes," she squeaked, "yes."

"Don't touch anything. I'm radioing the sheriff and I'm coming right out. Okay. Touch nothing." The line went dead.

Katie turned. Ruth was curled over into her own lap, shoulders shaking.

"Come on, Ruth," said Katie. "I'm taking you down to Grace."

Ruth had left the four-wheeler that Davy had taught her to operate in the driveway. Katie used that to transport Ruth. The cardboard box of pickle jars rattled in the back. With only the barest explanation, Katie returned to the farm arriving just as sirens roared up the dirt road leaving a trail of high rising dust.

Raymond arrived moments after the sheriff and his deputy. One cruiser parked in front of the house and the other pulled around to the barn.

Katie walked Lewis and Boyd through the chain of events with both taking notes. Raymond stood grimly in the kitchen, listening without interrupting.

While Lewis worked the inside of the house, Boyd went outside. Katie leaned against the sink, grateful for Raymond's solid presence. Through the window, she could see chickens pecking like nothing had happened and LG stalking one of the hens.

"Bonnie!" yelled Katie. "Where's Bonnie?" She dashed outside, calling.

Lewis raised an eyebrow to Raymond, who answered, "The pig."

Katie skid down the low bank toward the barn, practically bouncing off Boyd as she rounded the corner to the milking parlor door. Once inside, she hurried toward the free stall where she found Bonnie buried in the hay. At the sound of Katie's voice, the pig raised its head then quickly shied away. Katie advanced.

"Careful as you go," warned Boyd.

Katie wasn't listening. Something was wrong. She reached into the hay and the half-grown pig squealed and jumped away. Once she was free of the hay, Katie could see the ugly red mark on her hip. Someone had struck her, probably with a stick and most likely to shoo her away.

Katie growled. Raymond, who had entered right after her, pulled a lump of sugar from his pocket and offered it to the pig. Bonnie didn't even hesitate. While she crunched, Raymond examined the mark.

"Doesn't look bad," he said. "Didn't break the skin. It's a sure bet her feelings were more hurt than anything else. Yeah, you're a good girl." He handed her another lump of sugar before closing the door so she would stay inside. "I'll have Davy bring up some salve to put on it, more a band-aid than anything else."

Katie turned to Lewis. "Do you believe me now? I'm all done messing around. It's getting to be serious."

Raymond nodded in agreement. "My family is right here," he said. "My wife, my kids. Step up to the plate, man, or let someone else do the job."

Lewis had an ugly look. Katie was unsure if it resulted from her demand or Raymond's challenge.

"There's a forensics team in Montpelier," Lewis said. "I'm going to call them. I don't want you back in the house until I know whether they'll come out." He walked away from them up the lane toward his car instead of struggling up the slippery grass bank. Katie was still standing with Raymond and Boyd when they heard the squawk emitted from the radio in the sheriff's car.

After the sheriff confirmed someone was driving over from Montpelier, Katie and Raymond walked back to the Dean farm. Boyd would wait for the forensics tech.

"I don't mind the cats," he said, "but I don't have to handle the pig, do I?"

* * *

The adults sat around the Dean kitchen table sharing a pot of coffee after dinner. A half-hour earlier a green van bearing the State of Vermont logo had pulled up the road. Katie faced her farm, but from where she sat could see nothing.

"Why would anyone want a bag of soiled, unusable clothing?" asked Grace.

"How would they have even known it was in the house?" countered Katie. "Ruth and I were the only ones who knew it was there, right Ruth?"

"And Rick," said Ruth. Her fingers fidgeted with the cup handle as though trying to knit a stitch with the ceramic."

Initially, Katie wasn't concerned, then Ruth added, "We were talking about it at the chicken barbecue. I remember telling him, I thought you would throw it all away, but instead, you wrapped it up in a paper bag and put it on the shelf." Ruth nodded. "Yeah, and I said there were tears in the shirt I didn't think had been there before." She lifted her cup.

Around the table, three sets of eyes stared at her. Katie's jaw dropped.

"At the barbecue? Were you in the truck?"

"No, don't be silly. We were at the picnic tables and Rick was chewing on his third ear of corn on the cob." Ruth smiled, shaking her head at the memory.

"Which rooms were ransacked?" Raymond asked Katie.

"My bedroom, the kitchen, and the laundry room."

"Oh my," said Grace, "there were a couple hundred people there that day.

We were packed in tight at the tables. Anyone could have overheard."

Katie stood up. She needed to go up the road and talk to Lewis. At the doorway, she turned back to Ruth.

"Think about who was sitting around you," she said. "Make a list." She knew Ruth probably wouldn't remember anyone, but if there was the slightest chance, she needed to grasp at it.

Chapter Thirty

Katie was still shaky the next morning when she faced Ruth before leaving for work.

"Don't forget," Katie said, "when you get back from Monkton call me, okay?"

"Are you getting more stamps?"

"And copies," said Katie. She picked up her lunch and reached out to pat LG, but got a swipe for her trouble.

"KATIE, KATIE," Ruth came running out of the house. "How about if we stop on our way back and I pick everything up at the feed store?"

"That would be fine," she said, knowing Rick would be accidentally running into them in Monkton. Sliding behind the steering wheel made her muscles cringe. Even with the long soak after the forensic tech left, Katie ached. It was a sure bet today would be another hard-working day. With Rick not working, she had no way of letting him know what had happened the previous night. It had been far too late to call him by the time the forensic van pulled out, and Katie felt telling Ruth to keep it quiet would create un-needed stress. She was sure she'd find Rick at the farm when she got home, and he was going to have a burr under his blanket.

Cindy was running the service counter so Stan could work out in the sheds with the crew, sorting and putting everything to rights. Dan was running the lift as Katie was not qualified to do so.

"How long have you been doing this?" Katie asked.

"This time?" asked Dan.

"You've worked here before?"

"Yeah until I graduated high school a year ago. Then I went to work in Williston at the Home Depot. Same job as this, same money, one day I woke up asking why was I driving all that way every day?"

"True fact," said Katie. She was drinking the last of the water out of her thermos when she choked. Her brain asked a question and her throat stopped working.

"So, Dan, you've only been out of school for a year, you must still know all the jocks out at CVU?"

"Most of them," he laughed.

She swallowed, trying to slow her thumping heart. "What's the deal with all those pickup trucks with the monster tires?"

"Other than they can mess up the bottom of the truck, not much." He shrugged and swung back into the seat of the lift.

Katie leaned on the side; she wasn't ready for him to leave yet. He looked down, thinking she looked pretty good for an older woman.

"Everybody wants to be cool, right?" He pushed the starter.

It wasn't until quitting time Katie had a chance to question Dan.

"All these cool guys around here, they get their tires from Phil's or like, where?"

"Nah, there's a place over in Taft Corners called Recon Tire. Guy carries all these super treads. And he's the only guy around who can fix them because they're too big for a regular tire machine."

"Ah." Katie winked at Dan. "You guys are so sly."

The first thing Katie did when she got home was run to the mailbox. It was unrealistic to believe that letters only mailed the day before would have elicited an answer, but hope didn't seem to know that. Inside she found several flyers and more bills she didn't want to open. For some unknown reason, seeing her name on the envelopes distressed her. Cats fought to be the first one to exit the cat flap cut into the kitchen door as she walked around the house. She had seen them watching her through the windows, and when she didn't come right in the house, they wanted to be where she was. In the barn, she released Bonnie, who headed back into the scrub bushes before joining the parade behind Katie as she walked through the orchard toward the burial plot.

"I wonder what it would take," she mused. "To bring some of these apple trees back up?" At the burial plot, the deer path swerved around the granite post and iron pipe fencing. Katie left the well-worn path, stepping into the waving grass. "I'm going to have to come down here and mow this, aren't I, Gram," she asked. The four cats that had followed her through the orchard chased grasshoppers while Bonnie stood outside the closed gate, woofing her displeasure when Katie wouldn't let her in. After spending the time needed for her soul to converse with her grandparents, she left the fenced-in area. The path down to the brook was as well-trod as the section that ran through the orchard. Katie looked down the length, watching two cats wrestling in the sun-warmed meadow.

"Well," she said, "come deer season, it shouldn't be too hard to find one. It looks like whole herds have been going through here. Come on cats, time to go home. Let's go before the foxes smell you." Bonnie got to her feet and with her usual huffing voice complaining, trailed behind until LG ran to the forefront. After that, pig and cats vied for first place, dashing past each other and crowding close to the backs of Katie's legs.

* * *

Being home alone didn't bother Katie. She actually enjoyed being by herself. She hummed along doing this and that, leaving the milking parlor door open in the event a barn sale customer came up the road. She made sure there was a dollar's worth of change in the help-your-self cash box. Above the box, the big bell she had seen hanging on the Dean porch, and which Grace used to call her family, had been installed. *Ring Bell for Service*, the sign said. Katie reached up, wiggling the clapper.

"Ding-ding won't work today," she said. "Everybody's gone."

Back at the house, Katie poured lemonade, and with the last two cookies in hand, headed outside.

The telephone rang.

"Hello," said Katie.

"Is this the crazy cat lady?" demanded a muffled voice. Then the line went dead.

"Just some thrill junkie," Katie said to the cats who had gathered beneath the telephone, eyes on the cookies. After a leisurely break on the porch, Katie returned to the kitchen, opening the refrigerator trying to decide what to cook for supper.

The telephone rang.

Katie was there by the end of the second ring, but the line was already dead.

Supper was ready and staying warm on the stove before Rick's truck pulled in.

"It never occurred to me, you guys might eat out," Katie said. "This will keep until tomorrow."

"We haven't had supper yet," said Ruth. Once again, she looked like she had been rolling around in the dirt. This time she had a long scratch on one arm and several smaller ones on both.

Katie looked pointedly at Rick. His shirt was ripped, and there was a strong smell of gasoline and wood smoke on him.

He shifted uncomfortably, then started speaking in a rush. "OK, here's the deal. I think I found a lot to put my trailer on. It's going to take some work to get ready. Ruth and I have been out walking around, you know, checking it out."

"With a gas-fed fire?" Katie asked.

"Well, we might have poked around to see what might need to be done and ended up getting our hands dirty."

"And?" asked Katie.

"It's not going to be as easy as it sounds. Then I don't want to leave a mess for someone else to clean up, okay?" He frowned, face darkening.

"Okay." Katie held her hands up. "You know it's none of my business."

"Speaking of knowing your business, Ruth told me someone broke into the house yesterday."

With a deep sigh, Katie turned back to Rick. This time the displeasure on his face was not from her chastising him. Holding up her hand to keep questions at bay, she walked him through the events of the previous evening, right down to the part where she'd told Ruth about her possibly staying somewhere else.

"She said no," Katie reported.

"Yeah, that's what she said," Rick answered. "Oh, we stopped at the grocery store and I was talking to one of the gals there, she was telling me how you've been hitting on Dan."

"WHAT?" Katie's body went rigid.

"Yup, seems when I'm not around, you're all over him, asking questions, batting your eyelashes. All that stuff." Rick had a poop-eating grin on his face.

"He doesn't know I'm gay?"

"Yeah, I think he knows, but I don't think he believes it. It's like a barmaid wearing a wedding ring to keep the wolves back."

Ruth came back clean and ready for supper. "I think we should get a picnic table," she announced.

"Too late in the season," said Rick headed toward the bathroom sink. "Maybe next spring that would be a good idea."

Katie was considering the conversation she was going to have with Dan until she realized Ruth was looking at her.

"I have a lead on big tires," Katie said. Over Hungarian goulash and roll-and-bake biscuits she told them about her conversation with Dan. "I've been wanting to go over to one of the bigger grocery stores in Williston, I'm thinking I'll drive over Friday after work and see if I can find Recon on the same trip. What do you think?"

Ruth nodded. "Grace goes over every couple of weeks for her groceries. She's asked me a few times if I wanted to go with her. If it's a better deal to shop there, we probably should consider it."

"I can't quite place Recon Tire in the Taft Five Corners area," said Rick. He skipped dessert and coffee, leaving right after dinner.

* * *

CHAPTER THIRTY

The next morning Rick was already clocked in and rearranging stock when Katie showed up.

"I found Recon Tire," he said. "Whoever told you it was in Taft Corners was about five miles off. It's further west on the Williston Road. There's a section out there full of industrial dealers. Now You See It Body Works is in the same sub-division. I stopped in there. They handle a lot of off-road vehicle repairs and what have you."

"Last night?" asked Katie, surprise stopping any movement. "They were open at that time of night?" Then she paused. "What were *you* doing over there that late?"

"I wasn't ready to settle down when I went home, figured the ride would tire me out. But yeah, the body guys were there telling whoppers and sipping beer. I think they're hanging out there for lack of someplace else to go. They seem to be mostly young guys, the kind with a chip on their shoulder."

"The kind who are over-dosing on testosterone?" she asked sarcastically.

"Sometimes you're not very nice," he frowned.

"Am I wrong?" she asked, eyebrows raised.

"No." He sighed.

Chapter Thirty-One

Pulling in the driveway after work, Katie could hear the telephone was ringing. She dashed up the steps, fumbled with the key, and tripped on not one, but two cats before she got into the kitchen.

"Hello?" she asked, fairly sure the caller would have hung up by this time.

"Katie?" said a man's voice she didn't immediately recognize. "This is Grace's brother, Philip. Where are you, or actually what are you doing? Can you come over here right now?"

Katie's lips pursed; Philip sounded like he was on the verge of having some type of cerebral episode. Before she could answer, Philip continued.

"I'm at the high school," he said. "Just pull up to the main door, I'll be watching for you."

"Philip, it's suppertime, there's no school." But the telephone line was dead, Philip had already disconnected. "So," Katie said as she let LG into the house, "it looks like I'm going to school."

Even though the high school was in a north-easterly direction as the crow flies, to get there Katie needed to head southeast toward the village. Once in the village it was north, then east to CVU. As was the case when she had to drive somewhere, she was amazed at her ability to remember the area. She was still out of visual range when the sounds of a marching band drifted in through the open windows of the Subaru.

"Oh, that's why." As she pulled off the road, she could see the packed parking lots and crowds surrounding the football field. Ignoring the graveled walkway to the sports field, Katie circled the parking lot before pulling around to the front of the school. Philip was nowhere in sight. As she walked toward the granite stairway leading to the wide double doors, he exited the building.

"Okay," he said. "It's half-time, we should have enough time before the game is over and people leave. Your car will be all right there for a few minutes." His long stride took him past Katie, who turned, still unsure what was happening.

Running to catch up, she asked, "What are we doing?"

Philip stopped short. "After you came into my shop that day, looking for repair reports, I was talking to Grace. She told me about all the trash that's been happening up there. I never heard a word about any of that, but I don't like it. That's my sisters, my nephews. If there's some lunatic wandering around near where my family lives terrorizing people, he needs to be found."

"Well, I agree with that, but why are we watching football?"

"Not football. Well, it actually started with football." Philip started walking toward the field again. "I came up to watch Davy play. While I was wandering around, I ran into the guy who teaches auto mechanics. He and I play cards sometimes. A light went off in my head and I kind of asked him about repairs on pickups. He has a list, and it's not short. We trimmed it down to just front ends that would have happened this summer and are slated to be done in the class over the fall. I think you need to look at some of these trucks." He held up a piece of paper. "And I'm willing to bet most of them are in the parking lot right now."

The game was deep in the fourth quarter before Katie and Philip finished. They weren't able to find any that fit closely to the few facts Katie knew. Front end damage, blue or green truck, tires sized 285 or larger.

"Sorry Katie," said Philip, wiping his forehead with a red handkerchief.

"It was a great idea," said Katie. She moved out of the way as a few early birds lined up to pull out of the lot. Philip left while Katie was still standing, mesmerized by spinning tires as they went by.

But, she thought, *what if the repairs were done weeks ago? If some jock likes big tires, maybe his buddies do too. They might know about a wrecked front end.*

As quickly as possible, she moved around the lot, writing down the plate numbers of pickup trucks sporting over-large tires.

Deciding to bite the bullet, Katie drove over to the sheriff's office. Now that he had acknowledged some threat existed, maybe he'd be prone to playing friendly. It was a disappointment to find neither Lewis nor Marlie working that day.

"Is there anything I can do to help?" asked Boyd. Even he had put aside the disdainful attitude he had worn the first day she'd met him while he loaded the pig.

"No, I'm good," said Katie. "I appreciate the offer and I'll take a rain check if you don't mind?" She gave him a big smile, and he returned in kind.

Katie drove back out to the farm and found the barn sale had browsers. Dean's four-wheeled ATV was parked in front of the milking parlor door. Katie gave it a look as she went by.

Hm, she thought.

"Hey Ruth, how's it going?"

Ruth turned, her face flushed and happy. "Really good."

"Did you ride the ATV up from the garden?"

"Yes, I can't believe how easy it is to drive, and Davy doesn't mind. He's playing football today anyway," said Ruth.

"Yeah, I heard that. Are you going back down there or would you like me to take it back?"

Ruth gave Katie a two-minute lesson, reminded her to take the totes out at the house first, and went back to her customers. Bonnie was laying in the sun on the lawn. When she saw Katie coming, she jumped up and sashayed over, sticking her head in the tote Katie put down.

"I guess we're not leaving those on the ground, are we?" said Katie. There were carrot greens sticking out of the tote. Katie snapped them off, tossing the handful to a very grateful Bonnie.

Katie found Grace and her mother returning from the garden. Each pulled a red wagon stacked with wooden baskets. Leafy greens stuck out of several of the baskets. There were frequent stops to level the load as a stone in the path created a tipping issue.

"Grace, would you mind if I used the ATV for a little bit? I'd like to ride up onto the mountain."

"Absolutely," Grace said, "check the gas level before you go."

Katie cruised past her farm as quietly as possible. She could still see the glimmer of someone's car behind the house where the lane ran down to the barn. She didn't want to attract either Ruth or Bonnie's attention. The riding along went smoothly until she reached the area where the saplings were growing in. At that point, progress slowed considerably and stayed so until she had crossed over the top of the mountain and was close to the bottom on the Roser side. Leaving the ATV in the pines, she proceeded on foot.

She didn't have any plan, but more like an itchy, restless feeling. Irma had had an emotional connection to the property, which caused her to crawl far out on a limb to try to save it. Katie didn't have the same connection, and it worried her. Initially, Katie felt the need to save the property because of Gram. What if that was wrong? Just like the time she had spent in the hayfield when she first arrived, Katie was hoping time alone spent walking and looking would ignite a spark within her, or a resolution might present a clear picture of itself.

There were a lot of vehicle tracks around the sandpit, as well as footprints within, so someone had come out looking.

"Please," Katie prayed, "make an offer."

She found someone had pounded low stakes with hot pink plastic ribbons attached around the lot. Assuming the town surveyors had left them, she ignored them and kept walking. Where the sumac and bittersweet jungle had overgrown the cellar hole, which was actually more of a crawl space, someone had begun clearing. There was a large stack of brush to one side with a burn permit attached to a stick driven into the ground nearby. It was impossible to tell if some burning had already occurred on the site.

"What the heck?" Katie frowned. There were more little stakes on one side of the house. These were taller, thinner, and didn't have ribbons attached. Back near the sheds, the area around the well house was cut back. By this time the itchy feeling that she was missing something she should notice had turned into a slithering crawl up her spine. It was broad daylight, but felt as creepy as a moonless night.

"If someone stepped out of the woods right now, I'd be screaming and running for Houston," she said.

She peeked into the first shed. It looked undisturbed. Then she walked out to the road looking toward Charlotte village.

Ms. Deyak mentioned someone looked at a house lot out here. She didn't mean this one, did she? Katie wondered.

Remembering Cindy's interaction with the garter snake, Katie watched where she went. For this reason, she became more aware of the ribbon adorned stakes. The other ones were around the house only, but the ribbon bedecked ones seemed to be more spread out. They were only two inches high, easy to miss in the tall grass, yet they definitely seemed to be trying to provide a message. The meaning escaped Katie. In the meadow, she followed a deer path. Many of the birch saplings were quite tall, while the firs were perhaps only eight or ten feet. Her steps halted abruptly when she encountered another bright pink ribbon. With the tree growth, it was hard to follow the deer path with her eyes. She kept walking and found more ribbons as she went. She also realized that unlike other deer paths she'd followed, these were much straighter. Eventually, she ended up back at where the Roser barn had tumbled down over forty years prior. In the copse, a few old beams and a section of shaker shingle roof were still visible.

Katie returned to the ATV. She had come here for an answer and ended up with more questions. She'd seen a lot while walking around. However, she hadn't noticed the deer cam attached to a tree where the lawn turned into the forest lane leading to the sandpit.

* * *

"It's the weirdest thing," said Katie, putting biscuits on the table. "It looks like a bunch of people have been doing stuff. I just don't know if it's the same bunch doing it all or even what they were doing." She straightened up, looking out the kitchen window. "Except maybe the people in the pit."

Rick, who had come for supper again, held a plateful of chicken from the grill. He got all twitchy, and there was a guilty look on his face.

"I thought Ruth said she was going to be right back," he said, nervously turning toward the front of the house.

"Here I am," laughed Ruth. She held a small pie in her hands. "Grace made these with Georgia peaches she had delivered. I asked her to make a small one for our celebration."

Rick and Katie, who had taken a seat, turned to Ruth.

"We're celebrating?" asked Katie. "What?"

"While you were gone," Ruth grinned, "a man stopped in to see you. About the sandpit!"

"Are you serious?" Katie's jaw dropped.

"Yes. He's coming back, though. I told him you had to work, and he said he'd stop in after the supper hour, maybe tonight. Isn't that exciting?"

"Oh, my gosh," cried Katie.

Rick extended his hand across the table. "Congratulations," he said. "Are you ready for the interview process?"

"What interview?"

"The one where a prospective bidder asks what you expect to get and what the rules are."

"Yeah, well, I'd better call Cindy," grinned Katie.

* * *

Miles away someone else held one of Katie's letters, reading it over one more time. With fingers trembling in anger, she considered her next move,

"Remember that farm out on the Kitteridge Road we did the work up on?" she asked the man seated across the table."

"Yeah?" he said, never lifting his head from the New York Times crossword.

"Well, it seems the new owner is looking to develop," she said.

"Mm, we gave it a shot. There's a lot of potential there, particularly with the connecting piece in Parentville. A whole town road could go in there."

The woman sat back considering the man's reaction, dismissing the issue. There was a tape retrieved that afternoon in the recorder in her office. She

187

had already watched the tape twice. The images showing a woman walking around, a few men in work clothes, crawling over the log and going into the pit, and Katie meandering up the path, apparently mindful of where she stepped.

Chapter Thirty-Two

Katie was getting used to coming out of work and finding people leaning on her car. Today it was Sheriff Lewis. She opened her mouth, ready to tell him she knew her car still had Illinois tags, but he spoke first.

"Dennis told me you stopped in looking for me," he said.

So, Dennis must be Deputy Boyd, she reasoned.

She threw her lunch bag and thermos in the car.

"You ought to lock your car," he drawled.

"The lock on the driver's door doesn't work."

He shrugged.

"Anyway, yes I did. I was up at the CVU football game," no reason to bring Phillip into it, "and I noticed all the pickup trucks with big tires."

He looked interested.

"I didn't find one I could narrow down to what we think we're looking for, but my question is if I do, is there a way you could trace the plate for us without a warrant?"

"Depends on probable cause," he said standing up. "I can't go around checking plates willy-nilly or hand you the information. But if we have reason to believe the owner should be questioned, we can get that information."

"Really?" A tiny golden light burned in her chest.

"Yes." Lewis gazed off down the road. "Okay, consider the fact you are only seeing trucks that are interested in football right here in this town. What if it's not some young hot-shot? Or he's from another town, Charlotte, Shelbourne? It's not unusual for city kids to come out here and run amuck.

Maybe it's not even a kid, could be some guy trying to impress his girlfriend, or a beer party. There are a lot of reasons a truck was out there tramping around. The question is how they found that field."

"They came across LaPlatte Brook from one of the housing developments," she said.

"How do you know that?"

"I followed the tracks. They went out the back of the field, then across the pasture to the brook. I didn't go on the other side."

Lewis raised his eyebrows.

Are you impressed? Thought Katie, suppressing a grin.

"It's a long shot, but I'll go over, check around, and talk to some of those guys. Wouldn't get your hopes up though."

The glimmer dimmed.

Lewis was standing sideways to Katie, rocking slightly from foot to foot like a kid who had to pee. Her eyes narrowed as she wondered what else was circling inside his brain.

"Listen, Ms. Took..."

"Katie," she said.

"Katie, I've been giving considerable thought to the events that occurred the evening your grandmother passed away." He cleared his throat. Another employee pulled out of the lot. Lewis watched the vehicle go, but Katie watched Lewis.

"It was late in the day, coming on to dark. We'd had a lot of incidents in recent weeks of people out here joy-riding and destroying property, spooking livestock." He took off his hat, wiping his brow. "I may have jumped to the conclusion it was natural causes too quickly." He turned toward Katie.

"To be honest, my impression of Ruth has always been she was three ounces short of a peck. For that reason, I didn't believe I could trust her words. It didn't help I couldn't get a thought in edge-wise with her constant yammer and tugging at my sleeve. Then the doc was right there. He kind of took over, gave her some shot that dropped her to the ground like a sack of peas. Now I had a body and an unconscious woman to take care of. We got

Ruth into my cruiser, and the, ah, remains into Doc's van and left. Doc was pretty clear Irma had a bad heart; he'd been watching her for a while."

"Gram didn't go to the doctor here in town," said Katie. "At least I don't believe so. Ruth did, but I found a receipt in Gram's things for the clinic in Monkton."

Now Lewis's eyes narrowed. "You're sure?"

"I'll make a call," she said.

"I was sure from the way Doc spoke; she was one of his. He was there right out of the gate, I figured Ruth had called him after she called me. How else would he know to come out there, ya know?" Lewis's voice faded as his eyes drifted off. "Anyway," Lewis turned back to Katie, "I'm trying to reconstruct what I saw in the event I botched this. An apology won't make it right, but maybe it's not too late for me to dig out the truth."

"Did your office respond when the chicken coop burned?"

"I don't know anything about that." Lewis frowned.

Katie explained about a firebug torching the coop. Lewis opened his mouth, but Katie held her hand up, cutting him off.

"I've talked to Ruth a couple of times about this. Her story is always the same. The can is in the barn, but they both handled it so any prints have probably been compromised."

"I'll get someone over there to pick it up anyway," he said. "Don't handle it anymore."

After Lewis left, Katie went back into the feed store. Because most of the employees took a half-hour lunch and left at four-thirty, Stan was still inside manning the desk with one other employee to fetch and carry.

"Hey, Stan," said Katie, "can I use the telephone?"

Katie called the doctor's office, keeping her fingers and legs crossed until the receptionist picked up the line.

"Hi," said Katie, ready for the woman to slam the receiver down. "I'm Katelyn Took. My grandmother was Irma Moore." The words sped up. "I'm having an issue with the insurance company on my grandmother's policy. They want me to get her medical records for the last ten years. Can I get copies from you?"

191

The woman who didn't know about the altercation between Katie and the doctor put Katie through to the nurse. With Katie waiting on hold, the nurse pulled Irma's file, then came back on line.

"It seems," she said, "Irma hadn't been here in almost four years, got a tetanus shot the last time she was in. I guess her health was good. I can make copies if you'd like and mail them out, but it'll be tomorrow before I can get it done."

"That's fine," said Katie. "I appreciate it. Thank you." Katie's next call was to the Monkton clinic, but they were already closed for the day.

"I was right," Katie said aloud, getting into her car. "But what's with that whacked-out doctor?"

* * *

Katie wasn't the only one questioning the doctor. Even as she spoke with the nurse, Sheriff Lewis was asking the receptionist if the doctor could spare a few minutes.

"This way," the nurse beckoned Lewis into the doctor's private office. He waited only a few minutes before the doctor breezed in, closing the door behind him.

"Whew," he smiled. "I could use a break."

Lewis didn't smile. The doctor, intent on the candy dish sitting on his desk didn't notice.

"Listen," said Lewis. "Remember the night we went up to the Moore farm and found Mrs. Moore dead up in the field?"

The doctor went stone still. After a pause the length of a breath, he selected a gumdrop and without looking up moved to his seat.

"Yes," he said, shuffling papers. "It was a sad thing."

"It was," Lewis agreed. "I've been thinking about it some. You know, getting the call and hustling to get up there. Anyhow, in retrospect, it seemed like you were right on my elbow when I pulled in. I didn't call you; how did you know?"

"Yes, well, I believe the woman's friend called me. Probably right after she called you."

"Hm." Sheriff Lewis's eyes narrowed. "After hours and all, pretty surprising she got you."

"A lot of my older patients have my home number; seems they usually need me after hours." Giving a forced chuckle, the doctor rose to his feet. "Well, this was a nice break, but I have patients waiting."

"Yup, time's wasting," said Lewis, also standing.

He left the office well aware that the doctor hadn't once looked him in the face, and throughout the conversation, the man's shoulders had been tensed up around his ears.

Chapter Thirty-Three

Katie waited for Ruth to put her teacup down and sit.

"I need you to think carefully Ruth and tell me exactly what happened after you called Sheriff Lewis the night Gram died."

The fidgeting fingers, a hint Ruth was stressed, returned. They had discussed this before, and Ruth wasn't sure why Katie would want to talk about it again. Had she missed something Katie needed to know? Why was there a notebook sitting in front of Katie?

"Just relax." Katie leaned back in her chair, sipping her tea like this was any ordinary conversation. "I just want to make sure I remember everything you told me on the first day." She tapped the notebook, indicating she was going to take notes this time.

Ruth nodded. "Well, after I called Sheriff Lewis' office, he told me to wait here, and we rode out together. I was trying to tell him what I'd seen, but he kept shouting at me to get back in the car and let him do his job. Then, the doctor was there. It was like he just appeared out of thin air. I remember being surprised. He was talking to the sheriff. I heard him say it was Irma's heart. Hm...Oh, I remember asking him how he'd know, she wasn't his patient. I think I might have been getting frustrated. It was dark by then, but he was close enough to me so I could see him good. He looked kind of pained. Then he had hold of my arm, told me to sit down, I think."

"The next bit is fuzzy. I remember waking up on the couch and it was morning! There were cats outside crying to get in. It took me a while to get them all together and to make sure everyone was all right. Then I went for Irma's envelope on the refrigerator, but it was gone. I must have given it to the sheriff the night before."

"You don't remember the ride back from the hayfield, or lying down on the couch?"

"No, I don't. It must have been because of the stress. I can't believe I was able to sleep at all."

"Did you call the doctor after you called Sheriff Lewis?"

"Why would I do that? I could tell she was dead. If she'd been breathing, I'd have called 911."

"Were all the lights on when you woke up, Ruth?"

"The porch, the living room, and the kitchen were the only ones, I believe." Ruth touched Katie with icy fingers. "Did I do something wrong?"

"Absolutely not," Katie got up and wrapped her arms around Ruth. "I was worried I'd forgotten something, but we're good. How about I make one-pot chicken and tomatoes?"

While she was fixing supper, she compared Lewis's story to Ruth's. It was darn close. She stopped in the kitchen doorway to watch Ruth straighten up the living room; it was out of the question to believe Ruth's OCD would allow her to let the cats stay outside, sleep on the sofa, and leave lights on. *If nothing else, I would think stress would make her compulsive behavior worse,* Katie thought.

There were times Ruth said and did things that made Katie worry about what the other woman actually knew, but at that moment Katie was sure she had all the facts.

Chapter Thirty-Four

Katie made a conscious decision to discover what happened to Irma, knowing that stepping out of her comfort zone might make her a target. She shared her idea with Ruth so the other woman would be more aware of what was happening around her.

"No more walking to town, or leaving the house unlocked," she told Ruth. "From now on if someone tells me they knew my grandmother, I'm going to ask them when the last time they talked to her was and ask if she said anything about being scared."

"How will people know Irma was your grandmother?" asked Ruth. She was holding the tray filled with bowls of cat breakfast. When she stopped walking, the noise level around her ankles rose.

"I'll just tell them. I'm going over to the clinic in Monkton with you for your next visit this week. I'll stop at the post office and talk to the postmaster and her sub, the librarian, the vet, I'll make a list. If someone is willing to talk to me, I'm going to pump them for all they've got." She went back to lacing up her work boots. Just as she got ready to head out for work, Ruth rushed over.

"This is my extra notebook," she said. "I think you might need it."

Katie was true to her word. During her lunch and after work, she either walked over to other businesses or stopped as she drove past, opening the conversation by identifying herself and then following the thread. Even at work, she stepped up to people, shaking hands with a greeting that had sour men and harried women smiling back. It didn't take long for Rick to catch on. He took to telling customers his new assistant was Irma Moore's granddaughter. There were some who merely nodded and continued what they were doing. But there were others who remarked on Irma, offering condolences, sharing memories, and a few speculating on her demise.

"I heard a rumor," said one man.

Katie held her breath.

The man studied the ground. "It seems to me, there was somebody telling me she didn't just have the big one."

"Do you remember who?" Katie cleared her throat.

"Nope, I don't. really." He looked up a trifle sadly, but Katie smiled back letting him know it was all right.

Rick's big hand dropped on her shoulder. "Someone's gonna know something. Some small piece of information or thing that will tilt the world."

She could only nod. Later she stopped at Beauregard's hesitantly identifying herself to the clerk she had talked to on her first day back in town. The other woman didn't react as though she remembered questioning Katie. With a dejected sigh, Katie walked down the wooden steps, stopping short when she saw the deputy's cruiser parked next to her own car.

"Hey," said Katie.

"Hi, Katie," dimpled Marlie. "How're you doing?"

"Okay," said Katie, whose thoughts were miles away. It took her a few moments to realize they were standing in silence while she studied Marlie's features.

"You have interesting eyes," said Katie to break the silence. She immediately blushed as this was not what she had intended to say.

"I get them from my Micmac grandmother." Marlie batted her lashes.

"You should thank her," grinned Katie.

"With every sunrise," said Marlie.

"Only on the days the sun shines?" Katie blinked, surprised.

"Oh, small sparrow, the sun shines somewhere every day."

"I remind you of a sparrow?" Katie blushed again, unaware of her goofy grin.

"Actually, you remind me more of a persistent Blue Jay," said Marlie. "But that doesn't sound nearly as nice." Reaching out to run her finger along

Katie's cheek, Marlie smiled, dimples reappearing. Returning to the driver's seat of her cruiser, waving her fingers, Marlie pulled away.

***

"Katie." Ruth burst out the front door, racing across the porch. "You got mail. From two different contractors."

Katie's heart thumped. Then she was scrambling to get out of the car. "Let me see."

"And the guy that was here before came back, the dirt guy." Ruth was dancing around in hopping steps. The cats who normally trailed behind her gave her a wide berth.

"Well, I guess I picked a bad day to hang around in town, didn't I?" said Katie, reaching anxiously for the manila envelopes Ruth offered.

The original letter had provided the offering, the location of the property for inspection, and a cutoff date for offers. Katie tore open the first envelope. She had expected a letter similar to the one she had sent out. What she held looked more like a legal document.

"Is it good?" asked Ruth.

"I don't know," Katie replied, opening the second envelope.

This letter was like the first referring to yards of sand, gravel, mix, price per yard dependent on quality, numbers of truckloads, beginning and ending dates of removal, insurance, and security. Katie swallowed. Entering the house, she walked through to the kitchen, unaware of anything she passed.

"Katie?" said Ruth. She tried to sound upbeat, but there was still a nervous quiver in her voice.

"I don't understand what this means," said Katie. "Any of it." She sat down, still holding the letters. This could be something good, and if she didn't react, she could miss it. How to know?

"Cindy," she said. "I need to get hold of Cindy. Is this other guy coming back?"

"Yes," replied Ruth. "I don't know when."

Katie knew if the man coming in person spoke in the same language as the written missives, she needed to talk to Cindy first.

Cindy arrived about an hour later, having left Stan to clean up after supper and watch the kids.

"Okay," she said after listening to what Katie and Ruth had to say and reading through the documents Katie offered.

"First, anyone who comes in person? Agree to nothing, tell them you need to have the written bids in hand prior to the cutoff date. It's not fair to other bidders to offer deals, or even extra information. Anyone reputable will understand. Second, we need to go through each letter you receive and chart what they're offering in a way that's easy to compare."

Ruth jumped up, disappearing upstairs and returning with her notebook. She offered it to Cindy, who shook her head.

"No, I said I'd help, it's up to you to do the rest. What I suggest is that one of you does it, and then the other second checks to make sure you haven't missed anything. And last, it's time to get a lawyer to draw up the contract."

"I need a lawyer?" Katie's shoulders slumped. "How is that going to work? They'll want a retainer. I don't have money for that."

"I brought a list of lawyers that handle this kind of thing. Start calling, explain truthfully what you can do. Offer to have the closing in the lawyer's office. There will be an extra fee, but you're asking for a down payment. That means they can take their fee out that. Also, there are different ways to get paid for removal. I suggest that for the rest of this season, you get paid monthly."

"When you see the lawyer, he'll want to see all the stuff you got from the town, proof of ownership, survey information, all of it."

Katie told her about the letters she had received from the Charlotte planning and zoning board.

"And you didn't ask for this?" Cindy asked. "Well someone did, maybe there was a mix-up with a bidder who had questions. Who knows?" She shrugged. At that moment there was a knock at the door. Katie, who was closest, rose.

The man at the door introduced himself as the project manager for a Burlington-based contractor. He had additional questions. Cindy slipped out the kitchen door. After the man left promising to have his bid in before the cutoff, Katie spent a while sitting on Irma's bed. Ruth stopped long enough on her way to bed to say she had looked over the letters received and created a chart where they could record additional bids and compare the offers. Katie laughed softly, imagining what she'd find when she went downstairs. To her surprise, Ruth had done a very competent job and Katie couldn't find anything else to add. There were two additional pages left on the table, one the list Cindy had recited to get together for the lawyer, the other the project manager's questions and the small amount of additional information Katie had provided.

"There needs to be a page for Ruth too. That way I can keep track of how much she needs to be paid." Katie said to the cats lounging around the living room. A few blinked in agreement.

Ruth's ability to remember, record, and evaluate left Katie staring with a wide mouth at her notes. Rick had said Ruth's mind wasn't addled. Yet, so many people believed she was.

"It's like she's two people," said Katie.

Rick had given Katie a lesson in replacing window glass using the broken pane over the sink. Sitting at the table Katie looked out the new glass, she could see the top edge of the coop's roof and in the distance the mountain. Her mind drifted. Suddenly her guts clenched. What if that was the problem, what if Ruth was like two people? Not schizophrenic, but what if her meds or lack of brought out a darker shade of her personality? The hair on Katie's arms stood up. She had stopped locking her bedroom door, but in her mind saw the key turning in the lock again.

Chapter Thirty-Five

The smoking woman from Charlotte was having coffee with her town clerk friend the next day when the contractor who had stopped at Katie's house walked in.

"Good afternoon," he said. "I'm looking for a permit to remove sand here in Charlotte."

The woman carefully put her cup down, turning slightly as her friend approached the desk."

"You're sure you don't already have permits?" the clerk asked.

The woman didn't raise her eyes to watch, but felt her ears stretch open to listen.

"No," he said. "This is a new pit."

"Okay," said the clerk. "I'll be right back."

The smoking lady waited until her friend was in the zoning office before approaching the desk.

"Good afternoon," she said. "Can you tell me which pit you'll be using?"

Assuming she was another town employee, the man didn't hesitate. "On my paperwork, it says Katelyn Took."

When the clerk returned her friend was leaving the office. With a waggle of her fingers, the clerk turned to the man offering to answer questions on the forms.

Out on the sidewalk, the smoking lady hurried back to her office. She waited until her husband stepped out for lunch before placing her telephone call.

"Are you sure? I mean, you can use this right? Well, I'm just checking

201

because the price might be a little on the high side." She chewed her cuticle as she listened to the man on the other end of the call. He was adamant about his ability to make the Roser/Moore property pan out and what her cut would be.

The woman hung up the telephone. She should have to put more of an effort into gaining the piece of land while Irma was still alive. Now, she'd have to think of a different approach. Fortunately, no one else knew she was interested. She left a note for her husband letting him know she wouldn't be back that afternoon. She needed time to think and make a plan. There had to be a way to get hold of that property. Maybe if she could scare them enough to jump at the first way out, something right in their face while they were still shaken by something, maybe a threat? What, what to do? Her gaze went to the New York paper and an article of a problem happening in a southern state.

Driving out of town, she knew just where to find what she'd need. This time of day there would be no one around to hear her. Get it done now, drop it off later, come back smiling with a check in hand by lunch tomorrow. Yep, sign your name, honey, and get the hell out of my way. Laughing, she flicked a butt out the window and turned up the radio.

Chapter Thirty-Six

The sun rose in the east, sliding over the roof edge and down the side of the hen house lighting as it went and rousing the biddies. Ruth was at the sink, a skillet in one hand and a bowl of eggs in the other when she looked out the window. The nine-inch Griswold cast-iron skillet hit the floor ten inches from Katie's head as she was lacing her work boots. Katie jerked in the opposite direction from where the skillet was skidding.

Ruth didn't notice. She leaned across the sink, peering out, sure she wasn't seeing what was there and unable to close her mouth. The eggs landed in the sink and now runny yellow rivulets headed toward the drain. Her knuckles wrapped around the porcelain were stark white. She made a gurgling noise.

"Ruth?" said Katie. When the older woman didn't respond, Katie approached the window. She also gasped and pulled Ruth away before heading to the door.

"Stay inside," she ordered. Once outside, she moved with slow steps, one foot placed carefully in front of the other. Her eyes flashing from side to side as she approached the hen-house. Leaning against the small building was a roughly constructed scarecrow wearing a flannel shirt and cut-off jeans. The scarecrow had been partially burnt, and the tip of the stake forced into the dirt. Katie touched the blackened fabric; it was cool and there didn't appear to be any scorch on the outside of the coop. Backing away, Katie's eyes swept the yard looking for any damage. Other than the barn sale sign being tipped over, there was nothing. Her fear was as real as the warm sun's rays. This was an obvious threat, and she needed to call the sheriff.

Inside, Ruth was not in sight, but Katie heard a door upstairs slam. Unable to stop her fingers from shaking, it took Katie two attempts to get the call to ring through. The dispatcher wasn't able to tell Katie how soon the sheriff would arrive.

"For god's sake," she yelped. Frustrated, she slammed the receiver on the hook. Her next act was to dial the state police.

Less than fifteen minutes later Deputy Boyd pulled down the barn lane, parking near the hen house. A state trooper's vehicle followed Boyd, and eventually the sheriff himself. For the first time, the sheriff appeared honestly rattled. He walked up to the small group just as the trooper remarked that he believed this to be someone trying to frighten the ladies.

"No kidding," said Katie immediately regretting her rude tone. "Sorry," she said. "This is just beyond anything I can imagine. I don't however, think it's about both of us, just me."

"How's that?" asked Sheriff Lewis. He took a step closer. Katie fought the urge to move away.

"Think about it." Katie was curt, her anger apparent. "Ruth always wears a housedress, or a skirt and blouse, I've never seen her in pants. Someone dressed this scarecrow to look the same way I do every day when I go to work. Jeans. Women of Ruth's generation don't wear jeans."

The trooper nodded in agreement. He pointed out the only bit of evidence was a man's shoe print in the dirt Katie had left around the clothesline pole. The print was in a direct line between the over-turned sign and the scarecrow. "I have a camera in my cruiser." He squatted down, examining the print. "I think it's a shoe, not a boot."

"You mean like a man would wear to church?" asked Lewis.

"Or if he worked in an office or something like that," the trooper said.

While he went for the camera and Lewis checked on tire tracks in the yard, Katie took a chance.

"What size are your feet?" She asked the deputy.

"Nine."

"Could you put your foot right here next to the print?" she asked. "Yeah, be careful not to touch it." The print was easily an inch longer than that of the deputy. As she squatted to look at them, she realized the print was from a smooth-soled shoe. Definitely not a barn or work boot.

"What are you doing?" asked the sheriff returning with the trooper.

"Just looking," said Katie, rising to her feet. The trooper took several photos, then after wrapping the scarecrow in plastic took it with him. The deputy had already left, and now the sheriff turned to Katie. She was ready for him to guffaw the incident away, but the sweat circles had grown under his arms, and he rubbed a hand over his jaw.

"I don't like it," he admitted. "Keep locked up. You've got no neighbors out here to help keep watch. Nor a dog either."

Back inside, Ruth stood in the living room window watching the sheriff's car go down the hill.

"I made your lunch," she said. "I already took my medicine so don't bother asking. Don't forget to put out the barn sale sign."

Katie blinked, surprised. Earlier when she heard the door upstairs slam, she figured Ruth was hiding under the bed. The woman in front of her at that moment didn't appear rattled at all.

"Ruth, I don't plan on going to work," said Katie.

Ruth spun on her. "Yes, you are." She was angry. Her face was flushed, a thin white line rounded her lips. "You said you wanted to figure this out, and it might get dangerous. Well, it has, so either shit or get off the pot. You can't have it both ways."

Katie stepped back. Eyes wide, she stared at Ruth, unable to articulate her surprise.

"Don't look at me that way," stormed Ruth. Some of her rage had gone, but there was still enough left to urge her on. "I know you don't plan on staying on the farm. Well, I don't care anymore. I've done all I can, so figure out what you're up to. Now, get out of here."

Katie continued to stare at the older woman with narrowed eyes. "How do you know what I'm planning on doing or not?"

Ruth sighed. "You talk in your sleep. And you're loud."

Gulping back her guilt at Ruth's despair, Katie said, "Lock the door."

"No." Ruth turned to face Katie squarely. "I'll keep watch but I'm not hiding in a closet." When Katie picked up the brown lunch bag, Ruth added, "I hid the last time, and the time before that. I let Irma be my person, and I believe that's why all this is happening. I'm as guilty of her death as the person who killed her. I let the sheriff bulldoze her death under the rug. All this? All this evil around here? It's because I wasn't strong enough to stand up for myself years ago, or for Irma when she no longer had a voice. I will not hide again." Tears streamed down her face. She made no move to wipe them away.

Katie took a step toward Ruth.

"No." Ruth held up her hand. "It's time for you to leave or you'll be late. Go. I'm fine. Go."

Katie drove away, wondering at the wisdom of doing so. She couldn't let go of the image of Ruth's face.

"Rick," she said once back in the storage shed. "There's been another incident." When she was through, he took hold of her arm and dragged her into Stan's office.

"Talk to her," he demanded, shoving her toward Stan. "Tell her she has to stay somewhere else. It's not safe for either one of them."

Katie repeated her story to Stan, telling him also about the break-in.

"I agree with Rick," Stan said. "It's time to step back and figure out what's going on and let the police do their work."

"I'm not leaving," Katie said, stubbornly. "Ruth can go. She should go, somewhere safer. The sheriff is finally ready to do something." She looked up the street in the direction of Lewis's office. A sneer crossing her face. "And the state police know. Besides, where am I going to go with sixteen cats and a pig?"

"You haven't eaten the pig?" Stan asked.

"Can't," said Katie. "There's a rule. Ruth will be okay today. People are picking up their kittens today, so there'll be traffic in the yard. I stopped and talked to Grace on my way out."

* * *

When Katie pulled out of Fire Lane 61, a car was approaching from the west. The driver had intended to turn in, hand already on the turn signal lever, but at the sight of Katie, followed the young woman instead. Parked on the far side of the feed store lot, the driver watched Katie go into the shed. Before she was ready to get out of her vehicle, she saw Rick come out of the shed dragging Katie. The driver frowned. This wasn't what she had expected. She had no way of knowing that the police had been to the farm; she believed the women living there wouldn't have either the nerve or the brains to call for outside help.

"Well," she whispered, "don't think some old man will be of any help. For crying out loud, he looks like he can barely hold himself up."

Furious at both Katie and Stan, Rick slammed out of the office headed to his truck, and out of the lot. Stan shook his head.

"You're costing me money today, Katie," he said. "First you show up late, now you've got my best guy leaving with orders still to fill."

"I'm on it," said Katie.

The driver watched Katie re-enter the supply shed. There were trucks backed in and a younger guy going back and forth from the loading dock to the interior. The woman had selected a parking spot with a clear view of the shed. After several minutes she saw the young guy get into the company truck loaded with sacks and bales and pull out. When there was only one customer still parked at the docking area, the driver got out of the car. Adjusting her oversized sunglasses and tugging her short jacket into place, she mounted the steps.

"Katelyn Took?" she called out.

"Right here," said Katie, stepping from behind a pallet of stock. Wincing at the bright light and showing shadows below her eyes that shouldn't have been there, she asked. "Can I help you?"

"I represent a party who has an interest in purchasing a piece of property you own," the woman smiled.

At Katie's confused look, the woman added, "A man inside sent me out here. He said it would be all right." From there she pitched Katie, making it clear this offer had a short time limit attached. Though she would ideally have liked Katie to jump and sign, she took it as a good omen Katie didn't say no. When she walked away, Katie was reading the document, frowning in concentration.

"Another hick," said the woman to herself, opening the Cadillac's driver side door.

Katie's frown, however, was more about the improbable timing than the offer. When Rick returned, temper cooled, she didn't mention his leaving, or the pages tucked inside her lunch bag.

Chapter Thirty-Seven

Sunday Katie woke knowing she would have to decide about the offer given to her at the feed store. She hadn't said a word to anyone else about it. There didn't seem to be a reason to irritate the others until she'd thought it through. But the woman had been clear, Katie needed to call by nine the next morning with her answer. She still wasn't sure. It sounded good. Maybe she could just take the cats with her when she left. As near as she could tell, Irma hadn't stipulated she had to stay on the farm with them. She poured her second cup of coffee.

Even though it was still early, she put the barn sale signs out. It was barely nine when Ruth had her first customer. The man asked about furniture, and Katie duly opened the bay doors at the end of the barn. When the man's truck pulled away, there was a dining room table and four chairs strapped on top. Ruth was giddy with the fifty dollars earned and ran up to the house to put it away.

When she returned, Katie had set a pair of wooden porch chairs out.

"Maybe we should put two of the larger pieces in the milk house," said Katie.

"I agree," said Ruth. "I'll make room." She laughed. "If the customer can't see it, they won't buy it."

There was no way to maneuver the furniture through the barn, so while Ruth puttered, Katie selected the pieces she wanted to move. She had a two-wheel dolly found in the barn, but the uneven ground still made the process difficult. Panting with exertion, Katie leaned on a metal support. Her eyes flickered from one window to the next. Across four at a time, two

209

wide boards were nailed on the inside so the windows could open, but farm animals were kept away from the glass. None of the boards appeared to be loose. Though they were a sound idea, they limited visibility and incoming light. She prepared to wiggle back through to drop the bar that locked the double door closed when she heard Bonnie snuffling around. The pig had initially dodged around Katie's feet while she worked until Katie sternly sent her away. Now Bonnie was invisible, lost in the myriad of boxes and trash bags.

"Bonnie," Katie called. The only response was the excited woofing and small squeals. "Here pig, pig."

Still no response. Sure, that Bonnie was into something Katie wouldn't want her messing with, the woman followed the noise. She came to a small open space near the backside of the barn and less than halfway up the length. Bonnie was wrestling with something on the ground, but what caught Katie's eye and held her attention was a jumbled stack of wood pieces and a saw laying on the floor in the sawdust. The pieces were from two-by-fours similar to the inner framework of the scarecrow. A box of clothing had been dumped out nearby, leaving old shirts and jeans scattered around. Katie's hands shook. She steadied herself against a support, feeling the old whitewash turn to dust beneath her fingers.

What's going on? Who else besides Ruth would be in here? The taste of acid and bile rose in her throat. *How much of what she says is true? What does she really know?* The image of Ruth splitting into two came to mind. One version smiled sweetly, the other grinned like the devil himself.

Katie's brain commanded she drag Ruth back here and demand an explanation. Her heart, however, said the horrible thing she imagined was not true. Even though the evidence laying on the floor in front of her said the scarecrow was assembled here, the state trooper had said it hadn't been burnt on the side lawn where they had found it leaning on the hen house.

Bonnie bumped into Katie's legs, bounced off, and bumped her again.

"Move, Bonnie," Katie said.

The pig twisted and jumped before twisting again. The squealing volume rising.

Katie looked down and realized Bonnie had been playing with a piece of clothing and now had it wrapped around her head.

"You're such a fool," said Katie. Trapping the pig between her legs she freed the cloth. Holding it aloft, Katie realized it was the remnants of a Bolero jacket made of a Madras print with wide green bands along the edges.

"Talk about ugly," said Katie, looking for a place to put the jacket where Bonnie wouldn't be able to reach it. As she turned, the jacket passed close to her face and a cloying fruity perfume wafted near. "Yhew, again," said Katie. She shoved the jacket into an apple crate teetering on a pile of cardboard boxes.

Behind the boxes, the open pig door allowed the sun to shine inside. Katie approached the door, drawn by the light and a cooling breeze. As she stood on the concrete ramp, eyes traveling down its length, she noticed an area of discoloration near the bottom. Hunkering down she ran her fingers over what she thought was mold or rot, she came away with soot on her fingers. This was where the scarecrow had been burned. Furious, Katie went after Ruth.

"Can you explain this to me?" Katie pointed to the sawdust and saw, then taking Ruth's arm pulled her out to the ramp. "Or this?"

Ruth shook her head. She looked from one side to the other, then out into the orchard. Finally, she turned back to Katie.

"I can tell from the way you're talking, Katie Took, that you believe I have some idea how this came to be." Ruth squared her shoulders. "Well, I can tell you that I don't. If I had never seen that scarecrow, I'd believe this mess was left from something Irma was doing. And to burn so close to the barn? That's utter stupidity."

Katie couldn't relax. Her mouth was a straight line emphasizing the speculation in her eyes.

"You think I'm guilty?" Ruth's voice rose. "Really? Well, I tell you what. I don't have to stay here and worry that you're going to...to...I don't know what. I can leave right now." Ruth pushed past Katie, rushing back into the barn.

Katie let her go, following only when she realized the only way to secure the pig door would be to nail it shut. Returning moments later with a hammer and nails, she shoved on the warped door. Though the top swayed slightly, the bottom didn't budge. Grunting, she threw herself at the door and found herself sitting on the ground thrown backwards by the whiplash.

"How's that working for you?" asked a voice to her left.

Face blazing, she looked up at Rick. His face was dark as thunder. "Just came from the house," he drawled. "Seems Ruth is in a real tizzy. Did you throw her out?"

Fighting the urge to shout at him to shut up and leave her alone, Katie stood, dusting off her seat.

"No. I asked a question. She jumped to a conclusion. I didn't get whiny and beg for her forgiveness." Katie prepared to rush the door again.

"Whoa, let's start with this, then deal with Ruth." Rick stepped between Katie and the pig door. "Show me what you found."

She started with the scorched cement she had all but landed in and then took him into the barn. By his suggestion, they created a fence around the sawdust site and covered the scorch with a piece of canvas held down with rocks.

"This is getting out of hand," said Rick. "You called the sheriff when you found the scarecrow, so call again now."

"You're right," Katie said. "I'll call the trooper that took the scarecrow to come out and look at this. Protecting the evidence, as it is, is a smart move."

Near the tool bench, Rick found a sledgehammer, which he took to the bottom of the pig door. Four solid whacks and the bottom of the door was in place. Three well-placed nails and the top was locked in. The whole door was secured.

"Now," said Rick collecting the tools and handing them to Katie, "let's go see what we can do about the old lady."

* * *

Ruth was sitting on the top step of the porch with two tote bags beside her and Shade in her arms.

CHAPTER THIRTY-SEVEN

Katie bit her lip. Leaving Rick behind, she advanced.

"Look, Ruth," she began, "I might have been a little short-tempered, because, you know, of the stress. I don't know what I was thinking, how.." She didn't get any further as Ruth flew off the step and crushing Shade between them, threw her arms around Katie.

"I'm sorry," she hiccuped, "so sorry."

Katie's anger melted. "It's not your fault," she said. "I just don't understand how all this can happen with us right here. It's scary. I'm scared." She tried to separate Ruth, but the old woman wouldn't let go until there was a mewling cry. Shade wanted to be free.

The women moved inside, where Katie became aware Rick was carrying a canvas gym bag.

"What's that?" she asked.

"My stuff. I figured I'd bring it in seeing as I'm staying here for a few days, thank you very much." Rick dropped the bag beside the sofa.

"You just happened to have that in your truck?" Katie asked with a hint of sarcasm on the outer edges.

"I've actually been hauling it around for a while," he answered, offering her a candy-sweet smile.

"Well, if you're staying here, you can sleep in Irma's room," directed Katie. "The sofa is for sitting, not for tenants."

Rick's smile dissolved. "I don't want to sleep in Irma's room."

"It's that or with the pig," said Katie, walking away, intending to call the trooper.

Ruth grabbed Rick's bag and headed for the stairs.

"I'll just take this up for you." She smiled.

When the trooper arrived, he took pictures as well as both Katie and Ruth's statements.

"You can call the sheriff," he said. "He should probably see this, or I can send off a copy of my report to him."

"That would be fine," said Katie.

While she cooked, Ruth showed Rick the chart she had made for the contractor's bids. Katie watched beneath lowered lashes. Ruth was laughing, animated, and Rick attentive.

They're so cute, she thought.

During supper, Katie suggested Rick park his truck just below the driveway where it would be hidden from view behind the lilac bushes.

"That way," she said, "the only people who would know you're here are those that come up the road." After a moment she added, "Neither Raymond nor myself believe that's how the problem is getting here."

Rick nodded in agreement. "That's true."

The time had come for Katie to bite the bullet and talk about the offer to sell the farm outright. She brought the document down from her bedroom. Holding the papers between nervous, twitchy fingers, she told Ruth and Rick what it was.

Ruth sat with her hand over her mouth, eyes filled with tears. At the end of the table, Rick leaned back, speculating.

"What are you thinking?" he asked.

Katie tossed the papers on the table. She too, leaned back in the creaky wooden chair.

"I checked Ruth's list. This is one of the realtors we sent a letter to about the gravel pit." Her mouth was dry. "I'm willing to bet, either they have their own plans for the land, or they already have a customer who wants it. If I don't accept the offer before the deadline I gave the gravel companies, the price is going to go up."

"Katie?" Ruth's voice wavered, a thin sound from behind trembling fingers.

"If you do the math between this offer and Cindy's estimate on the gravel isn't anywhere near close." *I can't believe I'm saying this,* she thought. "I'm going to pass."

Ruth hiccuped; her eyes still tear-bright. Rick nodded, returning to his meal. He lifted his fork and asked, "What else?"

"As far as the contractors, I have two different lawyers who will accept payment when the contract is signed," said Katie. "A Joseph Costello and a Mark Morgan."

"Go with Costello," said Rick. "I hear he's tough but straight. I don't know about the other guy."

"Okay then," Katie agreed. "I'll call and tell him to put the contract together so we'll be ready. I want to close this deal before the Charlotte town clerk changes his mind about giving me an extension."

"We have cookies to have with our coffee," said Ruth.

Both Katie and Rick held up their mugs.

"Maybe tomorrow night," said Katie, mug in one hand and oatmeal raisin in the other, "you two could drive over to Williston and check out the big grocery store."

"Sure," smiled Rick. "Hey, how about we all go and we can have supper over there?"

Ruth smiled in agreement.

"Actually," said Katie, looking at everything around the room, except Rick, "I have a few things I want to, er, check out. You two could go, have supper, make an evening of it." She smiled broadly.

It was clear from the look on Rick's face; he wasn't buying her excuse. An eyebrow quirked up.

Katie smiled broader.

"Does this have anything to do with you putting your nose where it shouldn't be?" he asked.

"No." Her smile faded slightly. "I really do have something else planned. Just a little hello, how are you, thing. And I promise it's personal as in a friendly meeting."

Before Rick could question her further, Katie reached for the sale offer for the Roser property.

"You say somebody brought you this at the feed store?" Rick asked, nodding at the papers.

"Yes, while you were gone. Maybe twenty minutes before you came back."

"You didn't say anything about it."

Ruth had sat back down, concern etching shadows into her face.

"To be honest, I didn't know what to do about it. It seemed like weird timing, I mean with everything that's going on and all." She accepted the pages Rick passed back to her.

He shrugged. "It's possible this is just some Joe Blow looking to get on board. Or maybe he'd thought about it, heard gossip that you were being harassed over here, and figured he'd catch you when you were vulnerable and score."

Katie sat silently considering the papers ruffling them between her fingers.

"What are you going to do, Katie?" Ruth asked after a few minutes.

Dropping the contract on the table, Katie leaned back, a grimace on her face. "I'm probably going to be sorry."

* * *

Rick's plan the next day was to leave work, pick up Ruth, and head out.

"We'll probably be back by eight-thirty or nine," he told Katie.

At lunchtime she went into Stan's office to use the telephone.

"Hi," she blurted, nervous as soon as the caller picked up. "I'm calling to ask if you'd like to come over after work today for coffee and a little visit." She laughed to cover the quiver in her voice. "The kids are going out to dinner."

"Coffee would be fine. See you then."

Katie hung up the telephone, aware while her mouth was dry, her armpits were soaking through her shirt.

Shortly after Rick's truck went down the road, Marlie's car came up.

"I made coffee, but I have tea or lemonade," said Katie.

"Coffee's fine," said Marlie. "How about if we sit on the porch?"

Katie, who was just thinking, sitting in the living room, felt a little stiff, picked up the plate of cookies and her cup then followed Marlie through the screen door. As soon as they sat down, a few cats congregated, including LG.

"I should have warned you about the cat infestation," said Katie.

"And the pig." Marlie nodded toward the end of the porch.

Bonnie had followed LG and now stood with her nose outstretched toward the humans.

"No Bonnie. Stay." Katie ordered.

"Does she behave well?" asked Marlie.

"Not very," said Katie. She kept a stern eye on Bonnie until the pig lowered its rump to the ground.

"What shall we talk about?" asked Marlie sipping from her cup.

"To be honest, I hadn't planned that far, but you were upfront about where you came from and I'd like to tell you my three-line story."

"Just three?"

"I'd like to get away with that," said Katie. For the next several minutes she told about losing her parents, coming to Gram's, and then running away. "I only gave my heart once and got French-fried for it. I guess I'm kind of damaged goods."

"And you think you have a market on that?" asked Marlie.

Katie turned away, looking toward the lovers' lane. For an unexplained reason, she choked up. Suddenly Marlie was standing right in front of her. Katie drew a ragged breath. Marlie leaned forward until her lips touched Katie's. Only then did her hands run along the sides of Katie's head. The kiss was tentative, searching, then when no rebuttal came, more aggressive. Katie's head tipped back, accepting. She could feel the weight and heat of Marlie's breast against her own. Her hands reached up, caressing Marlie's waist and hips Katie wondered at the wisdom of starting this when Rick and Ruth could return at any time.

Suddenly there was a jarring slam from the side, a shrill squeal, and the smashing of glass. Katie's chair jerked, throwing both she and Marlie off balance. With Katie distracted, Bonnie seized the chance to sneak onto the porch. Unfortunately, the tiny three-legged table hadn't been sturdy enough to withstand the pig's weight as she reached for the cookies. Now she snuffled among the mess retrieving cookies while the cats who had scattered to the ground watched.

Marlie righted herself from the porch rail which had stopped her from toppling down among the cats.

"BONNIE!" Katie yelled.

Marlie laughed. "It's all right," she said, pushing the pig away from the glass. "Shoo, before you hurt yourself. Katie, we need a broom and dustpan. I'm afraid the plate and your cup both shattered."

Dutifully, Katie hurried into the house. "It's okay," she said over her shoulder. "None of the dishes here match, anyway."

Bonnie stood with her front feet on the lowest step, woofing mournfully as Katie swept up the cookie pieces with the glass.

"I think I got it all," she said to Marlie, who was moving the furniture back into place. "I'm so sorry."

"Don't worry about it." Marlie was still laughing. "It never occurred to me you would have a pig as a chaperon."

Marlie left a short time later, promising to return another time.

Chapter Thirty-Eight

K atie fed the cats and locked up the chickens and Bonnie feeling better than she had in a long while. Shortly after eight, Rick and Ruth returned.

Katie had once again spread the contents of Irma's file on Lawrence French across the kitchen table.

"What are you looking for?" asked Ruth. "You seem to study those all the time but I haven't seen one ah-ha moment."

"I'm trying to figure out why this guy was all over Gram. You said he was out here. Was it because of the farm or the Roser property? Neither one is overly large or flat enough to fill with houses and make a fortune. I don't get it. There's property all over the place that would be better, and there are farms, factories, whole towns practically that are going belly up. Wouldn't one of those be cheaper?"

Ruth circled the table to stand behind Katie. As far as the young woman knew, this was the first time that Ruth had spent any time studying the newspaper articles.

"I don't think this guy," Ruth pointed to French, "was the one causing all of Irma's problems. I think it was the toad."

"The toad?" Katie sat back, looking up at Ruth.

"Yes, when that man came to talk to Irma, there was a second man in the car." Ruth moved around the table and sat down. "French came up to the door and Irma invited him inside. I was sitting on the sofa and could see his car. While French was talking to Irma, the second man got out of the car and walked down around the backside of the barn. He was only gone a few

219

minutes, I watched him from the kitchen window. When he came back, he was carrying a camera which he must have had and I didn't notice at first. He got back in the car and waited for French."

"Do you think that was their plan?" Katie asked. "For French to keep Gram busy while, the other guy took pictures."

"I didn't have the impression French was trying to stall Irma," said Ruth. "He said thank you, goodbye, and left. I never saw him come back again. But the toad did."

"Why do you call him the toad?"

"I never knew what his name was. I don't think Irma did either. Every time he came around or she referred to him, she'd say the toad. French had a nice car, a nice suit, was clean and well sort of, polished. The toad was tall, kinda slimy-looking, and wore a cheap suit. The seat of his trousers was all shiny where the fabric hadn't held up."

Katie stared down at the newspaper articles with her hands, pressing the paper into the table. Was she searching for clues in the wrong place?

"Did the toad work for French?" she asked.

Ruth shrugged her shoulders. "Don't know. But if he was part of the deal French was offering, wouldn't he have come inside with French? If not for anything else than to know exactly what transpired?"

Katie had to agree. She had been behind the barn several times since her return and could clearly picture what was back there. "I can't imagine," she said. "what a few pictures would be good for."

Rick came out of the bathroom, towel drying his hair.

"What are you two clucking about?" he asked.

Laughing, Ruth went back to putting away the groceries she and Rick had purchased.

Katie pushed back from the table, her open hands indicating the newsprint on the table.

"You know all the articles I found in Gram's stacks that had circled articles were in newer papers?"

"How's that?" Rick asked.

Then Katie realized the files were something she'd only discussed with

Ruth.

"Somewhere along the line Gram started hoarding paper; newspapers, magazines, old envelopes, all kinds of papers. Every newspaper was folded the way they came, except for the ones that had articles she'd circled. Those papers were folded so the article was on the front. I cut them out and saved them before getting rid of the rest."

"There were local stories she kept," Katie peeked at Ruth. "Series about specific topics, and a pile about this same contracting company and its owner from Burlington."

"Let's have a look," said Rick. Over half a pot of coffee, Rick read each article without finding one item Katie hadn't already underlined.

"I agree there's probably something right here we need to see," he said. "But I've got no idea what it is."

Sighing, Katie collected the pieces, putting the file back in the cabinet. In the far back was one that held everything Irma had saved regarding George Beauregard; this wasn't the time however to bring that one out. Her fingers lingered on the file. She wanted to show it to Rick, but she knew that would upset Ruth.

"On the way back from Williston," said Rick as he sat on the sofa handing Ruth a glass of lemonade and her pill bottle, "we stopped at that body shop near Recon Tire."

Katie closed the file drawer, and shooing a cat off the rocking chair, sat down.

"There were only two guys there finishing up a job. I told them I was looking for a hot-rodder from Parentville who drove a pickup with big tires and had suffered front end damage."

"Rick said the guy had been horsing around and ran into his tractor." Ruth laughed.

"What kind of tractor?" asked Katie.

"Not important," said Rick. He gave me three names though; I think they're all either from here or Charlotte." He handed a piece of paper to Katie.

"I don't know any of these people," said Katie, reading the list over.

"Me neither," said Rick. "Are you going to look them up?"

"No," said Katie, "I'll give the list to Sheriff Lewis. I think this is more in his line of work."

Rick nodded. "You need a television in here," he said.

"And a picnic table," said Ruth.

"Yes," said Katie, agreeing to both.

Chapter Thirty-Nine

The next morning Katie drove into Burlington, arriving at the office of Joseph Costello before they opened at eight and staying until his secretary had made copies of all Katie had brought.

"He's probably going to have questions," the woman said. "Are you available by the telephone?"

"He can call me at work. They'll get me." Katie gave the woman the number and left. She made one other quick stop to leave the list Rick had gotten about truck repairs for Sheriff Lewis. Marlie was manning the desk, but there were other town residents waiting to see the sheriff, so no chance for a private conversation.

As soon as she arrived at the feed store, Katie went to Stan telling him why she was late.

"I was looking for you," Stan said. "I'm concerned about the scarecrow thing."

Katie shrugged. So was she, but Stan was her boss, not her father. She didn't want to burden him with her issues. Stan watched warring thoughts dance around on Katie's face. Cindy had voiced her concerns for Katie's safety, and Stan knew Rick had some too. But Katie was a grown woman who had thus far not asked any of them for help. When she turned away, he spoke again, not sure he was ready for her to leave.

"How's it going with the animal collecting?" He settled into his seat inviting her to continue.

"Good," said Katie. "So far I've escorted three dogs' home, trapped and re-located a skunk, disposed of two road-kill raccoons, and am currently seeking adoptive parents for a pig."

"Nice."

"Actually, the pig has eaten all the profits." With that, she left his office, and though Stan hadn't asked the questions he really wanted answered, he let her go.

Katie was finishing a grain order when Dan climbed the steps on the loading dock.

"Cops are here," he said. "Looking for you."

Katie went out into the parking lot where Lewis was talking to Stan. "Got a minute?" Lewis asked her, looking up. He waited until Stan walked away before continuing.

"I just got off the telephone with the state trooper you called about the burn spot out in back of the barn. I'd like to look it over with him, see what he has to say."

"Yeah," said Katie. "That's fine."

"Do you want to be there or can he and I just meet up out there?" Lewis asked.

"You don't need me," said Katie. "You can go into the barn by yourselves. I've already seen it." She paused. "Listen, Sheriff Lewis, Ruth will probably be around there. Please don't antagonize her."

"Noted," said Lewis.

Katie took a few minutes before returning to work to call and tell Ruth the officers were coming out.

"Why don't you go help Grace," she suggested. "Just so they can't get all sort of 'officer-of-the-law' all over you." For the rest of the day, Katie was edgy, expecting either Lewis or the state trooper to pull into the parking lot, sirens blaring and screeching brakes.

"I'm not worried they'll arrest me," she told herself, "more like they're going to call me a darn fool in front of all the guys and destroy what little credibility I have."

However, no one came. It wasn't until she got home and found the note Lewis left for her that she learned the mess in the barn and the burn spot were now official crime scenes, taped off, and to be left alone.

"Well, okay, then," Katie said.

"There's already a problem," said Ruth. She was sitting at the edge of the porch snapping late yellow beans and throwing the ends to Bonnie, who rooted through the grass searching. "When I got back up here, the police were just leaving. The state trooper took me down and showed me the places they were talking about. Not a half-hour after he left, I looked out the window, and Bonnie and the cats were playing with the yellow crime scene tape."

Katie felt her jaw drop.

"I put the tape back as best I could, but if she keeps collecting it, it won't last long."

Going into the house, Katie snuck out the kitchen door while Bonnie was still intent on yellow bean scraps. She barricaded the area in the barn, making it pig-proof, then built a wall of lumber around the burn. If the tape disappeared, the area beneath the tarp would still be marked out.

While she was working, the barn sale bell pealed. Coming around the end of the barn, carefully avoiding the weed patch Bonnie used as her private outhouse, Katie found Ruth bartering with an elderly man over a carton of three-penny nails.

"Fifty cents," said the man.

"Seventy-five, and I won't tell people you cheated me," said Ruth.

After the man counted out the change and drove off, Katie said, "Ruth have you seen your good customer lately? The woman in her boss's car?"

Ruth looked down the road. "No, I haven't. What a shame. She really liked to buy."

Katie wanted to ask Ruth to let her know when the woman returned, but she hesitated because she didn't want to explain why.

"You know," said Ruth fussing with her display, "I know when we started you and Rick, and me too actually, thought this was going to be a nickel and dime operation that didn't amount to a hill of beans."

Katie nodded in agreement.

"Well," Ruth grinned, "there's one-hundred and fifty-seven dollars and seventeen cents in the till."

"Wha-at?" croaked Katie.

"Yep," said Ruth. "Want to pay a bill?"

Katie sat at the table half an hour later counting the money Ruth emptied from the money bag.

"We'll be able to keep selling until snow flies," said Ruth.

"Yeah," Katie agreed. "Too bad we don't have an inside place to keep it up during the winter."

"You mean, like the schoolhouse?" Ruth had a crafty look on her face.

"Won't work, Ruth. Needs too much to make it decent and there's no heat." Katie heard her grandfather laughing silently in her mind. *Yes, I know you'd love that,* she agreed.

Chapter Forty

"The number of calls you're getting, Katie, I'm thinking of running an extension out to the shed," said Stan. He vacated his seat so she could take the call.

"Hello," she said, slightly breathlessly from her run from the other building.

"Katie? This is Sheriff Lewis. I have a car coming for you." He sounded gruff and before she had a chance to ask him what was happening, he added, "I have someone coming in for questioning and I'd like to have you sitting here before he arrives."

"Okay," she said. Outside, a horn blew and Katie went out to find Marlie waiting in the cruiser for her.

"So, what do you know?" Katie asked.

"Nothing, actually. Lewis has been chewing his spit for a while and I guess he's worked out what he wants to do." Marlie pulled out of the feed store parking lot. "He's not real good about sharing. Ever."

"I made some brownies if you're interested in coffee later," said Katie.

"Sounds good," Marlie answered, flipping on the directional for the turn into the town lot.

Sheriff Lewis was waiting just inside the door. Taking Katie's arm, he hustled her over to one of the waiting area's chairs.

"Sit here," he instructed. "Don't move and don't say a word."

The outside door opened. Katie looked up to see the elderly town doctor walking in. The man's smile disappeared when he saw Katie.

"Hi Doc," said Marlie. "Let me tell the sheriff you're here."

The doctor waved her back to her seat, and without knocking, walked

227

into Lewis' office. Katie sat quietly, trying to listen from across the lobby.

If I was in the town office, I'd be able to hear what was going on, she thought.

The meeting lasted for forty-five minutes, and though she could hear the harsh rasp of angry voices from time to time; she heard nothing else. When the door wrenched open, the red-faced doctor rushed out, looking neither at Katie nor Marlie. Lewis also appeared, looking disgruntled.

"Marlie will take you back to work," he told Katie. To Marlie, he said, "See you tomorrow."

"Well," Marlie said when they were in the car, "I guess I'm good for that coffee right now."

Marlie followed her home, then stayed for supper with Ruth and Rick. Though Katie waited, the deputy didn't speak of what had happened earlier at all. Later she walked down into the orchard with Katie and Bonnie, where the two women shared a kiss and a cuddle while Bonnie devoured the sour dropped apples.

"She's going to be sick," Marlie whispered.

"Her problem," sighed Katie.

Long after Marlie had driven away, and Katie had locked the cats in the house, and Bonnie was tucked in, she sat on the porch reflecting.

"What's up?" asked Rick, settling on the upper step.

"I wasn't planning on staying," said Katie. "I was going to sell, take the money, and run. Now, to be honest, I don't know what I'm doing."

"There's still cats hanging on," he said.

"Yes. Where's Ruth?" Katie looked through the screen. "She was awfully quiet at supper. Did Marlie being here upset her?"

"No," said Rick. "Shade passed away this afternoon. She's trying to be brave, but I think she's crying up in her room."

"Oh, crap." Katie walked silently up the stairs, tapping on Ruth's door and entering without invitation.

Ruth was already in bed, and though she feigned sleep, her cheeks and lashes were wet. Katie sat on the edge of the bed.

"I know you're faking," she said. "Tell me what I can do."

"It's done," said Ruth without opening her eyes. "I buried her this afternoon.

She can rest now."

"I'm so sorry, Ruth," Katie whispered.

"I know." Ruth's hand reached out, patting Katie's. "You're a good girl and were nice to her and I thank you."

Giving Ruth's hand a squeeze, Katie went to her own room wondering what would happen to the small orchard cemetery after she left.

Chapter Forty-One

Sheriff Lewis was brought up to believe a grown man didn't say he was sorry, never admitted to having made a mistake, and that anytime a woman opened her yap, he had the right to close it. Unfortunately, being of small stature, he had come up against a few rugged farm girls in high school that corrected some of his thinking. Martin Lewis was book smart, a trait Al Lewis didn't understand. When Martin had a chance at a two-year college scholarship, he took it. Al Lewis got loud and mean, so Martin moved out. It was as simple as that. He wanted to be a teacher, found three guys looking for a fourth roommate, got a job dispatching for the Rutland police, and left home. Martin's career choice changed, and eventually, he moved up from deputy to sheriff. There was still a little man chip on his shoulder, but his ability to consider his actions past and present had expanded. A perfect example was the incident with Irma Moore. It shamed Martin to realize a man he respected and trusted led him down a path of lies, the worst being Martin had gone with practically no struggle.

Katie Took's persistence was like a chigger under his skin. The more he dug at it, the more damage he found. Stepping up and telling Katie he would check further took nerve to admit he'd made a big mistake. But Martin was a man of his word, so when Katie left a list of trucks that could have been involved in Irma's death, Martin moved ahead.

Locally the football team was practicing daily after school. It was a place to start. Sheriff Lewis and Boyd drove up to the CVU football field and returned with Brent Thatcher and Colby Willis. Brent owned one of the trucks on the list. Colby was his glued-to-a-hip buddy. After Lewis pulled out of the office parking lot on his way to the school, Marlie took it on herself to call Katie.

"Park in the highway department lot," said Marlie. "Stay out of sight, please Katie. I could get fired for this."

Katie agreed and found a place in the town clerk's office where she could observe.

The boys rode back in separate cruisers, and Brent was still complaining about leaving his truck behind when he got out of the sheriff's car. Katie stood to the side of the parking lot window. She was holding the dog license ledger in her hands, but even Janice knew that wasn't why Katie was actually there.

Within minutes, two vehicles pulled in. An adult couple got out of one car and a woman out of the other. They exchanged words for only a few seconds before entering the building. Katie could feel a knot tightening in her stomach. From this point, she would know nothing until Lewis decided to tell her. It was more than she could bear. She decided to just walk into the sheriff's office and sit down. Maybe she'd hear something. Replacing the ledger, Katie turned and found Janice right behind her.

"Sit here," said Janice. She took Katie by the arm leading the younger woman over to her own desk and pulled out the chair. Once Katie sat down, Janice climbed up on the desk and slid open the cross-ventilation duct on the wall. She climbed down and sat at her assistant's desk with her work in hand.

Katie was sure Janice was trying to keep her out of trouble until she heard a man say. "You better have a darn good reason for involving my boy in whatever you're up to Sheriff."

Katie sat still, holding her breath.

"A crime has been committed; we want to talk to the boys. Colby is in the other office and I'll get to him shortly." Sheriff Lewis was not intimidated.

"This is ludicrous," said a woman obviously to the sheriff, and then more directly to the man "We should call Larry, get a lawyer."

"Shut the crap up about Larry and your swirly skirt crush on him."

"Don't you dare talk to me like that!" shouted the woman.

A young male voice cut in. "For crying out loud, can you two stop it? Why am I here? What about my truck?"

"Can we proceed?" asked Sheriff Lewis. "I have more to do today." He sounded bored, which raised the hair on the back of Katie's neck. For her, this was a soul-stopping moment, and she wanted him to feel the same way.

Lewis, however, seemed to have a different reason for negating the meeting.

"You don't think our time is worth anything, Sheriff?" demanded the woman. "You think that by embarrassing us in front of the whole community you're going to gain anything? Like more votes at the next election?" Her voice had risen an octave.

"Actually Mrs. Thatcher, I'm not concerned about votes at this moment. Also, the only way anyone in the community is going to know you were here is if you tell them. Now let's talk about Brent and his truck."

Mrs. Thatcher must have moved to say something because Mr. Thatcher spoke up.

"Just listen to what the man has to say, so we can get out of here," Mr. Thatcher growled.

"Brent," said Lewis. "Can you tell me where you were and what you were doing on July eleventh of this year?"

"He was…" began Mrs. Thatcher.

"The law requires a parent or guardian be present when a minor is questioned," Lewis cut in. "One, that's all I need. My questions are to Brent, to be answered by Brent. Thank you. Now, Brent?"

There was a pause. Katie held her breath. The voices were clear but low, as though far away, even though only four inches of wall separated them. However, if one person spoke softer, she would not be able to hear them.

"I don't know," said Brent.

"Are you sure?" asked Lewis.

"Ah-hem, as I was trying to say." There was no disguising the snide in Mrs. Thatcher's voice. "I have my calendar right here in my purse, and Brent was at football boot camp for the whole week."

"Overnight boot camp?" asked Lewis.

"Yes," said Brent.

"Is it local?"

"No, it's on the Dartmouth College campus."

"Did you have your truck there?"

"No. I had to ride on an activity bus from Burlington," Brent replied.

"I see," said Lewis. There was a pause before he added. "Thank you for your time, I'm sorry for the inconvenience. I'll have Boyd take you back to where you left your truck."

"Don't bother," said Mrs. Thatcher. "We'll take him."

There was a shuffling of feet and the Thatchers left without so much as a goodbye. Katie went back to the window and watched them pull out of the lot. Mr. Thatcher had his arm around Brent's shoulders. Mrs. Thatcher's back was rigid, her shoulders tense. She looked like she had every intention of making somebody sorry.

"Looks like she's got a ramrod where the sun doesn't shine, doesn't she?" asked Janice.

Katie didn't answer. Her best guess was walking away unscathed. She returned to the seat at the desk and listened for a few moments. If Colby was being questioned in a separate office, she couldn't hear. Katie didn't stay long after the Thatchers left. She was stopped at the end of the driveway when she caught sight of Colby and his mother exiting the sheriff's office in her rear-view mirror. The burning sting of tears forced her to rub her eyes.

"We were so close," she whispered.

* * *

Sheriff Lewis drove out to the house instead of calling with his report.

"I talked to all three of the boys," he said. "They all had alibis for where they were on the eleventh. I'm sorry, Katie."

"It's okay," she said. "You did what you could." A lead weight filled her chest. All she wanted was to sit down and not think about it anymore.

Ruth wanted to make tea, offered cookies or a grilled cheese sandwich. Katie waved her away.

"Come on, Ruth," Rick whispered. "Let's go for a little ride. Maybe we'll see deer in the fields."

They left Katie alone, and she made a point of going to bed before they returned.

Chapter Forty-Two

"KATIE TELEPHONE," barked the PA system.

Stan stepped out of his office after handing the receiver to Katie.

"Katie?" said Grace. "You need to come home right now. And Katie, don't say anything to Rick."

"On my way," said Katie. She knew Stan was still in earshot, just as she knew whatever had happened involved Ruth.

Exhaling slowly and relaxing the muscles in her face before turning back to Stan, she said, "Dog call. I gotta go, and it sounds like I might have to drive over to the vets." Her eyes made it up as far as the collar on Stan's shirt.

Stan nodded, unaware of Katie's inability to look him in the face.

"Got some heavy gloves?" he asked. "How about your snare pole? An injured dog can be dangerous."

"You know what the scouts say," Katie said walking around him, "always be prepared."

She found Ruth seated at the kitchen table with Grace dabbing at a bloody spot among the gray curls.

"Holy crap," said Katie. "What happened?"

"I fell down," whispered Ruth.

Over her head, Grace's eyes met Katie's. There was doubt in the brown depths. Stepping closer, Katie parted Ruth's hair.

"I don't think she needs stitches, but someone should watch her for the next few hours," said Grace.

"Ruth?" Katie walked around the table to face Ruth. "How did you fall down?"

"I tripped?" Ruth watched her fingertips tapping the tabletop.

"No, I mean did you fall forward or maybe to the side?"

"To the side," said Ruth. "Onto my side."

"Like this? On this side?" Katie dropped to the floor, lying on her left side. "Were you lying like this?"

"Yes," said Ruth.

Katie got back to her feet.

"You're lying to me," she said. "The cut is on the other side of your head. You didn't get hurt falling down."

A single tear ran down Ruth's cheek. Grace pulled the second chair to Ruth's side, taking her hand, while Katie leaned across the table, silently waiting.

"I was pulling some boards off the barn for a pigsty because Bonnie had started following me down to Dean's. I turned around. There was a...a ghost standing there. The ghost started yelling. It was really mad. I think I screamed and something hit me." By this time Ruth was sobbing. "I woke up on the ground."

Grace wrapped her arms around Ruth. "Shh," she said. "We're right here, relax, okay?" She turned to Katie. "The bell was ringing like crazy. I came right up and found Ruth standing underneath it."

Katie got Ruth a glass of water. When the sobbing stopped, she said, "Let's go have a look."

Behind the barn, Katie found a fresh stack of timbers and a crowbar. "Show me where you were standing, which way were you facing?"

Ruth moved close to the area where the collapsed section of the barn spread across the ground.

"Okay, where did you see the ghost?"

Ruth turned and pointed behind her.

"Right here? Okay, Grace, can you stand here?" Katie moved to stand close behind Ruth. "You were looking at the wood, you heard a sound?"

Ruth nodded.

"And turned." She was right against Ruth, whose upper body swiveled. Katie's movements followed Ruth's. In her peripheral vision, she could see

Grace. "What time was this?"

"I don't know, around nine, maybe or eight-thirty."

Katie raised her head, looking east right over the top of Grace's.

"Did you think it was a ghost because the sun glowed around it?"

"I don't know." Ruth sounded doubtful. "Maybe."

"Okay, I think it was somebody standing there and the sun shining directly behind him made the glow from this position, you aren't seeing a full clear shot."

"What hit me?" asked Ruth.

Katie squatted down looking at the items lying around, but it was Grace that pointed out a section of two-by-four with a small spot of staining on the end. "This, I think this is what hit you. My god, you could have ended up with a fractured skull."

Ruth sagged against Katie.

They went back to the house, and Katie called the sheriff's office. Boyd quickly drove out to the farm. He spoke with Ruth privately, examined the scene, diligently asking all the questions Katie had and more. He offered to take Ruth to the clinic, but she declined. While he sat at the kitchen table writing his report, Rick came home.

"A guy at work has a scanner, he said the police were up here." After looking at Ruth's injuries, he said. "I think you should see the doctor, maybe go to the ER."

"No," said Ruth. "I'm fine."

Outside, they could hear the buzzing motor of the ATV pulling into the yard. Davy knocked at the kitchen door. He and Billy were carrying Tupperware containers Grace had sent up.

"Mom sent supper," Davy said.

While Katie talked with the boys, Ruth called the cats. Rick, who was still feeling sore at having not been called when Katie had, followed Boyd outside. Rick's intent was to question the deputy.

"I'll take care of the chickens and feed the pig," he said.

"She's in the barn," said Katie, turning on the oven to heat the casserole Grace had sent.

"No, she's not. I let her out this morning," said Ruth.

Katie spun around. "How can that be? I haven't seen her since I got home."

Immediately, everyone rushed outside, calling for Bonnie. It was over an hour later that Billie circling on the ATV found her.

"I was just down there a few days ago with a hand scythe and the mower. I'm sure the gate was closed."

"Maybe she shut herself in," said Boyd headed back to his cruiser.

"No," said Katie. "The gate shuts from the outside, so if she was locked inside, somebody put her there."

Boyd changed directions in mid-stride, and with Katie at the lead, ran through the orchard. In the dim light of the September evening, they could see a well-trampled area outside the cemetery gate and where Bonnie had gnawed at the wood, attempting to be free. Boyd sent Davy back for the powerful flashlight in his cruiser, ordering everyone else to stop walking around. The beam of light showed a clear path from the cemetery toward the river.

"It's a deer trail," Katie explained.

"No," said Rick. "Deer walk narrow, one foot in front of the other, rear foot stepping in the front footstep, and in each other's tracks. This trail was made by someone walking foot side by side, lumbering. Even bears don't make a swath this wide."

Katie stared at Rick, then Boyd, then back to Rick.

"Are you saying," she asked, "a human being made this path, walking from the farm down to the river?"

Rick nodded.

"I'd say," said Boyd, "this person was running for dear life." The beam from his light faded as the hill dropped away to the river.

The path left by their antagonist was clear before them. Katie felt her heart sink and lay shivering in her gut.

Rick followed Boyd as the cruiser, siren screaming, tore down Fire Lane 61, back through the village, west on the Shelbourne Road, finally arriving at the closest point in the new development to the backside of Katie's farm. Katie had stayed near the cemetery and an eternity later saw their headlights pull into the work area across the river.

The workers were all gone for the day and there was no way to distinguish one set of tracks from any other on the dirt road, but the place of the river crossing was defined by bent rushes and trampled weeds.

"We'll be back out here first thing in the morning," said Boyd. "We'll talk to every man jack of them. Someone had to have seen something."

Rick returned, more determined than ever to move Katie and Ruth away from the farm. He found both of them sitting silently at the table.

The arguing went on for a long while until Katie's voice rose in anger.

"Listen up, the two of you, out of my house." She pointed toward the front door. "Nothing else will happen tonight, that's for sure. Ruth needs a decent night's sleep, and I need some peace and quiet. Just go. Come back tomorrow."

Cowed, Ruth went upstairs to gather what she would need. In the kitchen, Rick took a black magic marker and wrote his telephone number on the wall in letters two inches high.

"Nice," said Katie, surveying the damage after Rick and Ruth pulled out of the drive. Shutting off all the lights, she walked from room to room, the illuminated glow of the cats' eyes following.

"Don't get any ideas," Katie said. "You aren't all sleeping in my room." There was a soft cry from one of the older cats who was lying on the couch. Picking her up so she could lie down, Katie covered herself with a throw and left the elderly feline lying on her chest. LG jumped lightly up, settling against Katie's legs just before the woman dozed off. During the night, other cats climbed up until Katie was effectively trapped on the couch.

Chapter Forty-Three

"Katie." Ruth shook her arm. "Come outside and look at Bonnie. I think she's choking."

Katie snapped awake and rushed to follow Ruth out into the side yard. There she found the pig with her snout stretched out straight as far as her neck would allow while she gave off great dry, heaving coughs.

Katie pried Bonnie's mouth further open, and using a flashlight, peered inside. All she got for her effort was a whiff of bad breath and a splatter of mucus when the pig coughed again.

"She was like this when I let her out of the barn after Rick dropped me off. Maybe you should call the vet," Ruth suggested.

"I'm the only one here today," said Doctor Ronnie. "Can you crate her up and bring her over? If she's getting air, she probably swallowed something that's stuck in her throat. I don't think she's going to suffocate."

Katie offered Bonnie water, which Bonnie ignored. With Ruth's assistance, Katie rummaged around in the barn until she found some old canvas tarp. Using copious amounts of duct tape she then lined the cargo area in the back of her Subaru. It took both women to lift the squirming pig into the car.

"You ride in the back seat, Ruth," said Katie. "Try to keep her there." It was a nerve-wracking ride to the vet's office in Charlotte for all three.

The vet found the pig had eaten a fistful of burdock and had spines stuck in the backside of her mouth. Removing them proved to be easier than getting Bonnie back in the car. Thoroughly irritated, Bonnie squealed, snorted, and thrashed around, refusing to be loaded for the trip home.

"Give her a chance to settle down," suggested the vet. "You know, walk her around a little, tire her out."

Ruth had once again tied a rope to Bonnie's back leg and with a fair amount of trepidation, Katie followed the pig who ambled along behind the storefronts back toward the center of town. Behind the bank, Katie paused to see if another skunk had moved in beneath the back steps. She found the wooden structure had been replaced with one of concrete with no space under either the steps or the landing. Laughing, she continued on past the dumpster toward the trench. A hard wind was blowing, bringing in the next storm. Katie watched as small pieces of tar paper were picked up from the parking lot and blown out over the trench before drifting down.

"Hm," frowned Katie scanning the roof of the storefront and the bank. "When did they re-roof the bank?"

Even though the long grass had withered, drying to a wheaten gold bowing beneath fully ripened seed heads, Katie could see discarded items still littering the sides of the trench. Bonnie waddled over to the edge dragging Katie lost in her thoughts, with her. Bonnie's strength came as a surprise and momentarily upset Katie's balance, but it was the solid slam from behind that sent the young woman rolling head over heels toward the murky brook. As she somersaulted, Katie let go of Bonnie's leash. Freed from the restraining tug, Bonnie darted away.

Katie landed on her stomach inches away from the stony brook. The water was deep enough so a head injury could have resulted in drowning. It was the only vague thought in Katie's confused mind until a solid one-hundred-fifty-pound person landed on her back. Katie squealed in much the same way Bonnie had and though she tried to flip over, found herself pinned down while someone pushed her head downward. The ground was marshy, and a face plant would end in suffocation.

"Get off of me," Katie roared.

"Shut up!" The shoving pressure increased. "Damn it. You couldn't leave well enough alone, could you? Well, here's what you've got coming." There was another effort at shoving Katie down.

Katie levered her upper body up, trying to lock her elbows.

241

"Get off," she ordered again. Though the next minutes of wrestling back and forth was probably quite short, to Katie it felt as though she had been fighting for hours. There was no doubting the person holding her down meant for only one of them to crawl out of the trench, and it was not supposed to be Katie. The fingers of one hand flashed into view for a moment, showing bright red nail polish. The person fighting Katie was a woman! Katie could smell the stagnant edges of the brook, rotting plants, and something fruity and confusing. She cried out as her attacker pressed sharpened fingernails into the back of her head. Suddenly the weighted pressure was gone, and Katie was not the only person screaming. She heard a shrill peal of fear as the woman sitting on her was jolted away. A splash, and another scream and squeal.

Katie raised her head and saw a woman's legs and arms thrashing about in the brook and what looked like the rear haunches of a pig.

"Bonnie," Katie called weakly, reaching a hand out. Her other arm gave way, and Katie fell back to the ground. She heard the whisper of fabric rubbing on fabric near her head as someone rushed by.

"Get back, get back pig," ordered a man's stern voice.

"Katie," Ruth's arms wrapped around her. "Oh Katie, what happened."

"I fell, no, I was pushed." She rolled over, sitting up and spitting out grit which had splashed into her mouth.

Rick had hold of Bonnie's leash and was dragging the pig away from the woman Sheriff Lewis was helping out of the water. The woman was crying hysterically. Besides Lewis, a man Katie didn't recognize helped pull the woman up over the bank. Katie leaned on Ruth, trying to get up on her feet. Ruth held on to Katie but couldn't take her eyes off the man.

"Stay there," Rick ordered. "Let me tie down the pig and I'll come back. I'll get somebody to call 911."

"I don't need an ambulance," said Katie ineffectively, trying to wipe the mud from her front with muddy hands. "I just need to get out of here." Using her hands to help crawl up the bank, she followed the path of Rick and Bonnie. Ruth moved with her, assisting as she could. Once she was back on top, Katie stood with her hands on her knees, catching her breath. Across the drive, inside the office building, she could hear the woman wailing. When the noise quieted some, the sheriff came out the back door. A vehicle pulled in and two people, one carrying an oxygen tank, rushed into the office.

"Are you going to need rescue when they get done with Mrs. Thatcher?" Lewis asked.

"No," said Katie. "I think I'm good. I just don't know what happened."

"According to Mrs. Thatcher," said Lewis. "You were on the edge of the ravine and the pig shoved you over. She went down to help, said the pig seemed to be attacking you, and the pig turned on her."

"No," wheezed Katie.

An ambulance pulled in.

"I've got Boyd coming with a pig crate," said Lewis. "We'll need to take the pig. You know, vicious animal attack, possibly rabies."

Ruth gasped. Katie moved over to where a very dirty Bonnie was laying tied to the back end of somebody's car. Katie dropped to the ground, leaning against the pig.

"No. That's not what happened, and you're not taking my pig. How did you get here, anyway?"

"I was just coming out of Josh Burns' office," he said. "Katie, I have to quarantine the pig."

"NO!" Ruth shouted. Rick took her arm pulling her back, when he turned to speak to Lewis, Ruth moved further away.

While Lewis argued with Katie, Ruth ran back to the veterinary parking lot for the Subaru. When she returned, she and Rick got the pig in the back. Boyd still hadn't arrived.

"Take her home," Katie ordered.

"Now hold on," said Lewis. At that moment rescue exited the building with a stretcher. Mrs. Thatcher was strapped down, an oxygen mask in place, still keening about the attack. Unable to fight the impulse to look up, Katie caught sight of the woman just before a rescue worker covered her with a blanket. Katie jerked to her feet, running and stumbling towards the wheeled stretcher.

"KATIE!" yelled Rick. Both he and Lewis rushed after Katie while Ruth took advantage of the diversion to start the car and on screeching tires roared onto Main street and away.

Katie got just close enough before Lewis caught hold of her to reach out and grasp the corner of the blanket. As Lewis pulled her backward, Katie held tight, and the blanket fell to the ground. The heavy smell of Mrs. Thatcher's fruit-based perfume filled the air.

"So," Katie sneered at Mrs. Thatcher, who wore a mud-splattered shift of madras with bright green ribbon trim. "You left your jacket at my house, but don't worry, I kept it for you."

Mrs. Thatcher's wailing stopped abruptly, her face paled, and she fainted.

* * *

While the mud dried on her clothing, Katie explained to Lewis about the bolero jacket Bonnie had wrapped around her face in the barn.

"It was right near where the scarecrow was made. It gets hot in there sometimes with all the doors closed. If Thatcher took off the jacket, she probably forgot it. She wears a perfume that smells like some kind of berry, obviously Bonnie likes it. That's probably what made the pig mess with the jacket to begin with and chase Thatcher into the brook."

"Well, Bonnie didn't seem to like the woman much even if she liked the smell," Rick said.

"I don't know. Are pigs like dogs? Could she have been trying to protect me?" asked Katie.

"Who knows?" Lewis turned back toward the trench. Boyd pulled into the alley. He was driving a pickup truck with a large wood crate tied down in the back. "I'm going to follow the ambulance; Boyd will stay here. You," he nodded towards Katie, "go home. I'll be there eventually."

Chapter Forty-Four

K atie had a bath, as did Bonnie, who was then locked inside her stall with plenty of snacks. Fresh from the tub, Katie took a seat at the table with a cup of tea before her. Rick was pacing. His agitated movements coupled with Ruth's inability to finish a sentence grated on Katie's nerves. Out in the driveway, Stan and Cindy pulled in. They had the children with them and a tote of outdoor toys they poured out on the lawn. The children spread out, examining this new play area, and the adults followed Ruth inside. Before anyone could explain what had occurred earlier, Cindy started talking.

"Wait until you see what I found out," said Cindy. She spread several pages of typed forms in front of Katie. Her excitement was contagious, and Katie leaned forward. The others crowded around.

"I couldn't leave it alone, I was having so much fun," Cindy explained. "All this development is happening out here, you know? And while I was making a list of all the things you could do; I was talking to someone from college who stayed in the field. She was telling me about companies buying up, subdividing, micro developing; that means using the same piece of property for multiple projects. You sell the wood pulp, hardwood, gravel, then put in houses. Or scrap up topsoil, plant Christmas trees, and I don't know, raise beef cows or goats." The words poured out of her mouth, but Katie wasn't listening. She read the words on the forms, trying to decipher their meaning.

"Okay, okay," Katie said. "But what is all this?"

"Town government positions became intermingled between locals and newbies who didn't want to share their Eden's. They approached new independents trying to get started and hired them to assay the areas. Whole towns. The transplants wanted re-zoning, so the big farms on either side of their homes couldn't become housing developments or industrial complexes. Some of these start-up guys worked relatively cheaply, and to be honest, a lot of this was handled behind closed doors and written off to be something else. That part is complicated, so we'll skip to the good part." Once again, she flipped through the forms.

"Several towns on this side of Shelbourne, which," she looked at Katie, "has become a hoity-toity rich man's area, banded together. One firm they hired included a geologist and mineralogist."

"How about if we start supper?" Ruth suggested.

Cindy had come prepared to stay for supper with hot dogs, chips, and potato salad. Rick lit the grill standing guard as Bonnie who had followed the children up from the barn stood nearby sniffing the air. Watching the two men eye the pig eyeing the grill through the window made Katie smile. She pulled vegetables and goat cheese out of the fridge to add to their meal, unaware Ruth sat again at the table watching Cindy examine something she brought.

"Katie?" said Cindy.

"I'm sorry. What?" Katie half-turned, sheepishly smiling, embarrassed to have ignored the other women because her thoughts were elsewhere.

"I was telling you that one report I copied was the geo report for both the farm and your grandmother's old home," said Cindy.

Hip against the counter edge, Katie waited. Fatigue at the mere mention of the Charlotte property lowered her brow, making her demeanor appear sullen. Cindy was looking, but Ruth frowned at Katie's apparent disinterest.

"This report says the farm is good soil, well-drained and suited for crop growth and animal husbandry." She flipped to a second page. "The one for Charlotte says the northeastern section is fertile, however, the bulk of the property will be better utilized in excavation."

Katie stepped over to the table, pointing at the paper she said, "All they had to do was look at the land and what it was being used for. I'm sure they didn't dig any holes or deep wells that would take them more than a couple of feet down."

"That's true," Cindy said. "I agree with you one hundred percent. The deal breaker is that this is an *official* evaluation by a professional and licensed surveyor. Which means if you were looking to develop a piece of property and offered this report, you'd believe what you saw written here, right?"

"True." Understanding lit Katie's eye. "In other words, if you were looking for sand, you'd want the Charlotte piece." Then the light went dark. "But would you be willing to kill for it?"

"I'm sure I don't know," said Cindy.

"Another point to consider," said Stan, ushering the children ahead of him. "Is the development going in on Kitteridge Road. Charlotte says three acres per house. That's a chunk of land."

"Seriously?" Katie's jaw dropped. "Three acres?"

Stan pushed the children into the bathroom. "Wash," he said. Turning back to the women, he added. "Yes, so if you want to build houses and make money, you need a lot of land." Stan returned to the bathroom and the splashing and giggling therein.

"You're losing me," said Katie.

"It means if you own useless abutting land, you can incorporate that into the three acres and call it an association," said Cindy.

"This is all very interesting, assuming the murderer wants the land." Katie put a stack of plates on the table. "We don't know that for sure. Or even that there isn't something about the farm they want, and that's where I'm placing the money."

"Money is what the people who control the land want," Rick said. He put the platter of crisp hot dogs on the table.

Conversation ceased as the adults filled plates for the children, then helped themselves. Everyone found a seat in the living room.

"I should have fed the cats first," laughed Ruth pushing Simon away from the nearest child. Through the window, they could hear Bonnie woofing for attention.

"She touches that hot grill," said Rick, "and she's going to know about it."

They were just finishing ice cream sandwiches when Cindy's eldest son burst through the door.

"Cheez-it," he cried out, "the fuzz!"

"STANLEY JAMES," his mother exclaimed, immediately turning to her husband. "Where did he learn that?"

While Stan mumbled an excuse, Katie went to the front door and found Lewis on the porch chatting with the other two children.

"Ms. Took." He touched his hat. "I hate to interrupt you but I need a bit of your time to fill out this report."

Chapter Forty-Five

Katie opened the screen door to allow Sheriff Lewis in the front as the kitchen door closed. Outside she could hear the Stan clan calling their goodbyes as they loaded up and headed out.

"Let's start at the beginning." Lewis sat on the sofa, notebook in hand. "Why were you in Charlotte?"

Katie went through the earlier part of the day, the choking, vet visit, calming walk, and then the shove from behind, wrestling in the mud, and verbal threats. Lewis tapped his pencil against the notes he had written.

"Can you think of any reason you would have been attacked?"

"Who knows?" asked Katie. "I seem to have been under attack since I got here, and my grandmother too. Maybe she thought I was someone else, or she doesn't like pigs, or thought I was some kind of thief. She accused me of being where I shouldn't have been and," Katie gave a laugh remembering her attacker's words, "she's heavier than she looks."

Lewis was silent for several minutes, absently scratching the head of a cat brave enough to rub against the sheriff's knee.

"I probably shouldn't, but I'm telling you Delouse has threatened to get a lawyer and sue."

Katie heard one word, Delouse.

"Delouse?" she whispered.

"Yeah," this time it was Lewis who laughed. "I gather it's a family name. Most of us just call her Del."

Katie rose, to her feet trance-like. She pulled open the third drawer down on the metal filing cabinet, retrieving an over full folder she put on the floor.

Kneeling, Katie flipped through the articles she had cut from the paper. It was obvious she knew what she was looking for, and Lewis didn't interrupt even though he had questions. Her lips moved silently. Near the bottom of the stack, she came across a photograph of a lawn party with a long column of newsprint attached at the bottom.

"On August seventh of last year," she read, "Jacqueline and Lawrence French hosted a Robichaud family reunion at Rocky Ridges Golf Course. Assisting Mrs. French with the two-hundred-person event where her sisters, Delouse and Marie." Katie turned to Lewis, a question on her face.

Yeah," he said. "Delouse's maiden name was Robichaud. From South Burlington, I think."

Katie shook her head. "No," she said. "The point is Jacqueline French's husband, Lawrence, is the man I believe is responsible for Gram's murder."

"What are you talking about, Katie?" Lewis asked, his voice low and slow.

Still kneeling on the floor, Katie told Lewis what she had learned about the man who had visited Irma. "There was a second guy," she said. "Ruth described him to me. She might still recognize him."

Outside they could hear Ruth talking.

"I think," said Lewis. "We need to explore this further."

"Later," said Katie.

Lewis nodded and headed for the door.

"Wait just a minute Martin," said Rick. "There's something else you should know before you go." He looked over his shoulder to make sure Ruth had followed him into the house. "The other night after you talked to the boys, I went back to the body shop. I was upfront with the guys that work there, told them a crime had been committed and you'd talked to the young fellas that owned the trucks, but nothing came of it."

Rick cleared his throat. Katie waited; mouth dry.

"This one guy that handles the money? He said one of the trucks was brought in by a woman, said she'd been using her boy's truck and hit a deer. She had the repairs done and didn't want to go through the insurance."

Katie leaned back on the couch. Ruth sat beside her.

"Guy couldn't remember her name, but his bank deposit slip is a duplicate.

She paid with a check and the bank number and account number are on that slip."

Lewis stared at Rick.

There was conviction in the old man's eyes as he stared back.

"You didn't say anything," said Katie.

Rick turned to her. "This is the first time I've had a chance to talk to you. I've been fidgeting around since we got home. I was waiting for Martin." He looked at the sheriff. "I didn't screw this up, did I?"

"How did you figure this out?" Lewis asked.

"I didn't," said Rick. "Katie did. At least she had all these pieces, it was just a matter of getting them to fit together."

Sheriff Martin Lewis blew out his cheeks. He was studying his hands. It was clear he wrestled with something he knew. Finally, he looked up.

"The other day, Katie, when I had you come into my office? That was specifically so the doc would see you there. I sort of alluded to him that you were considering filing a complaint because of inappropriate actions on his part. I told him I'd been checking around and it seemed not all the facts on Irma's death added up, and I would be real sad to have to arrest him for murder." Lewis paused, the back of his neck darkening.

"First, he said he didn't know anything, I told him I could prove Irma wasn't his patient and Ruth hadn't called him. After that, he got real cooperative. Seems when he was in private practice, he had an affair with one of his young nurses. Her father found out, filed a complaint about rape. It was hushed up. But it's the reason he moved out here. That same nurse showed up in his office with her son about ten years ago. It was a shock to both the woman and the doctor. Anyway, this nurse, er, woman called him the night Irma died. She said there had been a horrible accident and he needed to get out there right away to clean it up or she was going to raise hell and back."

Through parched lips, Katie asked. "The nurse was Jacqueline Robichaud French?"

"No," said Lewis. "The nurse was Delouse Robichaud."

"Delouse Thatcher killed my grandmother?" asked Katie. It was an incredulous idea, but inside her mind, she could see all the facts adding up. "Is that possible?"

"Katie," said Ruth, "I've been trying to tell you, the man that was helping the woman out of the trench is the toad."

Katie blinked once. Unable to pull air into her lungs, she coughed.

"That's exactly what happened," Katie fought to get to her feet. "That woman killed Gram for a lousy patch of dirt."

Outside a cat left alone, gave a mournful cry.

"Not a word," said Lewis, "until I get a warrant."

Katie stood still while the other three watched her. Finally, she asked Lewis.

"Why were you there? In Charlotte. And you, Rick?"

"Burns is my tax guy," said Lewis.

"The bank on the slip is right beside the alley," Rick said.

"And that's where the nails came from too," said Katie. She dropped back down to the couch, head in her hands. "Go," she said, "go."

Lewis left quickly. Before the afternoon was over, he would need a warrant, and the bank slip, too. Ruth made tea, but Katie accepted the beer Rick offered first. One hour ticked past. Then another.

"Rick," asked Katie, "what hospital would they take someone from Charlotte to?"

"Mary Fletcher in Burlington, why?"

Katie got to her feet. "That's where I'm going. That's where she is."

All three ended up piling into the cab of Rick's truck. At the hospital, he pulled around to the emergency entrance. Once inside, Katie hesitated. What had she expected to find here? Delouse Thatcher strapped down on the floor? Bright lights shining on her, cops in bad suits grilling her? There was none of that. Patients filled the waiting area, hospital personnel moved from place to place, everything was subdued. A young woman at the desk looked up, smiled. Her mouth opened to ask if she could help when suddenly Katie heard a familiar voice scream out.

"GET YOUR HANDS OFF ME. You've got no right. Some dope-sniffing out-of-stater comes in here making accusations and you believe her because you're hot for her. You dirt-ball, men are all alike."

252

Katie ran toward the noise, Rick and Ruth close behind. Ripping the curtain open, Katie made eye contact with Delouse Thatcher as the woman fought against Sheriff Lewis and Boyd.

Delouse's mouth snapped shut and Katie's opened, but no words came out. Then Delouse wrenched free of Boyd, but stumbled to her knees because Lewis still held on. Looking at Katie, Delouse screeched.

"You don't get it, do you stupid, stupid girl? It's about the money. It's always about the money!"

"No," said Katie, one hand on Ruth's arm, holding her steady, "it isn't."

Chapter Forty-Six

A member of the hospital security staff pushed Katie and Ruth aside as he and two Burlington police officers filled the remaining space in the exam room. Katie stumbled as she moved awasy and would have fallen if Rick hadn't caught her and Ruth. He kept them on their feet while moving back along the corridor toward the electronic doors and then out into the unloading zone.

When Katie realized Rick was taking them outside, she fought against him. He had a good grip and though he let Ruth loose, knowing she would follow; he held tight to Katie.

"Let me go," she demanded.

"Outside," he hissed.

She continued to struggle, but he wasn't letting her free. Their struggle went unheeded as all other eyes were focused on the swirling cloth curtain and screaming mayhem they had left behind.

"Listen to me," hissed Rick, once the door closed behind them. "In about two seconds, the doctor will sedate her and then all those cops are going to step back and look around. You don't want to be what they see. It'll take at least a half-hour, but that doctor will say there is nothing wrong with Delouse. At that point, she'll be transferred to the police station." He pointed to the city police cruiser and the sheriff's car.

"This is how they'll leave. All we have to do is wait," Rick said.

Katie wrenched free of Rick's grasp. He stepped aside, making no effort to hold on to her.

"Okay," she said, holding her hands up in surrender. "We wait."

They brought the truck up from the public parking area and sat in the cab watching the emergency exit. Just as Rick said, Delouse Thatcher left the hospital in cuffs surrounded by police officers. The city officer placed her in the backseat of his car and with the sheriff following, they pulled into traffic. The lights were on, but not the sirens. Rick followed the cruisers, arriving at the police station moments after they did.

"Now what?" asked Katie.

"Now we give them a few minutes to get straightened out and we go inside," said Rick.

Katie sat in the truck, tapping her fingers against her knees, wishing she had a coffee. A light blue Lincoln pull into the lot. She immediately recognized the man and woman who left the car and hurried towards the building.

"That's Lawrence French and his wife." She pointed toward the couple.

Another car pulled in and the horn blew, stopping French. A short man in a dark suit climbed out and rushed towards French.

"I'm willing to bet, that's his lawyer," said Rick.

He opened the driver's door and Katie followed his lead. Once on the sidewalk, she fought the urge to run into the police station. Inside Katie, Rick, and Ruth found themselves in a small area with wooden chairs set in two short rows. Rick pointed toward the end seat furthest from the window where the desk sergeant was trying to assist the Frenches. From where she was sitting, Katie could hear Mrs. French, but see them only if she turned. The lawyer provided identification and was whisked away.

Another man hurried into the lobby. Two teenage boys followed him. He ordered them to sit down.

Ruth tugged at Katie's sleeve.

"The guy that just came in is the toad," Ruth whispered.

Unable to stop herself, Katie turned and stared at the dark-haired man at the desk. She had spun around just in time to see the newcomer shoulder Lawrence French out of the way.

"Watch yourself, Bob," growled Mrs. French.

The man ignored her. Instead, he spoke to the desk sergeant.

"My name is Robert Thatcher. My wife was taken to the hospital this afternoon. I don't understand why she was brought here. I demand to see her."

"It's okay, Bob," French said. "Calm down, we already got Delouse a lawyer." French had his mouth open to say something else, but Thatcher cut him off.

"We don't need anything from you," Thatcher spat. "It's your fault Delouse is in this mess. You're always putting grandiose ideas in her head. Leave us alone, hear me? Back off."

French silently took a step backwards, but Mrs. French swung around him and got right in Thatcher's face.

"The only thing we did was try to help her out." Mrs. French was wearing glittering jewelry from her hair to her ankles. Now, as she shook in rage, her whole body appeared to be on fire with sparkling lights. "My sister wanted better for her boys than you could ever give her." She took a step closer to Thatcher, but her husband put his hands on her shoulders, drawing her back to his six-foot-four-inch frame.

"Easy now," Lawrence said. "Let's not get ahead of ourselves."

"MY BOYS." Spittle flew from Thatcher's mouth. His eyes were on Lawrence French. "They are *my* boys."

The desk sergeant spoke and Thatcher turned toward him. The Frenches moved to the chairs, sitting on either side of the boys. Mrs. French rubbed the younger one's back and Lawrence sat with his arm on the back of Brent Thatcher's chair. Both boys were tall, the younger one dark like his father, the older one fairer. Katie blinked. Brent was Danish fair, just as Lawrence was. He also had a cleft dent in his chin, similar to Lawrence. Katie knew that facial feature was an inherited gene.

Oh my god, she thought, *this is like Peyton Place.*

She was still considering the picture before her when the desk sergeant told Robert Thatcher his wife didn't want him there; she wanted him to go home.

Thatcher was livid. He spun around to where the boys were sitting. One next to his aunt, fear on his face, and the other leaning back against Lawrence's arm. Thatcher's face had lost all color.

"Get. Over. Here," he ordered.

The younger boy jumped right up. Brent hesitated a second too long.

"He knows," Katie whispered to herself.

Thatcher dragged the boys out of the building. Katie heard the car roar away. Moments later Lawrence pulled a cigarette from his pocket, and he and his wife went outside. Katie fought the urge to follow. Then a voice behind her spoke.

"What can I do for you folks?" the sergeant asked.

Katie jumped up like somebody had stuck a hatpin in her behind.

"Sheriff Lewis," she choked out. "We're looking for the sheriff."

When Lewis entered the lobby, he shook his head.

"I should have known you'd end up here," he said.

When Katie spoke, he stopped her.

"Go home," he said. "This is going to take a long time. You don't need to be here if people start asking questions. I'll drive out when we're through." He went back through the locked door.

"I think he means like the press," said Rick.

*　*　*

Katie was exhausted. She went from leaning on the passenger door to slouching in her chair. Ruth made her a grilled cheese sandwich, but it sat untouched on the table beside her. LG walked beneath Katie's knees. The cat arched her back, rubbing against Katie. When there was no response, LG jumped into the chair, walked across Katie, and crouched on the wooden arm. Rick considered the cat. She was facing out, crouched to spring, and watching the room. Was she guarding Katie?

The evening dragged along. Eventually, Ruth went up to lie on her bed, while Rick snored on the sofa. Katie would doze for a few minutes, then jar awake. Every time she jolted back to awareness, LG would open her big yellow eyes and wait. Katie stared across the darkroom.

Memories jumbled in and out. The third-grade recital, where Katie wanted to sing but was rejected because she couldn't carry a tune. Irma had

257

worked with her continually for two weeks until Katie could sing God Bless America. It was still the only song Katie could sing without making people cringe. There was the time she'd fallen off the tractor and Poppa had run back to the house with her in his arms. Gram had cried at the hospital while the doctors set Katie's arm. Picking berries, gathering eggs, every sports game at school, and all the boxes of memorabilia Gram had saved.

Taking the money and running seemed far away right at that moment. Katie damned herself for the ten years she could have spent with her grandmother but had instead stayed away. Guilt stacked on guilt, creating a mountain of crushing pain. Eventually, she had no tears left. Her only movement the shivering of her huddled body. Lights shone through the windows. The sheriff had arrived. His vehicle was still rolling to a stop when Katie burst through the front door, Rick right behind her.

"Let's sit," said Sheriff Lewis. Exhaustion etched deep grooves in his face.

They sat at the kitchen table, while Ruth bustled around making tea and shooing cats.

Sheriff Lewis cleared his throat repeatedly before he got started.

Across the table, Katie sat on the edge of her chair. The only thing restraining her from screaming for information was Rick's hand on her knee.

"It took a while," Lewis began. "Same old thing, I didn't do anything wrong. I'm innocent. Eventually, she wore down and admitted to harassing Irma, here and around town. That's all she'd admit to; stealing stuff from the truck, harassing telephone calls, stuff like that. Then the detective got on her about the burning scarecrow and the old hen house. She got defensive, said it was her husband's fault. He wanted this big contract with Lawrence French to build tract houses. We let her sit for a while and called in both Thatcher and French."

Lewis rubbed his face.

"French said the Thatcher's came to him with the plan to own the whole mountain and build houses in both towns. Thatcher said it wasn't his idea. He couldn't remember exactly who had mentioned it first, but said he sat in on a meeting where French, his crew, and both of the Thatchers talked about it. We went back to Delouse with the tapes. She started screaming it was Bob's fault. He had promised the moon and only had the gumption for whatever was across the street. I thought she was off her rocker there for a while screaming her that boys deserved better. Her sister had it all. It should have been her."

"Her oldest son." Katie cleared her throat. "Her oldest son is Lawrence French's child."

Every head snapped in her direction.

"How do you know that?" Lewis was looking at her from under lowered brows.

"Brent looks just like Lawrence. Same build, same coloring, he even has the same dent in his chin. You don't get that by accident," said Katie.

Lewis nodded. "That explains a lot. Lawrence and his wife don't have any children. If Lawrence had an affair with Delouse and she had a child, Lawrence might be more prone to listen to what she wanted."

"And she wanted the land," said Katie.

"Yep, she did." Lewis waved away Ruth's attempt to refill his cup. "I think she became obsessed with it. She admitted to following both Irma and you, sneaking across the river, and being in the barn. You almost caught her at least twice."

Katie nodded.

"While she was babbling," said Lewis, "she admitted to the scarecrow incident. She said the pig snuck up on her and scared her to death, so she smacked it with a stick. Could be why the pig went at her. It wasn't until the detective stood up and told me to drive over and arrest Brent for arson on the hen house and murdering Irma that Delouse confessed."

"She said she'd done it all. The boy knew she was up to something because he could tell work had been done on his truck, but he didn't know the truth. Right about then she stopped blaming Bob and started putting it all on you, Katie."

"What?" said Ruth.

"She carried on about how you came back for no good reason and ruined her life." Lewis watched Katie. "I'm thinking you should know this because she's going to be raving at anyone who listens. You should be ready."

Katie picked LG up off the floor, holding the cat close to her chest.

"She's right, you know?" Katie said, her voice low and tired. "The part where I came back for no good reason. I forgot about my grandparents loving me, and how I loved them. I came back here to sell the farm, take the money, and party till it was gone." Her eyes went from person to person. She saw speculation in Lewis's, the sadness in Rick's, but Ruth held her the longest. There was disbelief and sorrow.

Suddenly aware LG was purring, Katie exhaled all she had suffered through the evening.

"That's not what's going to happen, though. This is my home, for the foreseeable future, this is where I'm staying. If we freeze our butts off this winter trying to scrape by, so be it."

Ruth was silently weeping. Lewis explained Delouse would stand before the judge in the morning charged on multiple counts including murder.

"Get a lawyer," he said. "You need to be protected too."

After he left, Rick stepped up.

"I have a confession too," he said. "I told you that Ruth and I were out puttering around a piece of land I was looking to rent. I didn't tell you that it was the house lot on the Roser property. You should know."

Before Katie could ask anything further, Rick left.

In the morning Katie called the lawyer who would help with renting the gravel pit. His colleague would represent her on the wrongful death case. She sat in the courtroom for three hours waiting for Delouse Thatcher to be brought in. Beside her on one side, her new attorney. On the other side, Ruth waited, hands in tight fists. Rick and Stan sat in the seats behind her. They didn't share a word, just waited, listened, and left. Being there didn't make the pain any easier. If nothing else, it reopened the wound. Now though, Katie knew there was a chance it would someday heal.

She went back to work the following day. The people at the feed store were silent, some giving her a pat on the back as they went by or offering an encouraging smile. Katie kept choking up.

"I feel so stupid, acting like a baby," she confessed to Rick.

"Man up, and take what support they can offer," he said.

* * *

Two weeks later, Katie sat in the lawyer's office with the representative for the company that would lease the gravel pit. She hadn't known what to expect but was pleased when she left with an initial check that would cover most of the taxes on the Roser property. On the way home from the tax collector's office, she noticed for the first time the swamp maples were turning to their fall colors. The sugar maples lining Fire Lane 61 were changing too.

The rocking chair on the front porch called out to her, but she sat on the step. Bonnie trotted over and flounced down, her back close enough for Katie's rubbing boot to reach. LG lay in the sun. When Katie reached out, the cat's ears flattened, and she showed sharp white teeth. A car pulled in. Marlie stepped out.

"Hey," she said. "It's my day off. You weren't at work so I came out to see if you were okay."

"I'm just headed out for a walk," said Katie, dusting off the seat of her pants. "Want to come?"

"Sure," said Marlie.

They headed down the lane with Bonnie and LG following.

"There's a story about this lane," said Katie, fingers reaching out to twine around Marlie's. "Years ago, the man that lived here had a sweetie that lived on the other side of the mountain."

Acknowledgements

Thank you from the bottom of my heart to all the people who sat and smiled while I carried on about my book. To my partner, my children, and my family. Marge Hakey, who read and re-read. Verena Rose and Shawn Reilly Simmons from Level Best Books who put up with me, and Harriette Sackler who sent my words along the path. My Fortin family, that gave me the roots for this book, and the people who are waiting to read.

About the Author

DonnaRae's writing career began in the seventh grade with derogatory descriptions of other students. It was also her introduction to public speaking and the start of training for the one-hundred-yard dash in track and field.

There were diaries, journals, two tiny columns in small-town newspapers, competition pieces for Toastmaster's International, and boxes under her bed filled with novels.

She currently lives just outside of town in the type of place where people feel free to drop off cats, kittens, cages of gerbils or white rats, and even the occasional farm animal.

CPSIA information can be obtained
at www.ICGtesting.com
Printed in the USA
BVHW031203200322
631487BV00001B/57